Chaos Emergence

Sabreena Rodgers

Kennedy,

As you prepare to venture into the vast expanses of life's journeys, I want you to carry with you the unwavering belief in your own greatness. Never allow fear to shackle your ambitions, for you are a remarkable and extraordinary young woman, deserving of every success the world has to offer. Always remember, whatever your focus, is what will manifest. I love you.

To every single one of you who have inspired me to keep going - thank you. Without you, none of this would even happen. To my team - you guys mean the world to me, without you none of this would even be fun, much less possible. From the Chaotically Unhinged conversations to the true family friendships we have made, I wouldn't trade it for anything!

Preface

It started as a story, passed on from person to person. A recollection of events, happenings, instructions. Then, mankind found a way to poison that. Leaving out the parts that did not suit their need at the time. Changing small details to favor an agenda. With the new knowledge of writing, stories were put down to preserve them. Mankind found a way to poison this as well, at times through interpretation, ommitance, or simply through summarization. It was found that if a piece of knowledge was too powerful, simply leave it out of the writings, and over time it would become forgotten. Today, mankind can explode entire nations leaving nothing but devastation behind. That, however, is not the real power. The real *power lies in the recording. The incident is only as powerful as the recording.*

Pronunciations

- Aria (are-ee-ah)

- Vega (vay-gah)

- Jaliah (jah-lee-ah)

- Riya (rye-ah)

- Ophelian (Oh-feel-ee-an)

- Nyterian (nye-tier-ian)

- Baren (bare - en)

- Tallon (Tal-on)

- Ethos (EE-TH-ose)

- Callen (Kal - En)

Table of contents

ARGUS. TRIBUNAL LEADER

ETHOS. CONNECTED TO BAREN

Vayu Clan

ARIA. CONNECTED TO OPHELIAN

VEGA. CONNECTED TO ATTICUS

GREYSON. CONNECTED TO ISADOR

Agni Clan

KATERINA. CONNECTED TO NYTERIAN

RIYA. CONNECTED TO ZURI

Jala Clan

JALIAH. CONNECTED TO KOBIN

CALLEN. CONNECTED TO KYSON

Prithvi Clan

ARCHER. CONNECTED TO LEXORA

TALON. CONNECTED TO SILAS

ANNALISE. CONNECTED TO CASSIUS

One

Aria

My bed is amazing, the one thing in this whole house that I did not go cheap on. I struggle with sleep most nights, so a good bed, good pillows, and good sheets - were my top priority when I moved in. I started here with barely anything. I thought it would be fun to sell almost everything I owned and start completely over. Like the ultimate spring cleaning, or New Year's resolution - new house new things - I told myself. I really love my bed, so why am I still desperately reaching into the depths of the darkness to find a sliver of sleep? I have turned, repositioned, stretched out for the cold spots, went pee, and repeated the process over a hundred times, and still - total failure. I worked hard today, hard enough to leave me mentally and physically exhausted.

Sleep should be knocking on my mental door, I shouldn't be searching for it, but here I am. It's stressful to check my phone for the time and see that the hours tick by leaving the window of rest smaller and smaller. When I do manage to get any sleep it's bombarded with wild and confusing dreams that feel so real they usually leave me wondering when I wake if I slept at all.

It's already 1 a.m. - I have to drag myself into the shower by 5 a.m. if I stand a chance to make it to work by 6. It's time to focus, I will not survive all day on my feet tomorrow if I do not find sleep! I lay as still as I possibly can, imagining each one of my limbs becoming limp, almost to where I cannot feel them as being part of my body. I let my ears tune in to the wind sounds rustling past the windows, as if it were a violin grazing the strings of sleep, creating an organic lullaby. I focus only on this, letting it consume every fiber of my being until finally, sleep finds me.

***

"Only here will you find your answers". The words echo within and around me, as if whispered by the very air. The scent of damp earth envelopes me, though darkness veils my sight. A mystical energy pulses around me, a gentle hum of power, poised to be grasped and released in an enchanting symphony of magic.

"Only here will you find the answers". The words echo once more, each time more distinct than before, resonating with a woman's ethereal voice—or so I believe. I teeter on the edge of wakefulness and dreams, unsure of my state. In the far-off horizon, a flicker of light appears, shimmering like the mystical border where the sunset melds seamlessly into the abyss of night.

"Only here will you find your answers, but first you must find your questions" They resonate once more. My fingers extend, gently caressing the ground beneath me; I sense the texture of leaves, the softness of

moss, the coolness of damp earth. Could I be outdoors? A distant shimmer, initially a deep honey hue, begins to transform into a fiery burnt orange. Suddenly, a burst of emerald green illuminates everything around me, casting an enchanting glow, and then—just as swiftly—plunging me back into shadowy obscurity.

***

I sit up, sweat seeping from every pore on my body. The only thing I can hear is my heart pounding in my ears only interrupted by the rapid breathing coming from my chest. I am clearly in my bed, inside my room - it was just a dream. I reach for my phone dreading to see the time since I'm pretty sure I only achieved about 10 minutes of actual sleep... 4:59... OK, so I managed to get almost 4 hours. It will have to do. I drag myself out from under my covers, placing my feet on the floor to get my bearings. The second I stand I can feel every bit of yesterday's work day still living in the soles of my feet. Today is going to be a long day.

I picked this house because it is only 6 minutes from my job. The job I've only been at for three days. It's a small house, but it's perfect for me, plus it has a yard. I would trade all the fancy apartments in town to have at least a small patch of grass for myself. Growing up with miles of woods at my disposal makes city living a culture shock for me, but when Grace Memorial offered me the day shift lead position on the surgical recovery floor I couldn't pass it up. Although I live in town now, with it's constant wave of commuter traffic and corporate coffee shops on every corner, I am only twenty-three miles from the national forest with abundant woods to explore on my off days. The job is worth it. My small town hospital at home did not even have a surgery floor to speak of, not unless you count the colonoscopies that the local primary care doc performed there as a surgery program. Healing has always been important to me, and surgery recovery is almost instant gratification. Not all patients who come through are quick recoveries, of course, some go through grueling procedures that take weeks or even months to recover from. There are definitely more quick recoveries than long ones. To watch a person who has lived in pain for years, get a hip or joint replacement, and then feel like a whole new person despite being cut into, is refreshing. Being a part of that recovery lets me be a part of their new beginning.

Walking what feels like two miles from my car to the front doors is all it took for the soles of my feet to remind me that I did not sleep enough to wear off yesterday's fatigue. Again, I remind myself that the job is worth it! I haven't made friends here yet, I barely remember names even, and home is eleven hours too far away to hang out with my old friends. The downside of striking out on my own. As I head for the elevators, the front desk receptionist waves me down. I know her name is Denise, I met her at my orientation, and she's one of those people you don't forget. She instantly makes you feel like family like you've known her your whole life.

"Darling, your badge was ready in HR, but I went ahead and grabbed it for you to save you the trip!" Her smile is so contagious I can't help but smile in return as I tell her thank you.

"How are you settling in? Moved in and all? I know you don't know people here yet so just let me know if you need any help and I'll bring my husband over to do the work while we supervise," she says with a giggle.

I thank her and head towards the elevators looking over my new ID. I know it's just a badge, almost every job out there has them, but this is the first one I have had that reads "Aria Ashton, RN, BSN". It's just a few more initials after my name, but I earned those initials all on my own and worked hard enough along the way to end up recruited to this job fresh out of school. It helps that I went to nursing school straight out of high school and got my LPN, which paid my way through RN school. To say it was tough is an understatement. Nursing school takes over ones entire life, leaving little time to do what normal young college people do. I sacrificed fun for focus, and in the long run it was worth it, I think. While the rest of my friends from school were off finding romance and — life, I was stuck in a book or a study session. There wasn't any time for romance, just like there isn't now, between twelve hour shifts and moving in to my new place. I guess eventually life will calm down and allow for those things.

The floor was hectic today; I barely managed to dash down and quickly devour a salad in the cafeteria. My energy is running on six cups of coffee, a salad, and half a protein bar. When I arrived this morning, there were eight new admissions from last night, in addition to the eight we already had, and nine patients scheduled for pre-op. Being the shift lead involves a lot of back-and-forth, meticulously checking everything multiple times, and handling piles of paperwork. With two hours left in my shift, I'm already fantasizing about my wonderful bed and the great sleep I hope awaits me. While wrapping up my last rounds, I get a call from the front desk. It's the hospital chaplain, requesting my assistance to accompany him to visit a patient on my floor who is about to undergo a lung transplant. Naturally, I agree. Being around a chaplain always brings me comfort and peace. Whether it's their non-judgmental listening or their soothing presence, I always feel uplifted after speaking with one. As we walk to the patient's room, I can't help but wonder why he chose to call me. It's not as if I'm known for my religious inclinations, or even known at all in this place yet. I set those thoughts aside as we arrive at the patient's room.

As soon as we step inside, I'm struck by the state of the patient. He's a young man, likely around my age. His complexion is pale and drawn, and his eyes appear to be searching for something. His breathing is labored, accompanied by the soft hiss of an oxygen tank. The chaplain introduces me to him, mentioning he might have some questions for me before the operation. The patient nods, and the chaplain leaves us alone. I sit down beside the bed, uncertain about what to say. The patient looks at me, and I can sense the intensity of his gaze.

"Do you believe in magic?" he inquires unexpectedly. The question catches me off guard. Normally, I'd chuckle and dismiss it, but there's an unmistakable sensation—a familiar hum—hovering just beyond my grasp, eager to be seized and yet ready to burst forth.

Two

Archer

I'm fairly certain I'm dreaming, yet I find myself in an unfamiliar darkness. This is the third occurrence, and each time it feels more intense. It's damp here, and the only thing visible is something resembling an eclipse. The first time, the moon-like shape was just a tiny sliver, but it appears to grow wider with each visit. Initially, I wondered if this might be death coming for me, as I've always lived with its shadow—diagnosed with cystic fibrosis at a young age, there are days I'm convinced my lungs are failing. Despite the darkness, I'm not afraid. In fact, I feel more alive than I have in years. In this mysterious place, which I believe is "deep sleep," I can breathe easily. I'm free from pain, and my body feels strong, rejuvenated, and powerful. There's a constant buzz of energy surrounding me, almost as if it's inviting me to interact with it. I have an intense feeling that I'm here to learn something important, though I'm unsure what it is. The ground beneath me feels cold and damp. Before I drifted off to sleep, I genuinely believed tonight would be the night I left this world for good. Yet, in this darkness, I sense the humming energy filling my body, purging the bad and making space for something new. It's as if it's replacing my failing lungs with something fresh. Like magic. Not the kind of magic from children's shows, but a potent force connected to the earth, weaving itself inside me and repairing me. It feels both warm and cold simultaneously, light and dark at the same time. I feel the power intensifying, and just when I start to believe this might actually be real, that I'm not dreaming, a sound slices through the air, jolting me awake and back into reality.

I wake up drenched in sweat, struggling to catch my breath. The noise is so intense, it seems to be emanating from within me. Then I realize it's just my phone ringing. I clumsily search through the darkness of my room to silence it. When I spot the number on the screen, my heart skips a beat—it's the transplant line. I believe I manage to say "hello," though I'm not entirely certain. The woman on the other end is calm and composed as she confirms my details and asks me to wait. Moments feel like hours, days even, and when she comes back on the phone, she tells me to report to Grace Memorial immediately for pre-op. This is the call I have been waiting for since I was young. I have had a hospital bag packed for years just for this. I cannot trust myself to drive, so I have had the apartment manager on alert since he offered to help. I grab my bag and make my way out the door and down the hall to his. Three knocks is all it takes for him to swing the door open, he doesn't ask questions, he's been waiting for this day just as I have. My family offered to move here to be nearby, but I was tired of being a burden to those I love. Instead, I found people less invested.

The moment I step into the hospital, the staff recognizes the reason for my visit. I'm a familiar face, frequently in and out of the facility. They escort me straight to the surgical floor and settle me into a room. When my doctor arrives, there's no need for him to go over everything again; we've been through this before and covered all the details then. I'm aware that every surgery carries risks, and a transplant adds even more. As always, the chaplain comes in to talk with me, helping me mentally prepare for the possibility of things not going as planned. He's an older gentleman with a genuine smile on his face. He sat by my bed and prayed over me. He asked me if I had any questions, but I couldn't answer. I know at this moment I am definitely awake, but the same buzz of energy fills my head, the same feeling I had in my dream. I guess since I did not respond, he said he would be back with a nurse to answer any questions I may have.

Once he exits the room, the buzzing intensifies, growing louder and more palpable, almost tangible enough to grasp. Outside my window, the first signs of dawn appear, though the sun has yet to conquer the darkness. Just when the buzz swells to a point where it feels overwhelming, a brilliant streak of green light flashes across the sky and through my room, somehow assuring me that everything will be okay. I'm aware that the chaplain has re-entered the room with the nurse, but I can't concentrate on them. The buzzing sensation is overwhelming, coursing through my body with such intensity that I'm unsure how much more I can endure. Then, someone touches my hand— SHE touches my hand. Instantly, the buzzing ceases, and I'm left feeling comforted. It felt as though the energy was trying to convey a message, attempting to connect me with her in some way, almost like a guide. In the depths of my mind, the voice from my dream softly urges me to trust her. The magical sensation from my dreams surges through me, momentarily easing the pain of my illness. The voice assures me that I was chosen, just like she was. While I could suspect the onset of a mental illness, there's an undeniable sense of reality to this experience—extraordinary, yes, but not an illusion.

The sensation grows stronger, as though anticipating my reaction, but I'm not following its guidance. The voice in my head becomes louder, drowning out everything else. It urges me toward her—not in a romantic, movie-like manner, but more objectively, as if guiding me to her. It's as though there's an unseen mission linking us, and she, too, is part of it. Could she be sensing it as well?

"Do you believe in magic?" It comes out before I can stop it, I instantly regret saying something so childish, until I realize she is looking at me like…like she felt it too.

Three

Aria

The atmosphere is charged with such intensity, it reminds me of my dream. I was managing to ignore it quite well until he asked the pivotal question. I glance at the chaplain, who remains by the door, seemingly oblivious to the electric tension surrounding us, and truly paying us no attention. If I were one of those romantic fantasy readers, I might interpret this charge as a sign of destined attraction. My imagination would fill with tales convincing me that I had unknowingly discovered my soulmate. That's not what the buzz is. It's something different. Something ethereal, out of reach but screaming to be held onto. I felt it in the dream, just like I feel it now. But I have to push the strange feeling to the side because, let's be honest, I am a professional at work, where I am expected to do my job, not chase dreams. We don't speak aside from his question. My hand remains on his, creating a wave of awkwardness that washes over me. To dispel that feeling, I do the only thing that comes to mind in the moment: I pray with him. I can sense tendrils of his pain flowing from his hand into mine. With my eyes closed, I pray for every step of his transplant to go smoothly. I hope he doesn't reject it, that his body thrives, and that he experiences rejuvenation.

As I continue to pray, the humming sound gradually returns to the room, softer and more controlled. I feel it within me, a tingling sensation traveling down my arm and into his hand. Perhaps I'm imagining things… I didn't get much sleep, and it's been a long day. I'm aware of the effects of sleep deprivation. I finish my prayer and open my eyes to find him looking at me. Is it fear? Confusion? I'm not sure what I see in his eyes. He asked me about magic, but I dismissed it, unsure of how to respond. I inform him that his transplant team should arrive soon and express my hopes for a successful surgery.

After finishing my shift, I move from one room to another, trying to shake off the memory of that encounter. It feels like it's trailing me, just beyond my grasp, insisting that I acknowledge it. Two hours later, the hospital's front doors slide open, greeting me with a cool evening breeze. Today dragged on, but every day seems endless. I still have enough time to run some errands before attempting to catch up on sleep tonight. Tomorrow is my day off, but it's packed with unpacking tasks so I can stop paying for that storage unit. I need to buy cleaning supplies because using window cleaner for everything is impractical. I also need groceries, as today's lunch is long gone, and my fridge only contains ketchup and milk.

***

I made a quick trip to the store, intending to pick up just the essentials, but somehow ended up returning with bags filled with unnecessary items—like many women tend to do on "grocery runs." After unpacking, I settle onto the bean bag that currently serves as my living room furniture and enjoy my dinner. My feet are grateful for the break. I glance around my new place and smile, knowing I need to eventually get some proper furniture, but it feels great to have a fresh start. I have tons of ideas for how I want my space to look; I just need to find the time to make it happen! Before I can do that, though, I need to sort through the stuff I put in storage. I mentally list the items I kept, estimating it will take me just half a day to sort them out tomorrow. When I began packing for the move, I promised myself that anything I didn't love or could easily replace had to go. So, I'm left with just the simple essentials. My bed welcomes me with a warm embrace as I crawl in, I don't think it will take much to fall asleep tonight. I close my eyes and lay perfectly still, allowing each part of my body to go numb, a trick I learned during a yoga and meditation class. It's raining outside which massages my mind and lulls me into a trance. Moments later, I am slipping into a perfect state of slumber.

"Here is where you find the answers, ask the right questions," the woman's ethereal voice whispers into every hidden cranny of my mind. I find myself once again beyond familiar walls, standing in a damp realm that smells of rich, recent earth—a scent that has grown strangely welcoming. The twilight now offers a clearer glimmer, undeniably a sunset, hinted at through a veil of mysterious trees. All around me, darkness reigns as if the dying light is light-years away, its gentle radiance unable to overcome the enveloping gloom. Yet, the darkness itself holds no dread.

"I don't know the questions," I murmur, my voice barely escaping, "Where am I?" as if that might be a stepping stone.

"Where you are is not of importance now. Seek out the right questions," the voice replies, carrying an enigmatic urgency.

"Who are you?" I counter.

"Who I am is an answer you are not yet prepared to receive, child." The word "child" reverberates through me like a soft yet stern chant, a signal that I have ventured into forbidden territory with my inquiry. A subtle warning—an echo of time wasted on aimless questions—I heed as I press on. "Okay," I stammer, bracing myself, "is this a dream?" My words hang in the air, laden with trepidation, praying that this question does not unburden more than it should.

"Yes, it is a dream, child, but humans are woven into a fate they scarcely comprehend, with the lie that dreams are mere illusions," she intones, each syllable seeming to pulse with a weight beyond its surface.

"What do you mean by fate?" I venture, only to be met by a long, enchanted silence—no nocturnal whispers, no rustling leaves, only the void of expectant space.

"That is the right question," she finally says in a tone softened by both care and warning. *"You are all ensnared by a condition that began long ago, where perception is the key to reality. Yet perceptions are mutable, and when they are unbalanced, transformations occur—reality itself is slowly compromised. This imbalance endures too long, and consequences stir on the horizon, yet there is hope for correction."*

"Umm, ok….How can it be restored?" I ask, the quiver in my voice mingling with wonder, fear, and…. confusion.

"Child, you are among the chosen, but it is not our purpose to enact change on your behalf—merely to illuminate the path ahead. Trials will arise, and your responses will reveal whether destiny has indeed found its rightful bearer. Remember to look beyond the confinements of your known world—the legacy of your history—and question every certainty. Keep your mind open to what lies

hidden, for a closed mind is the true peril of our condition."

Before another inquiry can take shape in my thoughts, the vibrant orange of the sunset abruptly shimmers into a luminous green, and a pulsating, magical hum envelops me. The buzz intensifies with every heartbeat, resonating deep within every cell, until just when I believe I cannot endure another moment of its overwhelming power—I wake up.

My eyes fly open. I don't move. I can't move. It was a dream, I mean the voice confirmed it was a dream. Are dreams some sort of reality? I'm on trial? Or wait, there will be trails? How will I know when it's a trial? Wait - hold on! I am smart, I make good choices, I am educated, and now I'm sitting here questioning my sanity due to a dream. But what if it was real in some form, and I failed because I was questioning it? Can I do both? Be smart and sane on the inside and feed into my insanity on the outside? I look over and see that it's seven am, it felt like 5 minutes but I somehow got a full night's sleep. So I'm not delirious from the lack of sleep. I am not alone, she said "one" of the chosen, and she must not be alone either because she said, "we."

I drag myself to the shower to kick off the day. Today's main task is to clear out the storage unit. I feel a bit different, possibly because I finally got a good night's sleep. The shower feels as refreshing as my bed did. I could stay here forever, but the small hot water tank reminds me I can't. I grab a towel, step out, and head to the sink. I dry off, brush my teeth, comb my hair, apply lotion, and perform the usual facial check for any annoying pimples. That's when I notice it. My eyes have always been grayish blue. Sometimes, depending on what I wear, they appear to change shades, but gray is their constant color. Now, there's a ring of green around the pupil, extending into the gray like brush strokes. Since I'm wrapped in a white towel, it can't be my clothing. That's something new.

My eye color is identical to my mother's, a striking gray that we both share. My hair mirrors hers too; it's a dark, deep brown, almost black but not quite, and as straight as a board. My father passed down his thin button nose and high cheekbones to me, and my long, thick eyelashes are unmistakably his, unlike my mother's barely-there lashes. As for my lips, I'm not sure where they come from—while both my parents have thin, small lips, mine are full and naturally pink. My friends often say I'm lucky and don't need trendy fillers. Both my parents have fair skin, which makes me wonder about my more olive complexion. It could be from my mom's dad, whom I never met. I throw on some old clothes and head out the door to check the storage unit off my list.

In just two hours, I managed to sort through all the items I had stored in the unit. I efficiently packed everything into the car, using the trunk, back seat, and front seat space wisely. Unloading it into the house took even less time. I meticulously unpacked each jar of herbs, cleaned them, and arranged them on the kitchen shelves in an apothecary style. Growing up, I often visited my grandma's house, and she's the reason I have this herb collection. She taught me which flowers to pick and save, their uses, and how to dry them. As a child, I was fascinated by how we'd pick flowers in a field and then have a tea party with tea made from those very flowers. At the time, I didn't realize that my grandmother was giving me my first lessons in medicine. I always thought my grandmother was full of magic, I would watch her while hiding in the doorway while she meticulously worked her herbs. Sometimes she would make movements with her hands that looked as if she were practicing some form of interpretive dance. The child in me concocted all kinds of magical stories up in my head, pretending that her hand movements were her way of working with the magic in the air.

During nursing school, I took an extracurricular class on cultural medicine which focused on natural healing methods. Teas and tinctures are the base of most lost cultural medicines, many using some of the same flowers my grandma and I picked. Ever since that class, I have made it a hobby to learn and collect herbs for treating minor aches and pains at home. It makes me feel close to my grandma again. She passed away when I was 13, I didn't even realize how much I loved her until she was not here anymore. I smile as I set the last jar on the shelf, stepping back and admiring my mini apothecary. The last few boxes are simple things, most going in the cabinet in the bathroom, or hung up in my closet. After another hour, I am done. Check box checked. I am officially completely moved in. It's only 2 pm so there's time to go browse the local thrift shops for some trendy home items I can flip to match the vibe I want.

Four

Aria

It's 2 am for crying out loud. Who could possibly be calling me at this hour? Where did I put my cell phone? I grope around in the dark, searching through the sheets as the ringing persists. The more time passes without finding it, the more anxious I become. What if it's about home? What if there's a problem? My hand finally reaches under the pillow, and I grab my phone, quickly pulling it out to see the hospital's number flashing on the screen.

"Hello"

"Is this Aria? This is Mildred, house supervisor at the hospital."

"Yes, is something wrong?"

"No, dear! Sorry to call at this hour! Bethany hurt her back and won't be able to come in this morning for her shift. I know it's your day off, but I was hoping there would be a chance that you would be able to cover her shift today?"

"Oh… OK, no problem, I will be there. I hope Bethany is OK!" I reply

"Thank you, dear, we really appreciate it!" Mildred says

I hang up the phone and sigh, "Welcome to healthcare." Mildred was kind about it; it was her first time calling me in. Anyone in the healthcare field knows staffing is short everywhere. I'm sure Mildred has to make these calls every day. Still, she was nice. I set my alarm for 5 a.m., hoping I can catch a bit more sleep. I need to use the bathroom, so I slide out of bed, keeping my eyes mostly shut to hold onto the drowsiness. Moments later, I'm back in bed and, thankfully, drifting back to sleep.

"*Child, there will be moments when you find yourself in realms where the line between truth and illusion blurs. Embrace the unknown, for it is through unknowing that you shall learn all,*" the voice whispers, ethereal and ancient. The sunset now blazes with an enchanting luminance, revealing more than ever before. To my left, a Japanese maple tree stands, its leaves a deep, enchanting crimson with golden fringes glistening in the fading light.

"*We are your guides along this mystical path, yet remember, the journey is yours and the other chosen's. Beware those who seek to sow seeds of doubt in your heart."* The voice, once omnipresent, now emanates from the direction of the tree, tender and nurturing. It resonates with a warmth that soothes my soul. My gaze is drawn to the tree, where something elusive catches my eye, though its nature remains hidden. The air is thick with a warm, earthy aroma, interwoven with a subtle floral scent that whispers of secrets yet to be unveiled.

"What is happening to me?" I implore, for I feel as if I'm teetering on the brink of madness, choosing favorites among the voices of my dreams.

"We have spoken, you are one of the chosen. Time is fleeting; we cannot afford to chase the same inquiries twice," she responds.

As if a veil is lifted, my vision sharpens, revealing her true form. Beneath the maple tree, she stands—an owl, yet no ordinary owl. She towers the size of a majestic horse, her feathers a pristine snow white, adorned with intricate golden filigree. The edges of her wings appear to have been brushed with midnight ink. Her eyes glow like amber, swirling with galaxies of shimmering starlight. The longer I gaze, the more hues unfold—waves of gold and green, dancing within the celestial swirl. She is a vision of terrifying beauty.

"My name is Ophelian, and I am here to guide you. Trust only in what your heart knows to be true, for this is how you shall fulfill your destiny."

I wake up, unlike the times before, I don't feel as if I was thrown from sleep but gently eased from it. I am a smart person with a good education. I have not made it where I am today falling for any old thing someone throws my way. Nor am I naive. So why am I sitting here allowing myself to feel like this is real, like this is normal? Everything inside of my being says it's real, but parts of my brain are telling me I am delusional. Suddenly my alarm fires off shaking me from my thoughts and instantly my muscle memory kicks in. I grab the phone and hit stop, making the fog horn quiet. I can muddle over this later, for now, I have a shift to cover.

***

Denise is smiling at me from the reception desk as I walk in the front doors.

"Hey, darlin! I didn't think you worked today?" she says.

"I'm covering a call out" I smirk back at her.

"Well, I hope your day goes smoothly! I just put on fresh coffee over there if you want some!" she says back.

"Aw, thanks, Miss Denise! Sounds like you're telling me I look tired!" I laugh.

"Honey, at this hour, we are all tired!" Denise says with a laugh.

I thank her and grab a cup before the elevator doors open up. I run through all the pre-op patients first to make sure they are ready for their procedures before moving on to my post-op patients. Three total knee replacements are first, they are easy, they are mostly still here for physical therapy to work with. I have one elderly patient who just had a colostomy placed, one female with a hip replacement due to a recent fall, and one post-op lung transplant patient. The elderly man was pleasant, with no complaints. The female requested some pain medication, she is feeling bad today. I pull her medicine out of the machine and take it to her before walking down to the next patient.

I read some of the details on his chart before heading in there in case I need to grab any supplies ahead of time. *Archer Brooks. 24 years old. 48 hours post-op. Admitting diagnosis: lung transplant due to cystic fibrosis.* Dang. 24 is young, but at least he got this done early in life — less time in pain. I quickly scan the doctor's orders: *wound care to surgical site qday. up to chair bid, turn q2hrs. o2@2l if stat drops below 90% ORA.* Typical orders for a patient 48 hours out, the only thing that strikes me as odd is that there are no pain meds ordered as needed, which means he is doing way better than expected.

As I place my hand on the door handle, I can already feel it, the buzz of electricity that has become familiar over the last few days. I remember - this is the patient the chaplain took me to. My heart picks up a few beats as the buzz continues to grow. I press the door open and look towards the bed. He's... well, he's different. I know it's the same guy, but he looks like the surgery breathed life back into him at an accelerated pace. I gather myself quickly, I don't want to seem rude, but I also don't want to freak my patient out by standing in the doorway gawking at him. I make it to his bedside, placing my stethescope to his chest. *Bilateral breath sounds even and unlabored.* I take mental notes. *Heart auscultation normal.* And that is when I see it *No redness or swelling present at the incision site* - there is barely even a site to document, there should be a vertical incision running over his chest, but instead, there is only a tan, muscular chest that seems to defy the very idea of surgery.

His skin carries a warm, healthy glow, and the absence of any visible scars or marks where the incision should be is perplexing. I can't help but marvel at the transformation, as I inspect closer, the contours of his chest reveal a perfect blend of strength and grace. The muscles ripple beneath the smooth surface, and I find myself momentarily captivated by the surreal scene before me. It's as if the surgery not only healed him but sculpted a masterpiece. I wonder if he notices the absence of the expected scar, or if this miraculous recovery is as much a mystery to him as it is to me. The air in the room hums with an unspoken question, and I feel the weight of curiosity pressing against my professional demeanor. As the buzz grows stronger, I can hear his heart rate increase. I pull my eyes off his chest and decide it best to walk away, I need to gather myself.

I walk to the door as I hear the memory of Ophelian in my ear. She told me what to do, is this part of it? Is this a test? Does he know? Is that why his heart rate increased? My hand is on the door handle and my body is halfway out the entryway when I make the decision to step outside of my professional self and possibly make a fool out of myself. I quietly shut the door and turned around, bracing my back against the door as if I needed it to hold me steady. His facial expression doesn't look like a confused patient, but that of a person who has been caught doing something. He knows.

"What is going on here? I know you feel that. And… and you're basically healed. You asked me. You… you asked me if I believe in magic. So I ask again. What is going on here?" I blurt out before I can even think of what I am about to say.

Five

Archer

There is a knock at the door to my hospital room followed by the entrance of a surgical nurse and my surgeon. "Archer Brooks, 24 years old, post-op lung transplant surgery. So far vitals, labs, and scans have all been normal, with no signs of infection or rejection. Breath sounds remain even and unlabored in all four quadrants. The incision site is healing well with no infection present" the nurse spits out to the doc.

"Mr. Brooks, how are you feeling today? Have any questions or concerns for us?" he asks.

I let him know I am feeling great in comparison to how I felt before the surgery. They let me know they will get updated scans and more routine lab work in the morning, and to keep breathing into the contraption on my table at least every hour, reminding me that I need to make the ball inside of it move to know I am doing it right. They smile and remind me to use my call light if I need any help as they exit the room. I'm to start getting from this bed to the chair tomorrow, which sounds like a simple task, but I know I will be sore. I do not want any unnecessary pain medications. I've lost too many people around me to the opioid epidemic to take a chance.

I have been careful with my body since I was a child. It used to annoy me that my mother was a health nut, but lying here in this bed, I appreciate her so much more for instilling healthy standards into my habits. Aside from the cystic fibrosis I have dealt with, I am healthy. I know that a transplant is not a cure, but it gives me more time. More chances to fight. The habits I obtained from my mom will always help me fight. Help keep me healthy enough to fight. I breathe into the spirometer thing until I'm too tired. I have a couple of hours of peace before the next round of nurses come in to check on me, so sleep it is.

***

The darkness envelops me like a familiar cloak, as it does each time I drift into slumber. It's become oddly reassuring, grounding in a way I hadn't anticipated. The dampness, once unsettling, now holds a strange allure. A deep, resonant voice echoes through my very being, *"Are you prepared to pose the questions?"*

"I am uncertain of what questions I should ask," I respond.

"Time wanes, and your strength dwindles, so I shall aid you this once. Soon, your vitality will return, for you have been chosen, and you hold significance. You shall not succumb to illness. This has been decreed," the voice intones, not as a suggestion but as a command to my essence.

"We required your presence here, through this journey, at this precise juncture to intersect with others of the chosen. We could have intervened earlier, but this was essential. Today, we have bestowed aid upon you, placing you ahead of others, so employ it to support them," another voice, tender yet firm, whispers.

A hush descends. I hadn't thought the darkness could deepen, yet it does. An ancient voice resounds, *"Child, you are among the chosen, but it is not our role to act for you, only to guide your path. Only fragments of your beliefs are true; others are woven into the human experience. Trials will emerge, and your response will reveal if our choice was just. Ponder beyond your reality, beyond the teachings of history, question all you assume you know, and embrace the unknown. The human condition favors a closed mind; seek support from your kind, but do so in silence."*

As the final word reverberates, a blinding light and resounding crash pierce through me, each cell in my body buzzing with energy —both soothing and unsettling. And then I fall... endlessly into the abyss.

I sit up searching for air, searching the room around me, forcing the air down into my lungs. The machines attached to me are beeping out of control, I don't know what all the numbers on the monitor mean, but I can see that my pulse rate is 118. The door bursts open and the nurses rush in. Everything happens in a whirlwind it takes me a moment to realize, I wasn't falling. It was the dream. My pulse slows down, air enters my lungs, and the fire that my body felt moments ago eases.

"Mr. Brooks, are you feeling OK?" The nurse asks me while she shines a light in my eyes to check my pupils.

"Yes, it was a ... a ...dream I guess" I stutter out. The beeping calms back down to an even rhythm and the team of nurses in my room look relieved. They remind me they will be right outside at the desk if I need them and show me the call light button.

I mentally go over everything that just happened. They are dreams. I feel crazy because they are just dreams. I have always believed in greater forces, God, angels, miracles, and such. I feel it in my bones that this is magic. Not silly kid magic with rainbows and unicorns, but an ethereal magic. Some would say to believe in God means you cannot believe in magic, but I feel differently. How could one believe that one would create this entire universe but put magic off the table? Come on! I would feel really stupid right now even contemplating all of this, if it wasn't for the leftover buzz running through my body. I can feel it, working and mending. I feel it in my new lungs, I feel it in my organs, tissues, bones. I sit up, no pain. I stand up, no struggle, no pain. I take a step, same thing. I walk, all the way to the bathroom with no struggle. I don't remember a time since childhood that I felt this... so strong. The feeling is overwhelming, and then I look at myself in the mirror. I look healthy, there's color in my face, my skin looks hydrated, I look... different. I did not realize all this time how much being sick has taken a toll on my looks. I am not one hundred percent myself yet, but as quickly as things have changed I know it won't take long. I look closely in the mirror, my eyes are different, not "I'm finally healthy" different, they aren't the same color as normal.

There is a gray color surrounding my pupil, bleeding its way into the deep brown of my iris. My eyes have always been deep brown, but with my health, they always appeared dull. The brown in my eyes is now deep and rich — healthy. It's the gray ring that is new. I peel off the hospital gown to look at my incision — it's almost completely gone. This is when the panic sets in. If the doctor comes in tomorrow to check me and sees that there's nothing to check...I will become a science experiment. They could accept it as a miracle that I'm performing better, but not that I was able to heal an entire chest incision overnight. I could leave - check out AMA, but the team has been so good to me throughout my treatment I couldn't put them through the worry. Hold it together Archer…. Think…. It's 7 pm. Unless there is an emergency, the doctor will not be coming into the room tonight. The night shift doesn't bother me too much, so there isn't much that could happen tonight. I can figure out what to do when morning comes, if it comes down to it, I will just have to slip out the doors. Sleep.

***

The sun is up.

My incision is gone.

There is no way to explain.

I need to get out of here.

I get up to grab my bag as the door swings open and the nurse walks in.

It's just the nurse, not the doctor, maybe she won't look. She looks familiar, I think it's the nurse that came in when the chaplain was here. Maybe she won't notice. I sit back down as she goes over the labs and scans they want to do today. She presses a cold stethoscope to my back and listens, telling me that my lungs sound perfect. She places it on my chest to listen to my heart, she looks confused, and she realizes there is no incision, she realizes I don't look the same as when she prayed for me. The buzz starts, and it spreads from my chest to her fingers on the stethoscope on my chest, her eyes widen slightly, and she makes eye contact with me. Her eyes…. The green in her eyes spreads from the pupil just as the gray does in mine, the same gray as the outer part of her iris. She doesn't say a word. She stands and makes her way to the door. She starts to walk out, and stops, closing the door and placing her back against it instead, facing me, confused.

And then, words pour from her mouth like water from a busted pipe. "What is going on here? I know you feel that. And… and you're basically healed. You asked me. You… you asked me if I believe in magic. So I ask again. What is going on here?"

Six

Archer

" I don't know," I say to her. I mean, honestly, I don't. If I tell her what I am thinking of, I will most definitely end up on the psych floor. I mean, voices in my head and hallucinations, psych consult for sure. "OK, well the way I see it is, no matter what is actually going on here, in about thirty minutes, your surgeon will be walking through that door to lay eyes on you himself. The second that he sees your chest — you become a case study. So, the big question is... what do we do about it?" She blurts out to me.

I can tell that she is freaking out, she's speaking a million words per second. But, she's right. "Tell me what you think I should do. Those doctors have been helping me for years, if I walk out the door, it will make me look like I don't appreciate everything they have done. If I stay, there's no way I can answer their questions without ending up committed for a grippy sock vacation in the psych ward." Honesty. The best policy.

"So then, tell me what's going on. I can keep our conversation confidential, no one has to know unless you're a harm to yourself or someone else, then I have a responsibility," She says, this time she's calmer.

"I have dreams. Dreams that feel weird. I haven't paid much attention to them, even though there were feelings in the dream that lingered over into when I was awake. And then, well, the voice in my dream basically told me I was healed. I woke up and, like he said, I was healed. There was also the day the chaplain brought you into my room, the humming, or electric feeling from the dream was everywhere in here that morning until you touched my hand." Honesty right? She will either walk out of the room and call a psychiatrist, or — there is a slim chance she will believe me.

"Um." She says while staring at the wall right past me. "OK, I don't think you're manic or anything. Or, maybe you are but to say that you are would be to say that I am as well. Sure - it could be a hallucination, but two people who don't know each other having the same exact hallucination cannot be a coincidence. I don't think. Right? I mean, if they haul you off for a psych eval they would have to take me too -"

"Wait, are you saying you know what I am talking about, or have seen it, or felt it" I interrupt her. "I'm sorry, that was rude," I say as I can clearly see that she is processing something, most likely the same thing that I am processing. She looks scared. She's beautiful though, which is not what I should be noticing right now.

"OK, first, do you have somewhere you can go? If you go home to a wife or family, they are going to question why you're out so fast. If you stay here we know where that is going." She says matter of factly.

"I have an apartment, been sick since I was a kid, so no time for finding a wife or making a family." I awkwardly reply. "The only person that ever pays attention to me is my apartment manager, he is who drove me in the other night, he wouldn't notice my chest, but he may want to check in on me."

"OK, you should go home. I can document all your normal findings, and you can slip out down the stairs, no one will notice right away. When they read your chart and see that there is nothing abnormal to report, they will freak out just a little less when they find your bed empty. Don't talk to anyone who knows why you were here, including your apartment manager" She says as she takes out a little notepad out of her pocket and scribbles something down. "Here is my cell phone number, I get off at 7, call me — or text me. If you're OK with that. We should meet up and talk about what's happening. The things you say you have dreamt, or seen, or felt - me too. And, I was told that I was *one* of the chosen, whatever that means, but that means I am not the only one and there is a chance that you and I are in the same strange boat." She hands me the piece of paper with her number on it, gives me a nod, and leaves the room.

I don't even hesitate. I get out of bed, prepared to feel the pain, but it doesn't come. I grab the few things I brought with me. I throw my clothes back on and peek out the door. Everyone in the hallway is busy scurrying through the halls, no one is even looking in my direction. I throw my bag over my shoulder and walk out of the room, being sure to make myself look like a visitor instead of a patient. The door to the stairwell is two doors down. I dip inside and make my way down the stairs without anyone noticing me. In all the hustle I didn't even think about the fact that I don't have a car here. My apartment manager drove me here. I open my phone to pull up the car service app and schedule a ride, 5 minutes later a white car pulls up to pick me up.

I walk into my apartment and drop my stuff on the counter. It's not even lunchtime yet. I have at least seven hours left until the strangest conversation of my life is going to happen. I am going to get some sleep.

"You have questions," intones a voice, its words hanging in the air as though spun from ancient enchantments. It is not a query but a declaration, resonating amid a forest that feels both timeless and otherworldly.

Here, magic dances through the air and murmurs among the leaves—a mystical woodland like no other. I lie beneath a colossal canopy where radiant sunlight filters through intertwining branches, painting the forest floor with flickering, dappled light. From every corner of the globe, trees have gathered in harmonious unity: mighty oaks stand shoulder to shoulder with graceful willows; tall redwoods share secrets with delicate cherry blossoms. Each tree, bearing the essence of its distant homeland, contributes to a living symphony of hues, textures, and evocative scents, whispering tales of faraway lands.

Beneath me, a lush carpet of vibrant green moss blankets the earth—its softness inviting gentle, measured steps. The moss cradles ancient mysteries in its cool, emerald embrace, as though nature itself had laid out a living masterpiece upon which every footfall becomes an artist's brushstroke. A subtle shimmer of gold drifts through the air; tiny, ethereal particles capture the sunlight, casting an otherworldly glow upon all that surrounds us. This magical luminescence deepens the forest's enigma, a place where dreams meld with reality. Delicate ferns, with fronds like whispered secrets, curl gently around tree bases, extending their verdant tendrils as if to share the timeless wisdom carried by the rustling leaves. In this serene haven, time seems to hold its breath, filled with a soft symphony of rustling foliage, distant birdsong, and the silent hum of unseen magic.

"Time is of the essence; speak your questions, child," the voice commands from somewhere near, its tone both urgent and enigmatic. "What is this place, and who are you?" I ask, my words suspended in the magical stillness.

The voice, imbued with the authority of an ancient guardian, responds with calm regality. *"I am Lexora, and you now dwell in the subconscious realm—the Arcane Nexium —a realm nestled between the present and the distant past, where the custodians of magic silently govern the recesses of our minds. It is a forgotten dream, a place once known to all but now sealed away. Yet forces beyond reckoning have swung open its gates, unveiling secrets and wonders long hidden, though only for the chosen few. Beware, for if this task falters, the gates shall close once more. Though our realm exists at the fringes of reality, it is the very source of the power coursing through your world. Centuries ago, history locked these gates, and the repercussions of that act now threaten your realm if left unraveled."*

"What is the task?" I press, yearning for further insight.

"I can only guide you," she murmurs, her tone layered with mystery and caution. *"Reveal not all, for if I bestow upon you what you are not yet meant to know, the task itself shall crumble. Listen well, child: you must seek your counterparts, for this journey is not for one alone. A chosen team awaits, and*

you must not speak of these matters outside your kind for the time being."

"How many others are there?" I inquire.

In that moment, as if emerging from the very mists of magic, she steps forward into the light. Her beauty is so profound that I nearly lose myself to wonder. She transcends mortal form, embodying the grace and raw power of a mythical tiger. Majestic and regal, she stands tall, her emerald green gaze locking with mine. A vision of purity, her fur is as white as untouched snow, adorned with bold, jet-black stripes that trace her untamed elegance. Intricate golden filigree winds over her form like divine art, enhancing her ethereal presence.

"I cannot reveal that, for it is forbidden by the laws of our ancient tribunal. In time, when the coven is complete, you shall know, for the hands of time themselves are in motion. AWAKEN."

Before I could even realize what was happening, a force pushed me back and the next time I opened my eyes I was in my room. I grab my phone and it's after seven, I grab the scrap of paper off the nightstand and dial the nurses number. I don't even remember if she told me her name...

Seven

Jaliah

I have to get my life on track. I've been in this city for two years, and I'm still working at the diner. I have tried to leave about thirty times, but every time I attempt to talk to Tim, the owner, I end up feeling bad since finding decent servers is next to impossible. Honestly, I probably make more in a week here than if I were to work at a department store or something. The diner is situated in a good place, with the hospital two blocks away on one side and the courthouse four blocks to the other side. We end up getting customers who know how to tip. Thankfully, we don't have to wear silly diner uniforms, as long as our lady parts aren't flaunted, Tim is pretty lenient on the dress code. Yet, there's only so many cups of coffee or plates of loaded fries one person can serve without going stir-crazy. I check myself over in the mirror one more time before I walk out the door. White tank top, red blazer, torn black shorts on top of opaque black leggings, finished off with a pair of zip-up combat boots. I fluff my hair, gloss my lips, and I'm out the door. I don't live in a fancy apartment, but it's far from the small, crowded foster home I grew up in.

My father was never in the picture; all I know is that he was a rich Argentinian man who never knew that he got my mama pregnant. The only thing I got from him was my soft, bouncy hair and lighter skin complexion. Mama worked hard to provide for me, but she passed away when I was seven. She had an autoimmune disease, so when she got sepsis from a procedure, her body couldn't fight. I see my mama in my eyes every time I look in the mirror, well, until lately. She always had soft hazel eyes that popped against her skin, Mama was beautiful. I've had some wild dreams I dare not tell anyone about lately. So many strange things have been happening, but the strangest are my eyes. My eyes aren't as light as Mama's were, but they were close. Now, there is a ring of purple around my pupils, and it looks like an artist brushed the purple delicately out into my hazel. I saw a man look at them in confusion last night at work, so I just smiled and told him it was my contacts.

I walk into the diner and see Shana drowning in customers, and of course, there's no busboy tonight. I throw my apron around my waist and get to work. My first table is a man and his wife, they are sweet, been married for 36 years the man tells me. My second table is a guy and a girl my age, maybe. I thought they were on a date at first, but if they are, it's for sure a first one. They look painfully awkward. She's in scrubs, so I assume she works at Grace Memorial. He is in a pair of jeans and a very fitted black t-shirt, it shows off every carving of his body perfectly. He is sitting of course, but he looks tall. I like tall men, not that I'm checking out this chick's date or anything. I have a habit of people-watching my customers, painting a story of their lives. Sometimes I bet the stories I paint are far more exciting than their real lives. She's not his sister, they look nothing alike, her skin is tan, not like from a tanning bed, like she was born that way. His is tanned too, but not as tan as hers. He is tall of course, maybe 6'2", but she looks to be around 5'3", give or take. She has dark straight hair, and he has light brown wavy hair cut short, but long enough on the top, that I can tell it is wavy.

"Jaliah — order up" the cook yells snapping me out of my people-watching trance. I grab the tray full of food and deliver it to the older couple, smiling and letting them know to wave at me if they need anything else, and that I will be right back to top off their waters. I approach the table with the young couple to take their order, "We'll have coffee for now" the girl says with a smile. I return moments later and fill their cups, that's when I feel it. The electricity that stirs in the air, like a magnet holding me there with them.

I've been dealing with this a lot here lately. I almost wonder if it is seizure-like activity, so I look at the girl. Scrubs. Possibly a nurse. I want to ask questions but as my mouth begins to move, my eyes lock with hers. She feels it too. Her eyes… they have a green ring just like my purple. I glance over to him… gray ring. I know what the dream people said, but that was in my dreams. Maybe this is a dream? Except, it's not, this is happening. They feel it. I feel it.

"Hi," the girl says, blinking in recognition that we all feel the connection "I'm Aria, and this is Archer. I think…" she pauses as if she is looking for the right words to say, "I think we were supposed to find each other." I don't say anything, I can't, I just turn and walk away, slightly in a panic, completely in confusion, but also, totally aware that this is real, and I am pretty sure she is right. It's what I was told in the dream. *One* of the chosen, not *The* chosen. I walk over to the counter where Shana is standing. I come up with a story that I must have eaten something bad and I need to leave before I spill my stomach contents on the customers. I know it leaves her overworked and understaffed, but there is no way I can focus on the customers right now. I tell her I will drop the ticket off to the table with the young couple on my way out.

I scribble on the back of the ticket for the two coffees, "Griffin Park. Three blocks away. Meet me there" and head over to their table. I smile and let them know I have their check and slide it onto the table and then make my way to the door. My body feels on fire, like if I don't escape right now I am going to combust. The doors open and the cool air hits my skin, caressing it with gentle wisps of freshness, calming down the fire under the surface. I walk straight to the park, no stops, no time to think, straight there.

I know I will have a moment to gather myself before they get here since they still had to pay. I find a picnic table and sit down, staring into the trees that surround the park. *"Close your eyes child"* I hear it - just as it has sounded in my dreams, except — I am awake. Might as well listen, since clearly I am, as they said, not alone in this. I look around the park first, to make sure it's safe for me to sit here like a weirdo with my eyes closed. No one is around, guess that makes sense, it's nighttime, and only weirdos go to the park in the dark.

I'm not asleep; I sense every whisper of reality around me. This time, I peer into the dream realm instead of lying within its grasp. The landscape unfurls as a breathtaking spectacle, reminiscent of Earth yet unlike anything I've ever encountered. It is as if every imaginable terrain has been seamlessly woven into an ethereal tapestry. Golden shimmers dance in the air, casting a magical glow over the surreal surroundings. The boundary between night and morning sky converges vertically at the center, defying the familiar horizontal divide. Before me stands a bear, extraordinary in size and splendor. Cloaked in immaculate white fur and adorned with intricate golden filigree, this magnificent creature exudes an aura of regal mystery. His piercing blue eyes rival the clearest sky on a pristine day, and in his presence, I feel as though I've met a being of unparalleled nobility and mystique.

"How can I be here if I'm not asleep? Every time I come here, I'm asleep—and you're a bear! And—I met people like me, they're on their way here, what's your name?" I blurt out, my thoughts tumbling into questions like a waterfall.

"Calm yourself, child. I am Kobin. You can see without dreaming because the power grows stronger as the chosen assemble. There is seeing alone, and there is seeing together. Trust the others; they travel the same path. More will come. It is vital that the cobal conceals nothing from one another, for secrecy will corrode the bond like a disease devours the body. I am here to guide, but not to lead. Trust your collectives."

My eyes open and I see Aria and Archer walking in my direction. I guess if I am delusional, I am not alone. If they thought I was just a crazy person, they wouldn't have come - I think. Aria and Archer sit down at the table and for the first few moments, none of us say a word. Aria breaks the silence, simply stating that maybe we should all share our stories and get on the same page.

So that is what we do. We've all been experiencing the same things, each learning a little more about what is happening. I tell them what Kobin said, about truth and sharing, seeing as one and seeing as a group. We speculate on translation and coming to the conclusion that while we don't know what is truly going on, it's something we all want to see through till the end. We know that there are more of us, and unless we keep getting lucky and bumping into others, we have to find a way to locate the others.

Eight

Journal of Truths

Article One:

In ancient times, the Earthly Realm and the Arcane Nexium were deeply intertwined, their fates connected by a delicate balance. This long-forgotten era saw a harmonious existence where both realms merged seamlessly. However, in this cosmic harmony, a dark dominion emerged—a sinister realm thriving on chaos and turmoil. Like a malevolent force, it drained the goodness from nearby realms, extinguishing their essence with its insatiable hunger for discord.

Setting its sights on the Earth, the dominion saw a chance to amplify its chaos. By linking itself to the planet, its malevolent influence would surpass all others. In the past, humans and beasts lived in mutual harmony, with beasts supporting humans and humans nurturing beasts, creating a peaceful world without chaos. But then came the encroaching darkness, a cunning and intelligent siphon of evil.

The dominion realized that using humanity as its ultimate weapon would lead to the realm's downfall by instilling a desire for power in human hearts. In this realm, perception shapes reality. By erasing traces of balance from history, reality gradually transforms. The once-majestic beasts that roamed the land are forgotten within the Nexiums, their memory fading from human consciousness.

Though whispers of that ancient era linger among a few, these stories are dismissed as mere myths, altering the perception of reality itself. The insidious dance between the Siphon and the Earthly Realm continues, a cosmic struggle where history's echoes are manipulated, and the fate of both realms hinges on perception and deception.

Nine

Vega

I shift the car into park and prepare myself for the chill in the air as I open the door. The nights have been getting colder here recently. I take my wallet and slip it into my back pocket, close the door, and walk toward the club while pressing the lock button on my key fob. Work was tough today, or so I tell myself to justify meeting Tuck for a drink. Honestly, I prefer the bourbon's company over Tuck's, but it's Friday, and this is our usual routine.

I nod to the bouncer and slip past the line, weaving through the crowd at the entrance. The club's bass thumps through me as I head into the main area. AJAX is the city's hottest spot, often packed to the brim most nights. Fortunately, playing poker with the owner every Tuesday earns me some special privileges.

"Hey! Look who's here, the mountain's own playboy!" Tuck shouts as I reach the bar. I've known Tuck since I moved here a few years back. He was a client at my dad's law firm, and his account was one of the first I handled. We hit it off quickly, bonding over our shared love of bourbon and women. Every Friday, we meet at the same bar, enjoy the same bourbon, and leave with different dates. Having my last name on the city's leading law firm makes finding a date pretty easy.

"Bro, you don't look your usual dapper self tonight! What's going on with ya, man?!" Tuck chuckles out as he slides a drink across to my spot at the bar.

I usually put more effort into how I look, but I haven't been sleeping well this past week. Strange and wild dreams have kept my mind occupied, even during the day. "Nothing major, just a hectic week with long hours, you know how it is," I say, blending truth with omission. Normally, I'd be in a stylish suit that screams wealth, with my hair perfectly styled, but tonight, I couldn't muster the energy. Instead, I opted for comfy yet snug jeans and my favorite dark green t-shirt, which fits just right. I go along with my usual chat with Tuck, humoring his unremarkable ideas. Typically, I'd be quicker with witty comebacks to his jokes, but tonight, I just don't have it in me. Choosing jeans over a suit should have been my cue to stay home. Even as I'm here, I feel like I should be somewhere else. I checked my calendar five times before getting out of the car, as if something inside is warning me not to be here or that something bad is about to happen.

"I'll be back in a bit, man. Just need to hit the restroom," I tell Tuck, though he's more focused on the tall blonde draped over his arm. No matter how upscale a club is, the men's restroom always reflects their poor hygiene. I'm not actually in need of a bathroom break; I just crave a moment of quiet. I hate to break it to Tuck, but I don't have the energy for the bar scene tonight, let alone for any woman who might end up in my bed. Catching my reflection in the mirror, I realize Tuck was right—I don't seem like myself tonight. I could have at least taken a moment to fix my hair. I turn on the cold water, wet my hands, and splash my face to perk up a bit. After giving myself a brief pep talk, I step back into the throng of people moving rhythmically to the music. Once upon a time, this scene made me happy. A sea of unfamiliar faces, pills to heighten the sounds and numb the emotions, bourbon to wash away my worries. Having been born into wealth, I never had to fret much about getting into trouble. This used to satisfy me. But perhaps not anymore.

"Hey, man! I'm about to head out, Tanya, or Tasha, not too sure on the name, but she wants to go for a ride if you know what I mean" Tuck says with a wink.

"Alright man! Same time next week" I say with a laugh, secretly feeling relief that I don't have to keep up the act.

"Yeah just hit me up! See ya!" He says as he heads out the door, draping his arm around the neck of Tanya….. or Tasha.

I wait a moment to give them time to clear the parking lot before I make my way out myself. I slide into the seat of my car and let out the breath I'm holding. As I reach forward to stick the key in the ignition, I hear a voice that has become familiar to me.

"You need to go. They are waiting."

His voice infiltrates every corner of my mind. I had started to become accustomed to it in my dreams, even coming to terms with it, but experiencing it while I'm awake is a new development. I have no idea where I'm supposed to go or who "they" are.

"Who are 'they' and where am I supposed to go?" I ask. "Actually, a better question—who are you? And how are you inside my head?" The irritation in my voice must be evident because as soon as I speak, everything momentarily goes dark. When the light returns, I find myself in the forest I usually see in my dreams. I'm face to face with what appears to be a falcon. He stands impressively tall, large enough for a human to ride. His plumage is bright white, adorned with intricate gold patterns that resemble jewelry. His eyes are golden, with flickers of fire dancing within them, and they seem to hold all the wisdom of the universe.

"I am Atticus, part of the Tribunal. My identity is less important than what you must become. I've warned you of the danger and informed you that you were chosen. More will be disclosed, but first, you must prove your worth. Once, our realms were interconnected, almost merging as one, but humanity unknowingly altered that connection. Now, the bonds between our worlds are weakening, threatening both of our existences. Before the windows between our realms closed, we left elements of our world in yours to eventually help repair these ties. Human minds were gradually manipulated, leading to a loss of knowledge. You and the others must unlock the mind's potential to comprehend more. Seek out the

others. Discover what we left behind. Begin your quest. Remember, time is running short; there's no room for trivial pursuits you call entertainment. I've observed you, Vega, and your mind is squandered on your so-called hobbies. You were chosen for a purpose, don't disappoint us. Everything begins in the forest beneath the mountain. Go there, and we will guide you."

He wraps up his speech, and before I can ask any questions, I'm jolted back to reality. I'm more confused now than I was in the dreams. My task is to locate others who were chosen —complete strangers to me. I need to uncover something left behind from a world I know nothing about, and find a forest beneath the mountain. Simple, right? I start my car and head home, knowing I at least need to gather some supplies… that is — IF I plan to entertain my own inner delusions. Once inside, I toss my keys onto the counter and make a beeline for my room, throwing essentials into my backpack as if I know what I'm doing. Clothes, deodorant, a toothbrush, extra shoes, chargers—I'm running on autopilot, just going through the motions.

I sit on the couch, running my fingers through my hair, trying to collect myself, and maybe trying to decide if I am crazy or not. I can't just hop in the car and drive aimlessly, hoping to land where I'm supposed to be. If I give in and go with this, I would have to assume I'm not insane, that this is real, and I truly had a conversation with a giant falcon. What other choice do I have? If I think about it rationally, I'll go mad. I grab an unused journal from the shelf to jot down my thoughts. I often buy elegant leather-bound journals when I see them, yet never write in them. At work, I jot down notes daily, but always on the old-school legal pads that are plentiful in the supply room. Somehow, I never want to waste the nice journals, but then again, leaving them unused is also a waste.

I quickly jot down every word I can recall from the falcon—Atticus—to preserve its message, then revisit each line to unravel its meaning. Perhaps, with any luck, it will reveal a hint about these so-called "others."

I decide to stop dwelling on the multitude of details all at once and instead focus on one aspect at a time: the woods below the mountain. I open my laptop and launch the GPS. I didn't grow up in this region—after my parents divorced when I was six, I moved to L.A. with my mom because of her job while my dad remained here for his firm. I spent long breaks and holidays out in these parts but didn't truly consider it home until after graduation. My dad did make it a priority to spend quality time with me; we went on countless local excursions as well as trips out of town and overseas. Being in the north means mountains are everywhere, and forests are equally abundant. Narrowing down a specific spot seems challenging, and driving all the options isn't a sensible use of time. As I scroll through the map, an inexplicable pull directs me toward a national forest that lies in a valley below a major mountain range. It isn't just a coincidence—the pull feels like a warm tendril linking my thoughts directly to that precise location. It's an overwhelming sensation that simply feels right. Fuck it. I guess I am going for it.

I pack my bag, toss my laptop inside, grab some extra cash I've stashed in a safe, and head out the door. Once I'm in the car, I set the destination in my GPS and hit start on the navigation system: six hours ahead. I open my email and send a "call-in" message to my dad, letting him know I won't be at the office because I'm chasing a promising lead on a case. Even though it's not entirely untrue, he will likely interpret it as a cover for "wasting my life running the country with random women, throwing money away, and using up all the drugs." With that, I shift the car into drive, silence all the internal doubts, and set off on my journey.

Ten

Aria

If you'd told me a week ago what I'd be doing at this moment, I would have laughed it off. Even now, as I'm in the midst of it, it feels unbelievable. While sitting in the park with Archer and Jaliah, I experienced a sense of doing something genuine for the first time. It's ironic because my daily work involves saving lives, and that's undeniably real. Yet, this feels ten times more authentic, both real and surreal simultaneously. I really don't even know how to explain it. I open the closet and take out the box of camping gear I had stored. It's strange because I parted with most of my unused items, yet kept this camping gear I've only used once. Apparently, there was a reason for keeping it, though I hadn't realized it until now, and also, I tend to collect camping gear for fun. I haven't yet figured out what to call the creatures from the other realm. They seem to be part of a tribunal, but it appears that we each have a different one. For now, I'll refer to them as our guides, as that's what they are cryptically doing. As a group, we have come to the following conclusions:

1. The beings originate from a realm connected to ours.

2. Our realms once flowed seamlessly into each other.

3. A being we refer to as the dark siphon thrives on the chaos and turmoil of a realm.

4. It feeds until that realm eventually collapses, some faster than others.

5. Our realm and the tribunal's realm once coexisted peacefully, with humans and animals living in harmony. During that time, magic was prevalent and normal, and most

animals were larger and more powerful than they are now.

6. The siphon turned its attention to our world, and because Earth has two realms—the realm of man and the realm of magic—it offered a significantly larger source of sustenance for the siphon.

7. The siphon doesn't need to exert its power directly; it simply introduces chaos, which humans naturally gravitate towards. Offering humans power to control others is how our world became what it is now.

8. The connections between the human and magic realms are weakening, and without them, humans will eventually destroy the Earth, causing the siphon to leave, but leaving nothing behind.

9. The magic realm has been trying, with limited access to our realm, to prevent us from destroying everything, but the balance has tipped in favor of chaos over harmony.

10. Nowadays, we dismiss the words and actions of magic as mere child's imagination or make-believe. This happened because we erased it from reality long ago, and if it is consistently excluded from records, it will eventually be forgotten. Children are born with open pathways in their brains, which allows them to believe in the remnants of magic, but we corrupt these pathways by omitting it from teachings. Essentially, we lost the ability to think independently and allowed corrupt teachings to dictate our thoughts.

We know a bit more now, but that's the overall picture. At the moment, our mission is to locate a forest that, based on our collective intuition, we believe is in a particular spot where we'll gather with other chosen individuals to retrieve a relic left behind by the Tribunal in our realm. They say mysterious things surround us—things we're unaware of—so who knows what exactly we might be searching for. I'm not anxious—at least not yet—because when we checked the map to decide on the destination, we all felt the same pull when we marked the location; it was as if we were all drawn to that very point at once. So here I am, packing my gear while everyone else does the same, and then we plan to meet at the park. Archer doesn't own a car anymore—he lost his driving privileges when his illness worsened, though thankfully that's completely resolved now. Jaliah does have a car, but it's too small for all of us to squeeze in. Since my jeep seats at least four, I was chosen to be the driver.

I toss my equipment into the back and head out to rendezvous with the others. Archer is the first to arrive, and I'm amazed at how transformed he looks compared to when I first met him in that hospital bed. His eyes are no longer sunken or dull; now they're vibrant and full of life. His skin has shed its pale, clammy hue for a warm, glowing tan, as if he had spent days relaxing by the ocean. He's taller than I remembered from the hospital, clearly a good height now. His clothes perfectly compliment his well-toned physique—something I never noticed during his illness. Perhaps it was part of the magic that restored him. His brown hair, shining with health, is styled in a carefree, perfectly messy way that nearly tempts me to run my fingers through it just to feel its soft texture. I look up into his eyes, taking in how the gray swirls merge with the brown, much like the unique dual color of my own eyes, and suddenly, an intense flush of heat courses through my body.

I avert my gaze, realizing he might have noticed me observing him. It wasn't so much ogling as it was checking for any lingering signs of illness, which weren't there. A wave of warmth sweeps over me as I think about how well his clothes fit, imagining what he looks like without a shirt, knowing there are no scars from his recent surgery.

"I guess since I beat Jaliah back, I get to call shotgun!" he jokes, thankfully easing the awkwardness.

Jaliah approaches from behind him, saying, "Dude, you can totally take the front seat. That way, I can have the whole back to myself for a nap. Aria, when you get tired, we can switch. That way, we won't have to stop and waste time," as she tosses her bag into the back and closes the trunk. As we reach the driver's side of the car, she nudges me with her elbow and jokes, "If you're done staring, we can leave."

"That's not what I was—" I start to protest.

"Oh yes, it was," she cuts in. "It's cool, I did too. I'm just more discreet than you." Jaliah is both cool and stunning, so honestly, if either of us were looking for a wild romance with the only guy on the trip, she'd likely be the one he'd choose.

***

Four hours into the journey, my eyelids grow steadily heavier. The exhaustion from a twelve-hour workday is hitting hard. Archer has done a great job keeping me alert so far; we've shared stories of our childhoods and belted out tunes like we were in a karaoke bar. But now he's dozing, and the yellow lines on the road are starting to blur. Meanwhile, Jaliah has been peacefully asleep in the back, undisturbed by our earlier noise. There's a rest area six miles ahead, and I'll stop there—maybe there's a vending machine with coffee. A quick stretch and a bathroom break might help wake me up. A few moments later, I exit the interstate and pull into the small rest area, noticing a few other travelers around. As I park the car, both of my companions remain blissfully unaware. I leave the engine running and gently close the door, hoping not to wake them, though part of me wishes someone would volunteer to drive. I spot the vending machines and, just as I hoped, there's a coffee machine. I watch in fascination as the robotic arm inside crafts the exact cup I requested, even placing it in the window for me to collect. I cradle it like a precious gift, inhaling its divine aroma. At this level of fatigue, any coffee would smell heavenly, especially since I'm accustomed to the burnt jet fuel we call coffee at the hospital. A guy, or should I say the Greek God of a man, comes up behind me and asks if the coffee is good, nearly causing me to drop my cup.

"It's good to me, but I wouldn't trust my judgment, I am pretty easy to please" I stammer out.

"Good to know," he says with a playful wink. My cheeks heat up as I realize exactly what I just said—and that he picked up on it. Now I want to find a hole and bury myself in it.

"I was about to hit a gas station, but at this hour, your chances of finding a fresh cup of coffee are pretty slim. This is the time when you only get coffee burned into charcoal at the bottom of the gas station pot, the kind that sears your esophagus on the way down," he remarks with a smile.

His teeth, face, and hair are flawless—wait, what's happening to me? That's the second time tonight I've been doing a head-to-toe appraisal like I'm reviewing a dating profile. Not even just one profile but two. Are my female parts trying to tell me something here? Get it together!

"Well, the trendy little robot guy in there made it fresh, so no burned esophagus—clearly, that means it's the better choice!" I say, suddenly regaining control over my wandering eyes.

I realize I'm still standing at the machine when he brushes past me to tap his card on the reader. He smells of amber and cedar, the enticing aromas swirling in my nostrils, making it hard not to breathe him in. There's also something familiar about him, although I can't quite pinpoint what it is.

"Have a good night, and I hope the coffee doesn't disappoint," I call out as I turn to walk away.

And then I feel it. That familiar buzz is unmistakable—it's in the air, on my skin, and echoing in my mind. At first, I blamed it on my "hot guy syndrome," but as it intensifies, I realize it isn't just that. I glance back, but he's steadily watching his coffee being made. What if... it's not entirely far-fetched to think I might run into another one of us, considering I've already encountered one member of the group in a hospital bed and another working at a diner. I walk slowly toward the jeep, taking mental note of the vehicles in the parking lot: a family buckling their kids into a van a few spots away, an older couple parked just across from us, a sleek black Mercedes a couple of spaces down, and an old truck that looks completely out of place on the interstate behind us. So, he must belong either to the old truck or the fancy car—and judging by his impeccable looks, inviting scent, and perfectly fitted clothes, I'd bet on the Mercedes.

My focus shifts when Archer climbs out of the Jeep, rubbing sleep from his eyes, with

Jaliah doing the same right behind him. Thank goodness I wasn't kidnapped; they would have snoozed through the whole ordeal.

"Did you sleep well?" I ask them as I approach the Jeep.

"My neck's a bit stiff, but given that I slept all twisted up, it makes sense. Not all of us had the luxury of stretching out in the back seat," he says, nudging Jaliah.

"That's what you get for calling shotgun, dude," she replies, stretching like a cat waking from a nap in a sunny spot.

"I need to talk to you," I say to Jaliah. "Arch—could you grab us some snacks?" I hand him my card.

"Eh—no one's called me Arch since my grandma was around, but I'll let it slide," he says, taking the card and heading toward the vending machines. Hopefully, that Greek God guy is still there; if Archer feels the buzz, we can rule out any girly crush feelings.

"What's up? Need some one on one time or something, I can get lost in the restroom or something" Jaliah jokes once Archer is out of earshot.

"Huh? Oh my God — no! There's a guy by the vending machine," I start before she interrupts.

"Girl, we just met; how do you even know I will make a good wingman?," she jokes.

I roll my eyes. "Not like that, weirdo. I felt a buzzing sensation when I was near him, so I sent Archer for snacks to see if he feels it too. What if…. you know… what if he is one of us?"

Eleven

Vega

I need coffee. Exhaustion had already set in, but the adrenaline from recent events was keeping me awake. However, it's beginning to fade. I consider stopping at a gas station, but I know the quality of coffee I'll find there at this hour. Instead, I'll head to a rest area; at least there should be an energy drink in the vending machine, and it's quicker than exiting the interstate. A short while later, I pull off the ramp and drive into the rest area, which is nearly deserted except for a few late-night travelers. I slip my wallet into my back pocket as I get out of the car. I feel relieved when I spot one of those modern vending machines that dispenses robot-made coffee. It's basically a fancy Keurig, but at least it's freshly brewed. As I approach, a girl is grabbing her fresh cup, so

I ask her how the coffee tastes. She is pretty, not pretty like the women I tend to meet in the clubs. Those women are on a mission, simply put — dress revealingly, find a hot rich guy, and try to snag a real housewife lifestyle.

The girl standing in front of me embodies effortless beauty. She doesn't need to dress up in a tight, skimpy outfit to catch anyone's attention. She's just the right height, with her long legs giving her an elegant stature. Her skin is naturally sun-kissed, not artificially bronzed. Her dark hair is casually knotted atop her head, a style that seems to require no effort, and if she's wearing makeup, it's undetectable. Snap out of it, Vega—she's eyeing you like she knows you're admiring her. Or maybe she's the one checking me out; I'm not sure. After exchanging a few words — coffee-related, of course — I slip past her to pay for my coffee when a familiar buzz fills the air. Instantly, the hairs on the back of my neck stand on end, fully alert. I'm rooted to the spot. She's leaving, but I'm acutely aware of her every movement. I try to keep my focus on the robot making coffee.

A few moments later, a guy approaches the snack machines beside me.

"Pretty wild how far we've come in the world of rest area coffee," he says, while watching the robotic arm slide my cup into the window.

"I was just thinking the same thing" I reply.

The buzz is still in the air, tingling along my skin like fragments of electricity trying to make the connection. I move over to one of the other snack machines in the line to look at the food choices.

"Is it just me or does night driving make a person willing to literally snack on anything just to stay awake" —Perfect, now I am making small talk with a stranger. This is what my life is becoming.

"Yeah, they call that eating away the boredom" he laughs.

The guy moves to the machine right next to me, his hands already full of random junk food.

"I got snack duty for the group — this is not exactly all mine" he laughs as he realizes how much food he is already holding.

The closer he gets the louder the buzz grows. I'm oddly uncomfortable at the moment. How do I ask another male if they feel a connection without sounding like I am flirting?

"This is going to sound odd." I trail off looking for the words.

"Nah trust me, after my day nothing sounds odd, and if you are about to ask me if I feel some weird buzz feeling that I am somehow familiar with — the answer is yes. I figured out about 30 seconds after walking up — I am pretty sure that's why my friend sent me up here on snack duty" he says.

Relief. Confusion. Wait… his friend… the hot girl? I feel stupid for even thinking that. Hot isn't the word. Words. My external words are failing me, while my internal ones are racing. I am just standing here in complete awkwardness which is very outside my character.

"Yep, I know what you're thinking right now, this must be the first time you've felt it outside of your own personal bubble. I was right where you're at man, literally this morning." The guy says when he realizes I am paralyzed with silence.

"Yeah" is all I can get out.

"Come on, meet my friends. Let's make this less weird, I'm Archer by the way." He extends his hand out as a formal introduction, which I take.

We walk over to his group, and of course, the coffee girl is part of it, and another girl who looks… intimidating. As if she might possibly slit my throat with a tiny hidden razor blade she has tucked away in her combat boots. Archer is a rather normal-looking guy, so it eases the possible throat slitting feeling. I learn that the coffee girl's name is Aria, which is just as beautiful of a name as she is. Scary Spice introduces herself as Jaliah, shaking my hand with a hard grip. She is taller than Aria with a cut-off old rock band t-shirt covered by an oversized flannel button-up, torn shorts, stockings, and the razor holding combat boots. She is thin, but all muscle, I am pretty sure she could almost take me in a fight. She is pretty too with coffee-colored skin, and curly hair that bounces. That's when I noticed a trait we all have, aside from the buzzing. Her eyes are hazel but with purple swimming from the inside ring outwards. Her eyes have a depth to them that screams fierceness, where Aria's grey and green show brilliance, and Archer's brown and gray show protection. I've always had a thing for reading a person's eyes, it is a necessity in my line of work. Their eyes can tell you the character of a client immediately, if they are liars, cheaters, or telling the truth. The difference is, that my clients didn't have eyes that spoke so loud.

"So it's safe to assume that you are most likely driving to a forest that is at the bottom of a mountain and that you had no clue where to go but for some reason, the map just told you" Jaliah pipes out.

"Yeah," once again all I can get out.

"I think it's also safe to assume you're still catching up and that we are the first people you have met that know this, or that you have even spoken to about this because you think people would think you have lost your mind" she says again.

"Yeah" — there it is again, apparently it is the only word I know.

"OK well, we will give you a minute, but you're going to have to catch up a little quicker pretty boy, and maybe find some of those things they call — words" Jaliah responds as she heads off in the direction of the bathroom just as Archer did.

"I don't think she likes me." I breathe out once they are out of ear shot.

"She isn't really this grumpy from what I have seen, I think she didn't catch enough sleep. But, in her defense, it is still a little new to all of us as well. Do you have an animal… in your dream I mean?" Aria says in a comforting and welcoming tone.

"I do, he's a falcon, he told me his name is Atticus" — finally words work.

"Cool. Mine is an owl, she's huge, her name is Ophelian" she says.

"So are birds the trend then" I say, trying to keep the conversation going.

"No, not really, Jaliah has a bear named Kobin, which I guess matches her personality, and Archer has a tiger named Lexora," she says, she seems nervous, as if conversation is happening to postpone the silence.

"Sweet" Jeeze, I sound like an idiot.

"So, we plan to drive through the night in that direction, which since you're here at this hour I would assume you're doing as well. Do you want to ride with us, or one of us ride with you to compare notes?" she says quietly.

I want to stay close to her, not sure how I will pull that off, but something inside of me wants to keep her near me. I don't know that I want to ditch my car at a rest area, and I wouldn't want her to ditch hers either. Before I can speak again Jaliah and Archer come back from the bathroom.

"Ari — I'm gonna drive since I got the most sleep, Arch is going to take the backseat and sleep. You can either ride shotgun or ride with pretty boy, so he doesn't loose his way like he has his words" Jaliah orders with a playful wink in his direction.

"Do you mind?" Aria turns to me and asks.

I try to control my response with a simple "Of course not" to not come off… excited. What is wrong with me? I don't get excited at the mere thought of a woman in my car, that's just another Friday night for me. But, here I am, hiding the excitement as she grabs her phone and slides into my front seat.

Twelve

Journal of Truths

Article Two:

When our mystical essence was drawn from the depths of human consciousness, a sense of ominous foreboding emerged. We envisioned a future where humanity, tangled in chaos and deception, would unknowingly orchestrate Earth's ruin. It wasn't their fault; chaos and deception were embedded in their very nature, like seeds sown in fertile ground. The environment was perfectly suited for this malevolence to thrive, as greed and power became insatiable driving forces, no matter how much was accumulated.

This path was a deviation from humanity's intended course—the creator's vision for the world. Over time, the once-glorious facets of existence became mere afterthoughts, with species either wiped out or reduced to shadows of their former selves. The sacred bond between humans and animals turned into a relationship of dominance and ownership, while the connection to the natural essence that shaped the world dwindled to a fragile state.

Faced with this inevitable fate, we of the tribunal were not mere spectators. We meticulously prepared for the impending future battles. Our mission was clear: allow humanity a chance without direct interference, while protecting ourselves, mankind, and the earthly realm. Fail-safes were carefully designed to maintain a delicate balance.

The mystical force remained, elusive yet ever-present. However, humans were unaware of its existence. Some stumbled upon bits and pieces along the way, but the misuse of these magical fragments diminished their inherent power. Those who wielded this power lacked understanding of its true nature, unable to control the natural magic available. As a result, magic became taboo, a mysterious force dismissed as madness by those who dared to engage with it. Throughout history, a few secret societies have practiced ancient magic in its purest form, always hidden from the public eye. Unfortunately, those who used magic for dark purposes lost their sanity and have been the ones shaping the general perception of magic all along.

The control of human perception became the ultimate power, where perception shaped reality. If humanity deemed magic taboo, it became so—an enigma buried deep within their understanding. We have watched this sickness over the years. One generation whispers about reality but never writes it, the next generation believes whatever the previous writes, therefore — dont write it, it doesnt exsist.

Thirteen

Aria

I climb into his car, probably the most luxurious vehicle I've ever been in. It seems to be packed with every piece of technology imaginable, things that people don't usually need but are luxurious to have. As the seat warms up beneath me, I feel my body unwind, and fatigue begins to take over. I'm not sure how many hours I've been awake, but I'm starting to feel the exhaustion.

"Would you mind if I take a quick thirty-minute nap?" I ask.

"Of course I don't," he replies with a smile, pressing a button on the dashboard.. "This should help." Immediately, the seat starts to massage my back, much like the ones at the nail salon, only better. He's trying to impress me, I think to myself, rolling my eyes where he can't see.

"Thanks," I say, as if it's completely normal for cars to give massages. But — it works, because a few moments later, I'm sleeping soundly without a worry in the world. Should I be worried, though? I mean, he is, in fact, a complete stranger; we are just trusting that those of us who are "chosen" are also good people. In the depths of my slumber, I hear Ophelian's voice. It's muffled, as though it's struggling to penetrate a dense fog. Initially, I can't discern her words, just the sound of her voice. I strain to concentrate through my sleepy haze as her voice grows louder, more insistent, more... frightened. Finally, I clearly hear her yelling at me to wake up.

I jolt awake, feeling the car suddenly braking hard. My mind takes a moment to catch up with reality as I try to understand what's happening. We're surrounded by pitch-black darkness. I can see the road, but it's as if a thick, black fog has engulfed us. "What is happening?" I ask, attempting to mask my panic.

"I don't know; everything was fine, and then it all went black. The others are ahead of us, but I can't see their taillights in this mess," he replies, trying to sound calm, but I can sense his panic in the air. I reach into my pocket to grab my phone, briefly noting that I managed to get over an hour of sleep, and I dial Archer.

"Hey, are you guys also in the dark?" he asks quickly.

"Yeah, looks like you are too," I respond.

"We've managed to pull to the side and turn on the flashers. You should do the same. There's a wide shoulder here, so you should be fine. If another car comes, they won't crash into you," he advises.

Vega moves the car as cautiously as possible, as if he's navigating through a dark hallway. I notice the temperature dropping; frost is forming on the windshield. The wind howls fiercely around the car outside.

"What is going on?" I ask both Vega and the others on the phone.

"We're as clueless as you are," they reply. My mind races through possibilities, dismissing them one by one. Let's be honest, black fog like this isn't something that happens in reality.

"It must be magic or something unexplainable. Let's stay calm and wait it out," I suggest, and everyone agrees. I place the phone on the dashboard, keeping it on speaker as we all sit in silence, waiting for the situation to pass. Frost eventually covers the entire windshield as the temperature plummets. Vega turns on the defrost and cranks up the heater, but it doesn't help. Something invisible taps against the windshield, then scrapes a line through the frost. Vega grabs my hand and locks the doors. "What the hell is happening?" he whispers.

"I don't know. Archer, what's happening up there?" I ask quietly into my phone.

"Just the temperature dropping, frost covering us, and we can't see anything," he replies. I glance at Vega as the invisible thing continues tapping on the windshield. He's scared, gripping my hand tightly, ready to pull me away at the first sign of danger. Suddenly, the tapping and scratching stop, and the frost begins to melt away.

A few minutes later, I spot the Jeeps tail lights in the distance. Vega notices them too, as he suddenly sits up straight. "Should we try driving to get closer?" he asks. "Yeah, archer, we're moving closer to you guys. How far are we from our stop?" I inquire. "We're about 30 minutes away. If we reach there, we can set up camp," Archer responds.

Vega shifts the car into drive and inches toward the tail lights. As we get nearer, the fog seems to part, not lifting or fading like ordinary fog. It's definitely connected to this journey. Archer and Jaliah start moving too, and after about a mile, we break through it. We all agree that reaching the camp is our best option for now.

Half an hour later, we arrive at the national forest. Since we don't need a permit for primitive camping and there's no burn ban, setting up tents and making a fire are our priorities. The sun will rise in a few hours, but we can catch some sleep before then. We each take on a task, and in less than twenty minutes, the camp is ready. Jaliah unpacks some supplies and serves us all a plate of food. The camping gear I've had stored for years has been incredibly useful. We consume the food quickly, soaking up the fire's warmth. Nobody speaks; I think we're all just processing the situation. There's a lot to sort out and discuss, but we've decided to sleep first and tackle it later.

We have one tent, but it's spacious enough for the four of us. Considering the whole black fog incident, it's probably wise to stick together. We gather our sleeping bags and blankets, not wanting to be far from one another. We position ourselves so everyone is within arm's reach in case anything strange occurs. Moments later, we're all asleep.

As soon as I drift into sleep, I awaken in the other realm, a place that now feels comforting and familiar. This time, all of us are gathered in a field encircled by the woods we usually find ourselves in. Our animals, or perhaps guardians, stand tall and protective around us, as if they are keeping watch. In the center of the group stands the largest elephant I've ever seen, his skin glistening with gold and adorned with intricate filigree. A crown of gold and black filigree sits atop his head, featuring a giant emerald at its center. He is truly awe-inspiring.

"I am pleased you have all come together. More will join you in time, but for now, this is your starting point. Each of you has met your counterpart, even though you may not realize it. Your counterpart has been with you since your conception, guiding your personality and ensuring your readiness for this moment. That moment has arrived. While you are safe right now, that won't always be the case. Remember, you are stronger as a group, and that frightens the siphon, the melevolent force that reaks chaos upon this land and feeds from it. The moment you united, it was felt, and as you grow in knowledge and numbers, it will only become more noticeable. The earth has gone

too long without our unity." He pauses to ensure we grasp his message.

"My name is Argus, the leader of the tribunal. It is an immense honor to meet you all. This is where your journey begins. Your counterpart cannot provide all the answers, but they are always accessible to you; you just need to call their name with intention. I wish you well, as the fate of us all lies in your hands," he concludes with a sense of gravity.

The dream world fades away, but it feels like ages before any of us stir. I'm the first to awaken, slipping out of the tent to tend to the nearly extinguished fire. I prod it back to life and start brewing coffee in the percolator. The sun is moments away from spilling into the night sky, lighting up the horizon and revealing the shadows that play around our camp. Finding a perfect spot to watch, I snugly wrap my sleeping bag around my shoulders and settle in. A rustle of earth behind me draws my attention, and I see

Vega approaching, also bundled in his sleeping bag.

"Mind if I join you?" he whispers softly.

"Of course," I respond with a drowsy smile.

"What brings you out here?" he inquires.

"I'm here for the sunrise," I softly reply. "For me, the best part of the day is when the sun begins to edge into the sky. Sunsets are nice, but they usher in the night, and I'm more fond of daylight. Night brings out shadows and eerie noises, but the sunrise seems to chase them away. Plus, I'm a nurse. We often tell patients that the first 24 hours are critical. If I can just help them make it until the sun rises again, it gives me a sense that everything will be alright. Even after a challenging night, the sunrise has a way of making things feel better." I gaze at the sky, waiting for the first light to appear. He watches in the same direction I am without saying anything.

"When I was a kid, I used to get these sudden night terrors. They'd scare me so much that I couldn't sleep, but if I clung to my blanket and waited for dawn, those bad dreams would disappear. That's when I began to appreciate the sunrise," he says, his gaze lost in the morning light.

"I love how it gradually colors the sky, as if telling the stars, 'Great job, take a break.' It's like the sky becomes a canvas, and the sunrise is Earth's way of preparing it. It might not be as grand as the evening view, but it sets the scene for whatever you can imagine, just like the day ahead," I say, my eyes fixed on the horizon.

"That was beautifully said, thank you for sharing. I feel like I'm losing control, not just with this, but with life overall. I did everything I was supposed to—I went to school, got my degree, passed the bar, joined the firm—but I still felt like I was spinning, searching for something meaningful. I felt guilty about it. I know people who worked even harder than I did and didn't make it, and they would love to have my position. Yet, I still felt lost," he pauses. "The way you describe a simple sunrise means more than most things I do in my life. Despite how silly it might seem, I'm happier in this moment. I feel more purpose now than I do every single day. I barely know you guys beyond what I've learned since last night, but I feel more connected to strangers than to people I see daily. This 'mission' gives me more purpose than my entire career or life."

"Well, I have a career with a purpose that I witness every single time I step into the hospital, but... this purpose feels so much larger. It's invigorating" I say as I look at him.

He's gazing at the sky, and the sun is slowly making its entrance, casting a soft glow on his handsome features. The sunlight highlights his tousled sandy brown hair, framing his head in a casually disheveled way. As I observe him, this stranger I find myself entwined with, I can't help but notice the sincerity in his eyes. His thick eyelashes would make any girl envious, and his lips are full and tinted with a delicate pink hue. He smiles as the colors of the sun mix with the darkness, and then he looks at me. I can literally feel my heartbeat in my fingers, and hear it in my bones. It's overwhelming me to the point I have to look away, but I can't. I'm completely lost, endlessly falling from the cliff inside his eyes. Not smart. I need to stop right now I tell myself as I force myself to look away. I don't know what this journey is going to ask of me, flirting with the thought of anything with the guy who I can totally tell gets all the ladies is ludicrous. I need to focus. I need to work on the task at hand.

I smile "I think the coffee is ready," I say in hopes of a distraction.

Fourteen

Archer

I wake up to the aroma of fresh coffee wafting through the air. It takes a moment to realize I'm sleeping on the ground in a tent. As I sit up and glance around, I notice Jaliah is still sound asleep, but Vega and Aria are nowhere to be seen. That's likely why I can smell the coffee. I'm still uncertain about Vega. Ever since meeting Aria, I've felt an unusual urge to protect her, despite the fact she was the one helping me. Vega seems to have arrived and set his sights on her as if she's some prize to win, and he strikes me as someone who usually gets what he wants. It's not my responsibility to protect her, but if he disrupts things with her, it could jeopardize everything we're working on here. For the first time since childhood, I feel energized and purposeful. I need this journey

—not just for humanity's sake, but for myself. Without it, where would I be? I never anticipated a cure, perhaps just a slight improvement to prolong my life, but I always had a finite timeline. Now, I'm uncertain of my future. Death could claim me tomorrow or in fifty years. I've never been able to think or speak like this before. So, anyone who enters the group and threatens — must leave.

I step out of the tent and see Aria pouring coffee into the tin cups on the makeshift table we made last night. She's wrapped in her sleeping bag paying close attention to her task at hand. I stand up tall and take a deep breath in, filling my lungs as much as I can, something I couldn't do last week. It feels beautiful. It is hard to even explain unless you know what it's like living the way I did just 48 hours ago.

"It's amazing to think that what you just did would have been impossible before," she remarks, almost as if she can read my mind.

"Yeah, I was just thinking that," I respond with a smile. She approaches me, offering a cup of coffee. "Mind if I listen?" she asks, gesturing towards my chest, and I nod in agreement. Without her equipment, she leans in, pressing her ear against my chest. Standing on her tiptoes to reach, she fits perfectly there. If I were to tilt my head slightly, my nose would brush through her hair. Despite already being close, she pushes in a little more, as if to hear better.

"You know I can't hear anything if you hold your breath, right?" she teases, making me realize I was indeed holding it. I exhale deeply and take a fresh breath. Her hand rests on the other side of my chest, her fingers tapping what seems to be my heartbeat, causing my heart to flutter slightly, and her fingers tap a bit faster. I have an urge to hug her, but that might startle her.

"How does it sound?" I ask as she slightly pulls away.

"It sounds... wonderful. Like a young, healthy pair of lungs. I'm not a doctor, but, Mr. Brooks, I think you're in perfect condition!" she declares with a professional tone. "Thank you, Nurse Ashton, I feel pretty perfect," I reply. I take a sip of the coffee and watch the sunrise. It's an ideal morning.

"Does someone want to wake Jaliah so we can get started?" I suggest, steering the conversation in a new direction. Soon, we're all gathered around the fire, discussing what we know—and crucially, what we don't. We all agree that we experienced a shared dream last night, where Argus provided us with additional information. We're aware that our mission is to find something left behind by the tribunal, but have no clue where to begin. What we do know is that we're stronger together; when united last night, we all dreamed the same dream. "Let's try something different. Everyone, come closer," Jaliah instructs. Her leadership skills shine through, even if she isn't officially our leader. She's straightforward and avoids idle chatter.

"Hold hands and close your eyes," she commands. We do as she says, but nothing happens.

"Maybe we need more than just physical contact and closed eyes. Let's focus on our connected...maybe?" Aria suggests wisely. We follow her advice. Within moments, Atticus, Lexora, Ophelian, and Kobin join us.

"Good. You've discovered something on your own," Atticus acknowledges.

"How can we assist you?" Ophelian asks.

"We're supposed to find something you left for us," Aria explains.

"Yes, but you must prepare your bodies and minds. This journey requires no physical travel. You're seeking the Golden Teacher, who will help open your mind and unblock pathways in your brain, even if temporarily, allowing your connections to flourish. This isn't meant to be what you humans call a college party, so approach it with respect. It was left for you to heal in ways modern medicine cannot. Sadly, it was misused and earned a negative reputation," Ophelian clarifies.

"Get ready, because the journey's success depends on how well-prepared you are. Hydrate well in advance. Avoid the junk humans call snacks; stick to clean, nourishing food. You each get only one, so don't be picky—chew it thoroughly. It won't taste pleasant, but if it were easy, it wouldn't be valuable," Lexora advises.

"Hold on, are you suggesting we eat hallucinogenic mushrooms?" Aria asks, astonished.

"Yes, that's right. Remember, we've already explained that perception shapes reality, and that's precisely why we're in this situation. You're hesitant because perception has made you fear things that used to be normal. So yes, eat the mushroom. Embrace its effects on your mind. Don't resist it. While everything good can also have a downside, resisting the magic will only invite chaos. You will all do this together, yet your journey will be solitary. Your connection will remain here, watching over you, ensuring your safety. We are not asking you to abuse substances, that is not what we are about. This is simply a catalyst allowing you to dive deeper into your magic, what has been inside of you all along, just waiting to be activated. We've brought you to this location for a reason—it's where the connection is strongest, and we can safeguard you. Is that clear?" Argus says as he steps into the circle, commanding our attention.

We all agree, exchanging glances as if we've been tasked with stealing the Declaration of Independence. As soon as we voice our consent, a surge of energy bursts from our circle, sending ripples through the meadow and into the trees. Our connected mention that we will be safe here, and back into the trees, disapearing from our sight. We assume that the burst is the magical boundary set to protect us. Aria takes out her phone to search for images of what we need to find, sending them to Vega and me. Vega and I draw the short straws and are assigned to the foraging team, while Jaliah and Aria set up camp for the night and our upcoming "trip."

"I have literally never done any drugs, not even pot," I say to Vega.

"Well bro, I've done it all, not that I am proud of it, but it was a way to escape reality, it could be said that I didn't always make the smartest decisions in life" Vega says with a laugh.

"So, you were born with money, you're a lawyer, you look like a God, and you're whining about life as if you needed drugs to escape reality," I say judgingly.

Vega doesn't snap back, he just simply says to me "Just because someone looks like they have a perfect life doesn't mean that it is happy. Money and looks do not make happiness, I'm sure you've heard that statement before. I mean, look at all the movie stars who get the spotlight in the media for drugs, suicides, outlandish behavior. Money doesn't fix everything man, sometimes it just makes the stupid shit more of a possibility."

He's right, and I feel wrong for judging him. We all have problems. I could have been a millionaire and it wouldn't have saved me from my disease, it took a group of magical animals to fix it.

"Sorry, that was rude. Thanks for bringing me back to reality. So - have you ever taken mushrooms?" I ask.

"Yeah, but it was more to get high, not a trip for purpose. Only the yoga-loving hippie people use it for *transcendence* as they call it, but if I really look and admit to it, there were times it helped me through things, I just didnt accept it" he says.

"Oooookay. Well - do you know what we are looking for?" I ask.

"Yeah, come on," he says while heading off into the woods like he has done this a hundred times. I drink from the water bottle Jaliah sent with me, they said to prepare, so that's what I do.

Fifteen

Aria

I'm not going to pretend otherwise; this situation goes completely against everything I've ever believed. I'm really trying to accept my circumstances, but experimenting with drugs was never something I wanted to do. After Jaliah and I set up the campsite, I took out my phone to search the internet for information and warnings. So far, I haven't found any documented risks when used responsibly, only the usual cautions similar to those about THC. Essentially, officials advise against it. I've treated patients addicted to synthetic substances and witnessed how it destroys their bodies. I've also seen the harm caused by alcohol, even though it's widely available. I've decided that being paranoid will only add to the chaos, so I'm shifting my perspective and viewing this as a therapeutic experiment. I've read studies where psilocybin was used for mental health and substance abuse treatment with impressive results, so I'm focusing on a therapeutic angle. If the "trip" goes poorly, the advice is to change your mindset, and that's what I'll do. Just as I'm coming to terms with our experiment, I spot Vega and Archer approaching the camp. Looks like it's time. Jaliah seems completely unfazed.

"Are you nervous?" I ask her.

"No, not really. It's not like we're about to eat a pound of it and jump off a roof. Plus, we have the supervision of animals—I assume they're watching from somewhere. Who could ask for more?" she jokes. I'm starting to realize that Jaliah has two modes: bossy and humorous. I suppose that's how she handles situations, and I can't judge her for that. Everyone has their own way. Archer comes over and takes a seat next to me, with Jaliah on the other side and Vega across from us. Archer scoots closer and asks if I'm ready, and I nod in agreement.

"Let's do it," Jaliah exclaims excitedly. Vega handles all the preparations, and before I can second-guess myself, it's done. Nothing happens at first.

"It takes a little while to kick in, just relax. When you start to feel it, let it happen. Don't try to be tough and resist it," Vega advises, looking directly at me.

I'm not sure how much time passes before I notice the grass swaying differently, almost as if it's dancing, and the trees are moving in harmony with it. Jaliah mentions she's starting to feel it too. Everything inside me says to lie down and relax, and I recall reading that if something feels good, do it; if it feels bad, change it. Just as I'm about to settle down, Archer finds a spot on the ground beneath our seat and gets comfortable. Whether it's the mushrooms or my need to feel grounded, I lie down next to him, using his stomach as a pillow.

I close my eyes and let the sensation envelop my body and mind. A comforting warmth spreads over me as vibrant colors swirl and dance behind my closed lids. Soon, the awareness of my physical form fades away, and I find myself drifting in a distant galaxy, merely a floating consciousness. The colors seem alive, as if they are breathing, and it's the most beautiful experience I've ever had. Typically, I don't dwell on past trauma, but in this mental landscape, every piece of trauma I've ever faced appears before me in locked chests, each one opening in turn. I expected fear to emerge, but instead, I felt liberated, as if the burdens I carried were released at that moment. With each chest that opened, an increasing sense of love filled my soul. I barely open my eyes to see I'm still in the same place, and the rest of the crew mirrors my expression.

The chests that once held trauma are now empty, replaced by steady streams of light filling them. It feels as though the light carries all the knowledge in the universe, effortlessly imparting it to me without any need for study. The sounds of nature around me are heightened; the rustling leaves compose a symphony in my mind, and I can hear every blade of grass brushing against each other in the breeze.

I run my hand along my arm, feeling every cell in my body respond to the touch. It's as though every part of my brain is activated at once. I'm consumed by shades of green, sometimes yellow, as if these colors are embracing me. My thoughts drift over the recent days, settling on Ophelian and the others. I sense their sadness and feel an urge to reach out and heal them. They remember a time when humans were more connected to them. Though they seemed to see themselves as superior, I now understand they feel sorrow and a sense of loss for the world that once was. I wish to comfort them, to absorb their pain just as the colors do for me. Time slips away as I lie on the ground, delving into my thoughts. I feel deeply connected to Archer, a closeness I've never experienced with another human, despite being galaxies apart. A hand gently touches my hair, filling me with emotions that overflow as tears. I'm unsure why I'm crying, but I manage to open my eyes enough to confirm the tears are real. Archer's hand moves soothingly over my head, like comforting a loved one in pain. When I look up at him, his eyes are closed, and he smiles peacefully.

Above us, clouds transform into every imaginable shape, dancing in the blue sky in celebration of daylight. My body fades away, and I find myself floating among the clouds, gliding from one to another in a joyful, gravity-defying dance. I feel my connection to Jaliah and Vega strengthen, as if I suddenly know everything about them and trust them completely, even with my life. Together, the four of us are united, strong, and powerful.

A sensation begins in my toes, warm and tingling, reminiscent of the excitement of our dreams. It travels throughout my body, eventually reaching my fingertips. It feels like pure power. Magic. Despite spending every Sunday morning of my childhood in a church pew, this moment is the most profound conversation with God I've ever experienced. Perhaps it was the conviction I attempted to suppress before this journey, but now, that conviction is gone. I'm uncertain how long this has been happening or how long it will continue, but I close my eyes again, savoring each moment of the surrounding embrace. The colors behind my closed eyelids dance and form beautiful images until the sensation gradually fades. When I open my eyes, reality almost returns to normal. The trees and earth still sway slightly, but my body is firmly on solid ground now. Though I remain lying on Archer's stomach, his hand is still tangled in my hair.

Jaliah lies within arm's reach, and Vega is just beyond her. There's a buzzing sensation that seems to start with one of us and flows through all of us, in an endless loop. I am filled with awe and adoration. I appreciate everything around me from the depths of my soul, experiencing life with a completely new perspective at this moment.

Sixteen

Vega

This wasn't my first encounter with psychedelics by any means, but it was the first time a trip felt like that. Typically, there's a sense of transcendence, but this experience was both transcendent and revelatory. I suppose the difference was that before, I always did it just to have fun with friends, without any specific purpose. I had never felt as connected to the people around me as I did during this trip. As everyone gathers around the camp, we're all sharing our experiences. It seems we all had similar journeys; each of us delved into past issues and felt a shared sense of connection. While they're quite open about the troubles they revisited, I hold back a bit. I admit that I worked through some things or at least became more aware of them, but I'm not really inclined to discuss the details.

After arriving here and experiencing what just happened, we're unsure about our next move, so we decide to stay put and camp out until we receive further instructions. We're primitive camping, which means no showers or electricity, but we have enough supplies to last through the night. Since we only managed to get a few hours of sleep, it doesn't make sense to move on until necessary. Archer points out that he spotted a creek with a swimming hole at the edge of the woods while we were foraging earlier, and suggests everyone could rinse off there since it looks clean. We all scramble to gather towels and supplies. If you forget that we're on an earth-saving mission, the bonding and swimming hole experience is just like a typical summer camp. I grab a change of clothes and the camp towel I'm glad I brought, and follow the group to the swimming hole.

Jaliah is the boldest of the group. Without a moment's pause, she jumps into the water from a large nearby boulder, taking only enough time to remove her flannel. She wades in wearing just her white t-shirt and a pair of shorts. Archer follows closely, tossing aside his jeans and t-shirt before executing a cannonball near Jaliah. Aria, a bit more reserved, laughs at her new friends splashing in the refreshing water. I consider diving in fully clothed but know I'll regret the weight of wet jeans. I toss them on top of my shoes before working my way out of my t-shirt. Just then, I catch Aria's eye.

"Are you joining in or just going to watch?" I tease.

With a roll of her eyes, she responds, "I'm right behind you," and starts slipping out of her jeans. I watch as she carefully places her pants in a dry spot, hesitating over swimming in her button-up shirt. Anticipating her need, I grab the t-shirt from my pile and toss it her way to catch her attention. "Maybe it'll be more comfortable," I suggest, just before diving in to give her some privacy. The water wraps around me, soothing the aches from days of camping. As I surface for air, I can't help but be mesmerized by her image. Her t-shirt slips off one shoulder, subtly revealing modest panties below as she ties her hair into a neat knot atop her head. I always thought she was beautiful, but in that moment, I pictured her exactly as she was—standing in my apartment's kitchen, ready to enjoy the breakfast I'd just prepared after disentangling from our embrace in bed. I've never imagined such a scene with anyone else who's ever visited; usually, they're shown the door at some point during the night. My morning routine remains unchanged, and having a woman linger has never been part of it.

My daydream is cut short when Archer launches another cannonball, splashing water between us and shattering my reverie. As the ripples fade, she slides gracefully back into the water. I join in the playful splashing and camaraderie—anything to mask the daydream lingering on my face. We spend what seems like hours in that swimming hole, goofing around like college kids on spring break. Eventually, exhaustion takes over, and we all end up lying on our towels in the tall grass, letting the evening sun dry every last drop from our bodies. We laugh, we swap stories, and once more, a sense of bonding emerges. Beyond my personal attraction to Aria, I genuinely enjoy the company of this ragtag group. There are no plot games, just four people hanging out. And then there's the magical excursion that awaits us, a mesmerizing adventure lying just beyond our current spring break lifestyle. Maybe we all needed a break. From what I've gathered, Aria has spent her life dedicated to hard work or attending school of some kind. Archer, on the other hand, has endured much of his life under medical care for a condition that's now vanished. Jaliah has been surviving from a young age; though her birth father is wealthy, both she and her mother have steadfastly refused his help, which is admirable. But her life hasn't been as sheltered as the others'; judging by her words, she's experienced her fair share of promiscuity in her youth.

At some point, we trailed each other through the field back to camp to begin dinner preparations. Just like the previous night, everyone grabs a role, and through teamwork we're eating before we know it. We gather around the fire, laughing as we let the food settle. Someone had remarked that we are more powerful as a group, and now I see it clearly. Even though I internally scoffed at the idea of bonding, it was necessary. We've come to know each other well enough to watch out for one another. Each of us feels responsible for the others—myself, even feeling that duty toward Archer, despite a tinge of jealousy. After dinner, we sit in silence, each deeply immersed in our own thoughts, yet all aware we're pondering the same question: What's next? Sleep beckons, but it's hard to move toward bed without a plan. Aria appears lost in contemplation, and I watch her from across the fire as embers flicker between us. Before I even see it clearly, I sense a subtle change in the atmosphere coming from Aria's direction. Then I witness something that can only be described as starlight: it floats gracefully around her, casting a dazzling array of shimmering, colorful waves. The radiant light extends outward, and as one of these waves passes over my skin, it leaves me with a sensation of warmth and energy. I notice that the others are equally captivated by the mesmerizing display, their eyes fixed on Aria as the light embraces each of us. Although I can't read the precise emotions of the others, I feel a profound sense of comfort.

It takes a while for the phenomenon to sink in, and we sit like children, eyes wide with amazement. Soon the feeling shifts from comfort to confusion—as if Aria is torn between choices, and we can sense her inner conflict. Then, just as quickly, the emotion changes again, this time to something like attraction. I glance around to see if the others are experiencing the same thing, and by the looks on their faces, they are. Jaliah, however, seems more concerned than Archer or I.

"Aria," she says cautiously. Aria snaps her eyes open. "Yeah? Sorry, I was lost in thought. Did you say something?"

We all remain silent, staring at her, not daring to speak. The moment she refocuses, the shimmering waves retreat from us. It's as if, against all logic, she shared her inner emotions with us, letting us feel exactly what she felt—almost as if she could control our emotions. Then, a burst of questions, ideas, and thoughts fills the air about what might have just happened. We don't rule anything out—after all, here we are, a group of strangers who have witnessed talking animals in both dreams and reality. It would be hypocritical to dismiss the possibility that we each harbor magical powers. Recalling the notion that we are stronger together, we gather around the fire and attempt to cast magic like the ones we see on television.

Naturally, nothing happens. Eventually, someone suggests that we join hands in a circle—an idea that seems straight out of Hollywood. We pull our seats in close and interlock our hands, but still, nothing occurs.

"Intention. I think we're missing intention," Aria explains. "When we ate the mushrooms, we were told to do it with intention. I'm not just saying to intend for magic—let's focus all our intentions on one thing and see what happens."

"Okay, well, the fire is dying down, so let's concentrate on making it bigger," Archer offers. We all direct our focus onto the fire, picturing its growth. As if by magic, waves of shimmering light emanate from each of us, swirling among the almost-dead embers, and before our minds can fully grasp what we're witnessing, the fire doubles in size—blazing with blue flames outlined in bright orange edges. We've just wielded magic!

Seventeen

Aria

Overwhelmed by the thrill of using magic, we exhausted our remaining energy. We agreed to get a solid night's sleep and start fresh the next morning. After extinguishing the fire and tidying up, we returned to our previous spots in the tent. As the night wore on, the cool air gradually thickened, making us grateful for the warmth of our sleeping bags. We exchanged some lighthearted chatter before drifting off to sleep. Being far from civilization makes the night feel even darker. The sole source of light is the moon glowing above us. Archer and Jaliah are sound asleep, their chests gently rising and falling. Vega, however, is restless, twisting and turning as though gripped by a nightmare. I lie there watching him, curious about what could be troubling his seemingly perfect life to cause such dreams.

I shut my eyes, hoping to drift off to sleep. At home, it's challenging enough to find rest, but in a tent with others around, I have no choice but to pretend until it becomes real. With my eyes closed, I replay the day's events. The magical encounter with mushrooms and the fun times at the swimming hole create vivid pictures in my mind. I remember Vega effortlessly shedding his spotless shirt, revealing a flawlessly toned body—every muscle on his chest, arms, and abs perfectly defined, especially the V that dips below his waist. Our eyes met, and for the first time, I truly noticed the stunning beauty of his. They were a captivating shade of green, shifting to a bright blue near the pupils, as if they could see right into my soul. Just before I jumped into the water, I caught sight of him swimming, water flowing over his back muscles, and his smile as he playfully splashed water at the others. As I sink deeper into my thoughts, a strong desire to be near him overwhelms me. I kind of want to run my fingers through his hair, tracing his skin. He is so close, almost within reach. As if he were reading my thoughts, his arm brushes against me. Feeling his fingers intertwine with mine, I keep my eyes shut, my heart pounding with excitement. Our fingers lock together, and I inch closer to him silently, unnoticed. Then, he pulls me nearer, granting me access to the spots on his skin I had just told myself I wanted to touch.

His breath brushes my hair, causing tiny shivers to run down my arms. His fingers, now liberated, glide up my arms, skim over my waist, and wrap around the small of my back, drawing me into a close embrace. I breathe in his earthy, natural aroma with a hint of amber. With his other hand, he gently turns my face toward him, tracing his finger along my jawline and into my hair. Despite this, I resist opening my eyes as a peaceful silence surrounds us, broken only by the steady beat of my heart. With a gentle nip on my lower lip, he seeks my consent, and my breath provides the answer. His hand, tangled in my hair, guides my lips to his. He kisses me softly at first, delicately exploring the limits of an invisible boundary. I respond by arching into him slightly, giving him the clear permission he desired. The kiss transforms from a tentative touch to a passionate storm, surrounding me completely. I keep my eyes shut, lost in the intensity of the moment.

The hand on my back remains gentle, contrasting with the fervor of the kiss. It roams over my back, sides, and stomach, mapping my body while carefully avoiding the more intimate areas. A longing arises within me, I want his touch everywhere, urging him to cross those boundaries. I reciprocate the exploration with one hand, mapping his body in return, while the other cradles his face. I fear letting go might end this moment. My fingers trace the defined muscles of his abdomen, lingering on each ridge with a gentle touch. I count the contours, my fingers pausing on the V shape above his pants, imprinting the sensation in my memory. His hand moves below the waistband of my pajamas, descending slowly, which my body eagerly welcomes. He doesn't move too fast, instead, he gently brushes his fingers on the skin between my pants line and my center, teasing me until my body cannot hide my need any longer. I arch into his hand, letting him know I want him. His fingers move along the center, gradually exploring the warmth, swirling and teasing until I am breathless. My racing heartbeat is likely evident to him, and I press into his hand, inviting him to continue further. He reads the moment perfectly, and just as I near the peak, he bites my lower lip, leaving me utterly undone.

Afterwards, my body feels like a cluster of electrified nerves, both sensitive and yearning for more of him. He retracts his hand to a safer distance, but keeps his hold on me. Drawing me nearer, he kisses me passionately before easing into a softer rhythm. As the intense sensations in my nerves start to fade, he places a gentle kiss on my forehead, silently leading me into a restful sleep.

***

I open my eyes and guess it's around 5 am. My body is on an internal schedule, set to wake up at this time every day. Sleeping in is unfamiliar to me. Suddenly, a wave of heat washes over me, and my heart pounds rapidly. The memory of last night stirs up embarrassment. Please let it have been a dream! I'm lying in the same position I fell asleep in, facing Archer and Jaliah, who are still sound asleep. I turn over as quietly as I can and see Vega also sleeping soundly, curled up in his sleeping bag with no signs that I intruded into his space. I silently slip out of the tent and head out to watch the sunrise. I reflect on last night's events. It felt completely real, yet there's no evidence it happened. Not that there would be much proof anyway. If I had woken up nestled against him, that would have confirmed it. I recall being close to him when I fell asleep, but that's not how either of us were positioned when I woke up. Maybe I dreamed it, or perhaps my dreams are just that vivid.

Oh God, if everyone felt what I felt around the fire last night, if the tent incident was actually a dream, what if they all experienced it? I can feel a queasy feeling bubbling up in my chest. If they even slightly hint at the fact that they felt my emotions, I will literally find a hole and bury myself in it. I feel a twinge of regret imagining Archer feeling all of that. I don't quite know why I feel this way, but it's there. I'll just act like nothing happened and see what unfolds. For once, I wish the sunrise would hurry up and push us into the day with as many distractions as possible. I actually wouldn't even mind a slight hurricane, or tornado — anything to skip us from last night to tomorrow.

I hear the tent zipper and see Vega emerging to take the same spot beside me that he did yesterday. Act natural. Nothing happened. I try forcing my body to listen as every fiber in me stiffens, aside from my fidgeting hands.

"Good morning! I thought you'd be out here waiting for her," he says.

"Her?" I ask.

"The sunrise, it has to be a 'her'; guys aren't that beautiful. Did you sleep well?" he says with a smile, adding a wink. Fuck... was that a flirtacious wink? Was that a "last night was cool" wink? Or maybe it was a "Aria, you are delusional and making up fantasies in your head" wink? I want to disappear, cease to exist. I. Am. Mortified. Crazy part is, I really could have dreamt that.... these days I can't tell the difference between dreams and real life anyway.

Eighteen

Archer

After the day we had yesterday, it's no wonder I slept so well. Like the previous morning, Aria and Vega are already awake, while Jaliah remains fast asleep. Drawn outside by the allure of fresh air and coffee, I step out.

"Good morning!" Aria greets me, handing over a steaming cup of coffee.

"Morning! Did you sleep well?" I respond with a smile. Her smile instantly drops, as if she has seen a ghost... only for a brief moment because she quickly collects herself before she responds. "I did, more exhausted than I realized. I slept like a log," she replies. I glance around but don't see Vega.

"Where's Vega gone this morning?" I ask. Not that I really care, but he is not in his usual spot, soaking up Aria's energy.

"I think he headed back to the swimming hole, but I'm not positive. Anyway, I've been thinking, and I might have a handle on this magic thing. If you're up for it, we could do some practice," Aria suggests. At this moment, I'd do just about anything she asked, just to spend time with her. "Absolutely," I agree with a grin.

We find a spot on the grass and sit down. Aria is initially silent, as if deep in thought. She starts discussing her theories, suggesting that magic is something inherent within us, always present but previously untapped because we neither knew how to use it nor believed in it. She believes that accepting what was happening, even though magical creatures led us to that realization, unlocked our potential because we began to believe. She explains how her online search about the mushrooms led her to read more. She discovered that psychedelics can open blocked neural pathways in the brain. With a newfound belief in magic, even if initially hesitant, and the opening of these pathways, we became capable of wielding something humans had long forgotten.

Aria mentions that whatever magic she exhibited last night by the fire wasn't intentional. She doesn't believe intention causes magic but rather guides it. While we have the ability to use it, it's the right intention that directs it. Her theory becomes uncertain when considering what exactly we can do—whether each person has a unique power or if we all share the same abilities with one special one. The more we discuss it, the more it resembles comic book scenarios. We decide to practice, though we're unsure where to begin. So, we choose to pick up from where we left off yesterday when Aria made us all feel what she was feeling, but this time, aiming for more control. She asks me to hold her hands, believing we're stronger together. The sensation of her hand in mine quickens my pulse, and I'm almost certain that's my own reaction, not magic. She tells me she'll choose a feeling without revealing it to me, and if I sense it, we'll know it's effective. I have to shift my focus away from the thought that I might fall apart in her hands at any moment, or else I'll ruin the entire experiment.

The morning air is cool, and it seems to be getting colder by the minute. Despite the stillness of the wind, a chill steadily grasps me. I briefly consider that we should keep the fire burning if we want to continue practicing, but then it hits me—the cold isn't just natural; she's causing it. It's her magic. It's more than just a sensation; actual snowflakes are starting to form around us. Her magic creates a snowy circle about five feet wide. I'm utterly amazed, while she has no idea she is doing this. Her eyes are closed, concentrating deeply. A snowflake lands softly on her eyelashes, and she opens her eyes to witness the magical scene she's created. She smiles, releasing the sweetest laugh I've ever heard, filled with innocence and wonder, as if every childhood fantasy just became real. Inspired, I decided to try my own ability, hoping to amplify the energy. I concentrate intensely, and the snow flurries transform into a heavier snowfall. I imagine that if we all focused together, we could conjure a blizzard. I open my eyes to see Aria, overjoyed as she watches the snow swirl around us. The snowy circle now extends slightly beyond five feet, so I aim to expand it further, signaling to Aria to do the same. In no time, the entire campsite is blanketed in a thin layer of snow.

I catch movement out of the corner of my eye and realize it's Vega returning to camp. At first, I detect a hint of jealousy in his demeanor, which oddly gives me a bit of pleasure. But when he sees me watching him, he gestures toward the snow as if to ask whether we're responsible. I return an enthusiastic nod. He approaches and slips into the circle, taking Aria's hand with a subtle show of possession—just enough for me to recognize he's staking his claim, though not overt enough for her to notice. I allow him to join, reluctantly offering my free hand as well. I know that if we're going to work together, I'll have to ignore the edge in his tone.

I mention that Aria has figured out our intentions are guiding the magic—thoughts set into motion enhancing the snowfall around us. He catches on quickly, I must admit, because moments later, the steady cascade of magical snow intensifies. It's so cold now that I wish I had a jacket on. I look up and catch Vega staring off into the distance, as if he's starving and has spotted a juicy steak on the table. Since he's facing the tent, I follow his gaze to see what has captured his attention. Jaliah has finally woken up; she climbs out of the tent wearing sleep shorts that barely cover her butt, showing off her long, caramel-colored legs. It's obvious why Vega is fixated—she's wearing a thin white crop top without a bra, and with our snowstorm covering much of the camp, it's clear she's cold, her nipples visibly showing through her top.

A flush warms my neck and I immediately turn away. Aria notices Vega's stare, but it doesn't seem to bother her; perhaps it's just a one-sided infatuation on his part. "Good Morning! Come join us!" Aria calls out cheerfully. "You chose snow even in the cold? Why not start with a five-star breakfast instead?" Jaliah teases as she reluctantly steps into the circle. I suppose she's right—of all the choices, we went with something cold. She joins between Vega and me; at least I'm no longer holding his hand, though I secretly hoped she might slide in between him and Aria.

"I'll play along, but could we try something warm instead of this snow?" Jaliah suggests. "I think some folks in the circle enjoy being chilly," I reply with a laugh. After an eye roll from Jaliah, we shift our focus to summer rain—the kind where it rains while the sun still shines. It's the best sort of rain. We channel the magic from deep within our minds, through our hands, and into the air. Gradually, the snowflakes transform into cool raindrops, dissolving the white layer covering the ground. Vega lets out a chuckle and remarks, "Well, Jaliah, it does appear warmer now," casting a teasing glance at her damp white crop top. "If I didn't want them noticed, I wouldn't have suggested the rain, Captain Obvious, — Plus don't even act like you're not internally drooling over the wet t-shirt contest I am clearly winning." she retorts, giving him a playful wink.

"So we can manage water weather; let's try something more challenging," Aria cuts in with a subject change. Is that irritation I detect? "Alright, what are you thinking? Maybe something a bit steamier?" Jaliah replies with a raised eyebrow, hinting as if she knows something the rest of us aren't aware of. Aria blushes briefly but quickly regains her composure. "Steam still counts as water weather," Aria says with an unamused look.

"How about we focus on fire," I propose.

Everyone agrees, though Vega can't resist adding another suggestive comment. We direct our energies toward the smoldering fire, which quickly turns into a blazing bonfire. We need more challenges; this has been easy so far.

Nineteen

Jaliah

I'm not quite sure what's happening with this group, but the sexual tension is so thick that a chainsaw couldn't even cut through it. From what I've gathered, Aria is interested in Vega, but she has something for Archer, too. Archer is into Aria, while Vega sees her as another conquest. It's tempting to dive in and stir things up myself. Maybe I'll pursue Aria as well, just to spice things up, though it's not typically what I go for. But I'm not against it either. And yes, I wore the white shirt on purpose. The whole magic thing is actually working out for us. Even though I was initially doubtful, I'm secretly loving every minute of it. Working at the diner was just a stopgap, after all. I've spent most of my life just getting by. Here, I'm surviving in a new way. I'm not working, but

I'm warm at night, my stomach is full, and I feel safe—at least for now. That's been my existence, so not much has changed, except everything.

I'm eager to delve deeper into this magic. If we crack the code, I might never have to work in a diner again. I've decided to motivate our quirky group to try more challenging tricks. This time, we're aiming to make the wildflowers in the field bloom. It requires more concentration since the field is vast. After about thirty minutes, we're surrounded by a sea of vibrant colors. We then move on to trees, covering them with moss and vines. We split up to see what we can achieve individually. While we can still manage the same outcome, it takes longer, and our magic only extends to our immediate vicinity.

I concentrate on crafting a plush chaise lounge right here in the field—a space where I can finally recline and appreciate our not-so-intense labor. It demands some effort;

unlike working with nature, this creation isn't effortless, yet I manage to pull it off. Aria comes over, clearly impressed with my idea, and makes herself a blanket nearby. As she lies down, she focuses on the drifting clouds, subtly shifting them so the sun can bathe her skin in a warm glow. Vega approaches next, eyeing the empty spot beside her on the blanket, but I channel all my magic into expanding my chair just enough to invite him over, gently patting the vacant space next to me. He settles in, then uses his own magic to conjure a footstool, positioning himself so he can elevate his feet.

A look of irritation crosses his face when Archer claims the seat next to Aria. Archer, undeniably the sweet one, contrasts sharply with Vega, who exudes a dangerous allure. I can't tell if his danger stems from his notorious heartbreaker reputation or the possibility that he has stumbled upon someone capable of breaking both of their hearts—and remains blissfully unaware. I'm completely caught up in watching the drama unfold. The downside, of course, is that if both end up enamored with the ever-perfect miss, my chances of any romance during this mission vanish. We pause to savor our handiwork until a distant rumble breaks the calm. Dark shadows stretch from the treeline like reaching arms, exuding an ominous vibe. Thunder churns within these shadows, and lightning flickers beneath them. None of us budge as the storm creeps closer, its thunderous growl intensifying with its approach. Then, from the cloud emerges a skeletal shadowed hand, snatching Aria by the throat and hoisting her off the blanket in a flash, leaving her no time to escape or even cry out.

I stand paralyzed, uncertain of my next move, and Vega shares the same frozen uncertainty. I mean — it is a fucking shadow hand… not like we are used to this. The thought races through my mind that it could be a test, but the blue tint painting itself across Aria's lips makes me think differently. If it is a test, Vega and I are failing, because we cannot even move. But Archer reacts instantly: he conjures a glowing white saber with his magic that cleaves through the hand, causing it to dissolve and allowing Aria to drop back onto the blanket. In an instant, the darkness recedes, and the air around us settles into an eerie stillness.

"What the actual fuck was that, and a lightsaber? Seriously, Arch? It worked, but still..." I exclaim in utter disbelief. "It just came to mind! I always dreamed of having a real lightsaber like Skywalker's, so that's what I thought of. Besides, none of you were doing anything," Archer retorts. Suddenly, everyone starts talking over each other, bickering about who did what and who should have done what, when a deep, resonant voice floods both the air and our very being above our commotion.

"ENOUGH."

Instantly, we fall silent, our eyes fixed on the enormous golden elephant, Argus. His tusks arc gracefully from his mouth, ending in sharp points that could easily pierce us with a single misstep. Standing behind him are the others, all connected and watching us with clear disapproval. "We appreciate that you took some time for yourselves last night. We're even more pleased that you discovered your power so quickly. It was against our tradition to teach you, yet you managed to find it on your own and even practiced with it. The dark shadows you saw were not truly dangerous—they were simply us testing you. Only one among you passed the test. To survive what lies ahead, you must learn to work as a team far better than you did now. Real threats out there are far more formidable, and a lightsaber won't be enough. We know that it wasn't comfortable, Aria — but the real threat has much higher consequences than what happened here."

Argus continues, "In truth, you are stronger together. The more separated you are, the weaker your powers become. Now that you've found them, they'll always be accessible—even if weaker when apart, they remain within you. But you won't be able to overcome the challenges ahead without staying united. As we have mentioned before, there are others out there as well. It's time for you to seek them out and join forces. We have looked into your souls and examined your intentions, and you have been deemed trustworthy enough for this truth. The others are not a threat to you, for they, too, have been entrusted."

At that moment, an Ophelian steps forward and places a small package before us. Aria picks it up and carefully unwraps the cloth surrounding it. Inside is a simple crystal amulet, pulsing with an inner magic. "Use this to guide you. While it isn't what humans would call technology, it is equally powerful. It will lead you to where you need to go. Guard it well, for in the wrong hands, its power could turn against you," Argus instructs.

Atticus adds, "Pack up camp, continue your journey, and remember to restock supplies when you can—you'll need them. Magic alone won't solve all your problems; there's much more for you to learn. You've only just begun to scratch the surface. Also, know that your power is directly tied to your mind. The purer your intentions and the wiser your mind, the stronger your power will be."

The Tribunal leaves us with those words of advice, and we stand in silence for a few moments. Vega is the first to take action, moving towards the camp to gather our supplies. I almost feel a little bad for him. He watched Archer step up and save the girl he is pining after, and then got scolded by Argus for freezing. It is like when you rub a puppies nose in thier own piss to teach them a lesson. At least that's what he looks like as he begins packing up. He had decided to leave his car at a storage unit he found online in the next town, concluding that traveling together was the best option. We carefully pack our belongings into the Jeep, leaving the non-essential items in the trunk of his car. No one speaks while we pack; I think we're all a bit shocked. It's a lot to take in. We had been out there playing around, not considering our safety. If that darkness had been the enemy, Aria might not be with us right now. Honestly, it is a hard hit to the chest to think that we do not even really know what our enemy is capable of, or what to even watch for in our enemy. They admitted to testing us then, but there was no talk of testing us when that black fog came on us the other night. What if our enemy has been watching us the entire time? Kinda makes me feel stupid for prancing around with my tits on display like a college girl at a party this morning.

"That's everything—let's get going," Archer announces, suddenly seeming like the most mature one in our group. We quickly make our way to the storage facility to leave Vega's car. The place gives off a shady vibe since we're technically still in the National Forest, but there's a tiny town with just one stop sign nearby. The silence has become unbearable after a while, so once we've finished dropping the car and all load into the Jeep, I play some lively music to lift everyone's spirits. "Stop!" Aria suddenly exclaims. I lower the music, about to tell her to quit sulking, when she adds, "We need to turn here; the amulet is blinking that way." Oh. Good thing I held back my usual sharp remarks.

Twenty

Katerina

My legs feel so numb that the only thing guiding me forward is the crunch of gravel beneath my feet. It's been an incredibly long and tiring year—actually, more like two years. Everyone seems to think they know exactly what to say, convinced their opinions are the correct ones. I've always wished I could make others understand my feelings, wanting to shake them until they get it. At least, that's what I thought I wanted—until last night. My life has been one trauma after another. I thought I was managing by compartmentalizing everything, tucking each issue away in the storage space of my mind. Sure, I tried talking to people—friends, family—but no one truly understood. They'd suggest seeing a psychiatrist or a counselor, label me as crazy. I even overheard a family member snark out, "It's such a shame, she was so wonderful when she was little." They just don't get it. They don't understand.

I suppose my mind doesn't function like most people's. It's been battered to the point where it can't operate typically. Yet, I believe many "normal" people are just pretending. I know this because I was one of them until I couldn't maintain the fakeness any longer. It's incredibly difficult to act like everything's fine when your mind is clouded with darkness and turmoil, when you can't feel joy in situations where others do with ease. "You need to try harder"—I've lost track of how many times I've heard that. Seriously, do they think I haven't considered it? Do they think this is what I wanted or dreamed of becoming? When children were drawing pictures of doctors and veterinarians in kindergarten, did they imagine I was depicting someone struggling with mental instability? Of course not! So, I stopped discussing it openly and handled it in my own way. The stress is intensified when you come from an ideal family living in a flawless, grand Southern-style house with white columns and a picket fence. Your father, a Senator, dislikes having his leisurely cigar gatherings disturbed by the issues of his problematic daughter.

I was doing well until my mom was killed two years ago. The darkness I descended into shattered all my control. The investigations, the media, the uncertainty, the grief—it was the perfect storm. The toughest part is seeing both sides of myself. The person I aspire to be and the darkness within me. The overwhelming darkness pulls you in so deeply that the light becomes invisible, and you start believing it would be easier to end it all. Do people think imagining their own death is enjoyable? It's not. Being completely shaken and torn apart by your own thoughts is even more terrifying. I have nightmares about my nightmares.

When the dreams began, I couldn't discern whether they were new nightmares or pleasant visions. It had been ages since I experienced dreams like a regular person. Instead of feeling fear in the dark, damp place where I found myself during these dreams, I felt at ease. I was accustomed to darkness, and this one wasn't as foreboding. Meeting Nyterian for the first time should have frightened me, but it didn't. My mind had been a scarier place, making the dreams a welcome respite. Initially, I dismissed them as mere dreams or my mind's way of soothing me, but once Nyterian appeared in my waking moments, I started to take notice. She is straightforward and direct, yet kind, with words that are gentle and comforting to my soul. She is beautiful, Large for a fox, but petite like me. Her appearance is as black as the dark recesses of my mind, adorned with stars that glimmer like the night sky. She also has a unique style, wearing gold filigree jewelry on her ears, delicate ear chains, and a small gold piece on her forehead. Her bright blue eyes stand out against her dark fur, effortlessly piercing through the barriers I erect to keep others away.

She has been a comfort, even as cryptic as she is, I get the sense that she may be the one creature in existence that understands me. This whole ordeal with magic and whatever journey I've supposedly been chosen to do was easy for me to believe. Maybe it's because my brain is messed up, but it's the first thing that has eased my mental pain for as long as I can remember. Since the dreams started, I have not thought about life ending one time. If it takes some mystical journey that could possibly be a hallucination to make thoughts of suicide go away, I will take it.

Nyterian assures me that I'm not alone on this journey; besides her, there are others like me. I assume she means others dreaming of magic, not those haunted by dark thoughts. So here I am, with my essentials packed in a backpack, walking along a gravel backroad without a clear destination. I suppose I'm guided by intuition, if you could call it that. I feel better, even stable, which is an unusual sensation for me. I've always believed there was more to life than what we can typically perceive, and it seems I might have been right. It's as if the chaos in my mind finally has a focus. I just need to keep going and not exhaust myself. I think I've been hiking for two days now, not solely on back roads, but without a car, walking is my only option. Last night, I set up a small camp to rest, and my mind was overwhelmed with information, as if a thumb drive had been plugged into my brain, uploading its contents. I'm fairly certain that at one point, magic was flowing from my body into reality, but let's keep that under wraps for now. I have no interest in becoming a science experiment, having already been prodded by enough doctors in my life.

I take out my cell phone, making sure not to overuse it since I don't want to drain the battery while I'm out in the wilderness. It's now 10 am, meaning I've been trekking for about four hours this morning, only pausing to drink water or when my body insists on a rest. Deciding it's a good time for a break, I drop my gear and sit down, leaning against the massive trunk of an oak tree. I had packed six peanut butter and jelly sandwiches before setting off, and now only two remain. Starving, I pull one out and split it in half just to tide me over. I kind of wish I could see the look on my Fathers face when he realizes I am gone, but that is petty of me to think that way.

After finishing half of my sandwich, I repacked my things, readying myself to continue my hike when I heard a car in the distance. Since veering into the national park yesterday afternoon, the only living creatures

I've encountered have been animals. It might be a park ranger, but asking for a lift is pointless since they're heading the other way. I resume walking so that when the vehicle passes, they'll just see another hiker out here.

As the sound of an approaching vehicle grows louder and draws near, a strange sense of exhilaration stirs within me, pulling me away from the dream world. Suddenly, I hear rustling leaves to my right; I spin around and spot Nyterian. "I know how hard it is for you to trust, but you need to trust me now. They are your people," she says softly and confidently before slipping away into the underbrush. Keeping my attention fixed on the vehicle's sound as I continue hiking, I eventually see a black Jeep drawing closer, slowing down when its passengers notice me. The buzz of excitement intensifies.

"Hey! This might sound weird, but any chance you are out here on a mission to save the world or something like that?" calls out the girl behind the wheel through the open window. Recalling Nyterian's words to trust, I reply hesitantly, "Umm. Yeah. I guess that's what we could call it."

"Awesome! We were told to find you! " the driver exclaims as she turns off the Jeep and leaps out. She extends her hand in greeting. "My name is Jaliah, and these are my friends —Aria, Archer, and Vega," she adds with a proud nod toward her companions. Every one of them looks as if they belong on a social media feed. I introduce myself and shake each of their hands, feeling a flush of red spread across my cheeks as I shake hands with Archer and then Vega. The heat intensifies when I notice Vega lingering on the scars that mark my wrists—reminders of the shadowed past I once called home. "Let me guess: you guys have some invisible — or sometimes visible — animal guides telling you what to do, and magic is real?" I blurt out, attempting to divert attention from my arms.

The whole group erupts in laughter, clearly amused by the absurdity of my remark. Archer casually takes my backpack, indicating he'll stow it in the back, while Aria gestures for me to claim the front seat. As we drive off in the direction our collective instincts point us toward, we exchange stories—filling each other in on what we've learned over the past few days.

It turns out that they had all met a few days ago and spent time camping in a forest a few hours away. I also learned that our animal friends, with their adventurous spirits, led the group through what felt like a magical mushroom hole. Even ancient creatures know how to enjoy themselves. For now, we're heading in a direction without a specific destination. Since it's still early afternoon, I assume our animal guides will show us the way by nightfall—or perhaps we'll just keep driving. I have people now. People who accepted me without concern for my past mistakes. People who understood me without needing to hear about my previous struggles. Four strangers who offered me acceptance without judgment. For the first time in my life, outside of family, I have people. I can't quite express what that makes me feel, but it's certainly not a dark or frightening feeling. Hope. Purpose. Happiness—emotions I thought I'd never find again. I know my family loves me, and I had friends who cared deeply, but they couldn't help me through the scary moments. I had to face those alone, find my own path. I'm thankful to everyone who helped me out of the drowning waters, but I still never felt like I belonged.

It took magic to pull me out and magic to find my people. Sitting here now, I know my story isn't over. I hope that if darkness ever returns, I can look back at this moment to guide me out. These four strangers have no idea what they've done for me, and that's the best part.

Twenty-One

Aria

Thankfully, Ophelian and the others are offering us more guidance, as if our connection with them is strengthening each day. Without their help, we would never have found Katerina while wandering aimlessly. I can sense she's very guarded, likely because she's experienced a lot. She reminds me of a sweet puppy at the shelter that's had a rough start but pleads for love and care. She's probably a year younger than me, with a sweet, shy voice. She's about an inch shorter than me, with delicate features. Unlike the rest of us with darker hair, Katerina stands out with her almost white, long blonde hair reaching her waist, fair skin, and deep blue eyes. I've noticed we all seem to have a distinct color ring now, and hers is white. Her style is a bit edgy, reflecting her personality:

she wears black leggings, black boots, a black long-sleeve shirt with lace-up sleeves, and a black nose ring in her septum. When I meet people, I usually take a moment to observe them, and though I can see she's experienced some challenges and often dresses in dark colors, I don't believe that defines her entirely. She appears to be sweet and kind, and though she may have been hurt in the past, perhaps expressing her inner struggles through her fashion, a person is more than just their troubles. It can be difficult to distinguish the two, but shortly after joining the group, I noticed her beginning to open up and flourish.

She shared with us about her connected, which is unlike the ones the rest of us have. We assumed all the connected were familiar animals, all mostly white with a golden touch. However, her connected is a fox, as dark as the night sky, with stars speckling its body like the evening sky. It suits Katerina perfectly, with her petite features and dark exterior, yet she describes the fox as gentle and sweet. This revelation showed us that not all the connected are the same. Switching gears — I keep trying to push aside the confusion about whether my encounter with Vega was a dream or reality. If it was real, I feel embarrassed for letting myself get involved; that's not typically me. But if it was just a dream, does that mean I secretly want it? Maybe I do, but I don't want to disrupt the group dynamics either.

Which brings me to my current dilemma: I gave up my front seat to Katerina, and Jaliah is driving, leaving me stuck in the back seat between Archer and Vega. I'm not into casual flings, and Vega seems like just that. I crave deeper connections in any relationship, and while we all share a strong bond, I'm unsure if Vega is what I want. Archer, on the other hand, is sweet and fits the kind of person I'd usually be drawn to. I wasn't even looking for anything before all this, then Archer sparked my interest, and now Vega complicates things, making me feel like a teenager again. Archer fell asleep about half an hour ago, and now his head is resting on my shoulder. Meanwhile, Vega's hand keeps brushing against mine between us. Granted, a jeep doesn't offer much space in the backseat, but every time he touches me, warmth spreads from my stomach to my cheeks. I'm pretty sure he noticed and is now doing it deliberately. I am literally falling into the "why choose" trope that I typically hate when I read a romance book. I guess I never liked reading them because something inside of me is always screaming "just choose", yet here I am. I am also not a "player" so the whole trope is outside my typical behavior. I need a distraction. Immediately. I ask Jaliyah to stop so I can use the bathroom. "We're literally in the middle *bumfuck you got a pretty mouth*. Can you hold it? We're not likely to find another town for at least an hour, but also — you could get kidnapped by the banjo boys and put in a frog stew out here," she responds sarcastically as ever.

I assured her that I could handle going into the woods on my own. A few moments later, she parked the vehicle and turned it off. Vega stepped out to let me exit. He offered to accompany me to ensure nothing bad happened, as if the banjo people really might kidnap me while I was taking a bathroom break in the forest. "No thanks," I replied sarcastically as I headed into the trees. I found a secluded spot where they couldn't see me and kept watch in their direction to ensure no one was looking. Something in the distance caught my eye—a small, flashing light, like sunlight reflecting off a mirror. I pulled up my pants and moved toward the flash to investigate. As I got closer, it seemed to move further away. I should have turned back to the car, but I was entranced and couldn't let it go.

Eventually, I reached the source—a shard of broken mirror lying on the mossy ground. I picked it up, puzzled over how it ended up there, and then realized I had wandered much farther than I had intended. The car and my group were nowhere in sight. A wave of disorientation hit me, muddling my sense of direction until I couldn't recall where I'd come from. Perhaps I should have accepted Vega's offer after all. The forest morphs before my eyes, with pine trees transforming into oak, grass overtaking the mossy earth, and vines sprouting where none existed moments ago. Each step I take in what I believe is my original direction results in the forest shifting again. Now, evergreen trees stand where the oaks were. I persist in moving the same way, but every change in scenery alters my course. Reaching for my phone, I realize I left it in the jeep, and panic grips me.

I attempt to use my magic to stabilize the forest, but as soon as I move, my magic is overwhelmed, and I find myself surrounded by unfamiliar trees. Fear clutches my heart tightly. I hesitate, not wanting to move, but knowing I must. Perhaps if I keep walking, the forest will eventually revert to the starting point. However, this doesn't work. The landscape continues to shift, making me feel like I'm venturing further in with each step. I stop, certain that my movements are worsening the situation, and then notice a change in temperature. Ahead of me, a dark figure emerges, resembling a hooded black-robed shadow. Dark tendrils extend from all sides, as if they help the creature navigate. "Maybe this is another test from the Tribunal," I say aloud to myself. The mention of the tribunal provokes a deafening scream from the creature, which rushes toward me, fear pounding in my chest.

I glance at the shard of mirror in my hand and notice the reflection doesn't match my current surroundings; it shows the forest as it was when I first exited the jeep. Adrenaline surges through me, and I hold the mirror up, seeing myself reflected amid the normal forest. I maneuver to spot the jeep in the reflection, hoping that if I get close enough, my magic will be strong enough to draw me back. I step forward, only to realize that the image I see is a reflection — forcing me to move in the opposite direction. I must trust this mirror likeness to be my guide as I physically step backward. One foot follows the other as I retreat, and I notice that even the woods seem to change in reverse, as if the entire scene is unfolding backward. A shadow draws nearer, compelling me to continue my retreat. Chaos—this must be the Siphon the Tribunal mentioned.

The faster my heart races, the more rapidly chaos approaches. I take a deep breath, trying to steady my pulse, and it appears that this slows the chaos a bit, though I'm too weak to calm myself completely. Frustration brings a solitary tear streaming down my cheek as I force myself to keep moving backward, retracing the way I came. Yet the Siphon speeds forward, closing in second by second. I struggle to suppress the overwhelming fear, quickening my pace until I stumble over a hidden root and crash onto the ground. In that moment, the jagged shard of mirror lacerates my palm before striking the tree's root and shattering. Panic surges as I realize I can no longer guide myself to safety. I shut my eyes and call out for Ophelian, but the connection is muffled and unresponsive. Now the dark shadow of the Siphon has reached me, and I find myself crawling backward as desperately as I can in a futile bid to escape. Agony radiates from my injured hand as blood stains the ground, while fresh, burning tears stream down my face. We were naive to think we understood this magic, never once pausing to consider the danger. If we hold such power, what might the Siphon possess? If it can reshape the very earth, why did I ever believe I had control?

The dark shadow now hovers above me, its tendrils slithering around my arms and legs, pinning me in place. The bands of inky black burn into my flesh like acid. "You feeble human, you are no match for me," it hisses. "Your fear is delectable—that is all I require from you." Its words seep into me like poison, stirring the terror within my soul.

"What do you want from me?" I manage to scream.

"Your fear nourishes me; it fuels the chaos that sustains me. Your foolish band of misfit animals and humans believe they can defeat me—how stupid," it hisses. "Join me, and I will reward you. Your meager powers are quaint, insignificant beside mine, but with me, you could have so much more." Its tone shifts from venomous hissing to a strangely alluring seduction. "You cannot imagine what you might become at my side. I can offer you power, even pleasure—I could make you a queen," it declares. As its form begins to emerge from the shadows, it appears as every woman's deepest desire incarnate. I remind myself that evil does not always manifest in ugliness, yet it remains inherently evil.

Fear swells, and I can sense he relishes it. The tendrils constrict around my wrists, while others brush against my face, then trail down my neck and body. Tears stream down my cheeks. I am utterly helpless. "I cannot compel you to join me; you must do so of your own will. I already know you will, so why delay the inevitable? Stand by my side, claim your throne." I refuse to abandon everything that defines me to embrace the darkness. My entire career has been about guiding people away from it; I will not become what others dread. He doesn't truly know me. He's merely playing with me.

"You think I don't know you?" he says, tilting his head in an animalistic manner. "I understand you better than you comprehend yourself. I know what's deep within, what you keep buried, what you'd never admit even to yourself. That's why I came for you. Now, JOIN ME!" His words drip with anger and malice. Even the ground beneath trembles in fear. I feel trapped between joining or dying. I will not join. He doesn't understand me. As I think this, his anger vibrates around me. Just when I am certain he will end me, an arm wraps around my waist and pulls me away, plunging me into darkness.

When I finally gather the courage to open my eyes, I see Vega, carrying me away from the darkness. The forest is normal again, and the chaos has dissipated. As the adrenaline fades, I break down. Tears pour from my eyes, and my body shakes with sobs. Vega looks towards the jeep, and I follow his gaze; we are out of the group's sight. He sighs, sets me on the ground, then sits behind me, pulling me into his chest and wrapping his arms around me. "Let it out," he murmurs softly. After every tear has fallen and my chest finally stops heaving, I manage to speak. "Thank you," I say. "You don't have to thank me," he answers. "How did you know to come find me?" I ask. "I promised I'd wait for you, but then Atticus came to me and said to go get you—he said you couldn't escape on your own. He didn't offer any more details, but when I found you, you were far out there, trembling on the ground. It looked like you were having some sort of seizure, so I grabbed you and brought you back to the group for help. Just before you opened your eyes, Atticus told me it was the Siphon." Vega's usual snarky tone is absent now; his concern for me is unmistakable.

A quiet silence hangs between us for a few moments. I look up and find him gazing into the distance. "What are you thinking?" I ask. "I think we haven't taken this as seriously as we should. What I saw resembled a seizure—how long has this been happening? We have a diagnosis to understand it, but what happens if it strikes again when I'm not there to pull you out?" Every word he speaks is filled with genuine concern. In this moment, I see him in a new light. He was attractive before, like a playboy male model, but now he seems so much more. The silence lingers as we both absorb everything. I hear Jaliah calling for us in the distance, and I shout back that we're coming. I remain seated with Vega wrapped around me like a comforting guardian. "We should head back and inform the group, you know," he says quietly. "Yeah," I reply, but when I look up at him, the worry etched on his face is overwhelming. I turn my body to face him fully, taking his face in my hands and whispering "Thank you," before surprising myself by pressing my lips softly against his.

At first, he hesitates, but then pours all his concern into that kiss, pulling me closer and claiming my mouth as he refuses to let go. His hands slide around the small of my back, pulling me into a straddled position over him. He continues kissing me, his tongue softly exploring mine. Then, he slips his arms under my hips and stands up, holding me securely against him. I wrap my legs around his waist, clinging close as I run my hands through his hair. His touch remains respectful, never crossing any line that might shift this moment from being one of sincere care. He gives me one last kiss, drawing it out as if to show me he's stopping reluctantly. "We should go; they're waiting for us, and we don't want to worry them more," he says with a hint of regret. "Okay," I agree. "Can you walk, or should I carry you?" he asks, making me want to linger in this moment a bit longer, but I know we must move. Not only because our group awaits us, but also because the danger that sought me is lurking, and we shouldn't provoke it again. I assure him I can walk, and he sets me down while still holding onto me as we return to the group. I'm almost tempted to bring up the incident in the tent the other night, but I choose to leave it be. What occurred here was vastly different from whatever I might have imagined in the tent. Even if it was real, we've moved beyond that now.

Twenty-Two

Archer

I woke up in the back seat of an empty Jeep, surprised that I slept so soundly I didn't notice everyone else leaving. Jaliah and Katerina are sitting on a log in front of the vehicle, sharing some jerky from the food bag. The Jeep is hot, suggesting we've been stationary for a while. Aria and Vega are nowhere in sight, which irritates me. Vega's constant shadowing of Aria, like a dog after a female in heat, secretly bothers me. I step out, stretching from head to toe and adjusting my neck.

"Hey, sleepyhead," Jaliah calls out.

"Why didn't you wake me up?" I ask as I walk over and sit beside her and Katerina. They explain that we only stopped for Aria to use the restroom, but she must have gotten turned around, so Vega went after her. Naturally, he played the hero. This jealousy he's stirring up inside me is unfamiliar and unsettling. I need to redirect my focus, but that's easier said than done. I grab the piece of jerky from Katerina's hand and pop it into my mouth.

"Hey - that's rude!" she protests. We sit there, bantering about all the random events of the past few days, momentarily forgetting that part of our group is still out in the woods. "If we want to make any progress tonight, we should hit the road; it's already past four," Jaliah says, checking her watch. She gets up, brushing dirt off her legs, and calls for the others. Aria responds, so she's no longer lost. We pack up the food and start the car as Aria and Vega return from the woods. Vega has his arm around Aria, more supportive than flirtatious, so I let go of my frustration. They get in, telling us we need to find a place for the night and have a talk. We drive for another two hours in silence. Aria sleeps with her head on my shoulder and her legs draped over Vega's lap. His hand, gently stroking her leg, continues to irritate me.

"Hey, I noticed on the map there's a town about ten minutes ahead with a motel— maybe we should rent a couple of rooms," I suggest to the group. They agree, and a heavy silence resumes. Eventually, we pull into the parking lot, and the rundown motel barely looks like it should still be operating. I double-check the map; it's the only option unless we're willing to drive another hour. We decided on a room with two beds so we can all stick together for safety. Even though the place looks sketchy, at least it has a shower. Vega leaps out, heading for the lobby, then quickly spins back to remind me to stay by Aria's side. What the hell happened out there?

Before long, he comes back clutching a key— this motel is so old that it still uses traditional keys for the rooms, the kind with the plastic keychain with the room number on it. I really hope the interior has been updated to something modern, or at least clean. We unload our gear from the back of the Jeep, secure the vehicle, and head into our room. Once inside, it's not as bad as it appeared from the outside. One really can't judge a book by its cover. Settling in, it's time to find out what happened—what's really going on.

"So, are we going to discuss what just occurred?" I ask Vega. Everyone abruptly stops what they're doing and gives me a look that makes me feel like the villain. "I don't mean it rudely; I'm just genuinely worried," I clarify. They each grab a sandwich from the small pile Vega had picked up from the lobby vending machine, and we form an almost circular seating arrangement on the beds and floor.

"I can't speak for what Aria saw—we haven't even gone over that yet," Vega begins, nodding in her direction. "But Atticus approached me after she'd been missing for a while and urged me to look for her, he said the Siphon had her. I headed into the woods in the direction I assumed she'd taken, but she wasn't there. I eventually heard her calling in the distance, so I rushed over. When I found her, she was lying on the ground, jerking—as if she were having a seizure. I picked her up to bring her back, and eventually she came to, just needing a moment."

Concern etched on everyone's faces, Katerina asks Aria if she'd ever experienced a seizure before. "No, it wasn't a seizure. It was the Siphon. I noticed something in the distance, which turned out to be a shard of broken mirror, and once I got closer, the forest started to change. It became disorienting and led me further into the woods," she explains. I could see the fear in her eyes as she recounted how a dark shadow had come for her. Even when that same dark figure had appeared in the field with us, it had targeted her specifically. We had assumed that the shadow represented our connection testing us, but maybe that wasn't the case. Perhaps, with all of us together, it was deterred, but when she was alone, she was vulnerable.

I noticed the terror in her eyes as she described how a dark shadow had come for her. Even when that same ominous figure appeared among us in the field, it seemed to target her specifically. We had assumed the shadow was simply testing our connection, but perhaps that wasn't truly the case. It might be that when we were together, its attention was diverted, but when she was alone, she was exposed. We concluded that the only way to get answers was to consult those who were connected to us. So, we summoned our animals through our magical bond. One by one, they manifested in the room.

The Tribunal reminded us that we must always be prepared for moments like these. We asked them why the shadow was singling out Aria, and their response was vague. "There are always several ways a story can unfold. It might be that Aria is a key element in the version that best meets his needs," Ophelian commented. Aria visibly tensed at this statement, as if she knew more than she was willing to reveal. Atticus then stepped in, reminding us that "just because a story *can* unfold a certain way does not guarantee that it *will*. Ultimately, you are the one who controls where your story leads." With those words, she appeared to relax a bit. Perhaps she had seen her own demise in the ensuing chaos. The Tribunal continued, urging us to remember that we are stronger when united, an idea they had expressed before. I interpreted this as meaning that by sticking together — at least in small groups — we could fend off the chaos. With that, they advised us to sleep before they departed. We all agreed that if we were to separate, we should do so in teams of at least two. Jaliah announced she was going to shower and, since we were just outside the door, she didn't require anyone to watch over her. We consented on the condition she'd leave the door unlocked should anything happen. "I have zero shame in leaving it unlocked for you perverts," she says with a wink.

After everyone took turns in the shower—some of us missing out on warm water—we decided to push the beds together and pile in, ensuring that if anything occurred, we'd all be within arm's reach of one another. Most fell asleep quickly, but having spent so long sleeping in the car, I found myself pleading for sleep to find me. Katerina had curled into a small ball between Aria and me, and I couldn't help but laugh softly at her, since she had asked us to call her Kat, which was exactly how she looked at that moment. The room was dark except for a sliver of light streaming through a window from a street lamp outside. That light danced over Kat's face, revealing a beauty in her features that I hadn't noticed earlier. Her skin was fair in contrast to her ashen blonde hair. I observed her eyelashes fluttering as if she were in the midst of a deep sleep, her brows furrowed and lips pressed together. She appeared frightened, as though in the throes of a nightmare.

Soon after, a small whimper escaped her perfectly pink lips, and I caught sight of a glistening tear trail on her cheek. It couldn't be the chaos because we were all together, so it must have been just a bad dream. I fought the urge to reach out, but ultimately, it overcame me. I moved closer, draping my arm over her and pulling her into my chest. "It's okay, Kat, it's just a dream. I'm here for you," I whispered into her hair. Her body relaxed, and she drifted into a calm sleep. I didn't let go, just in case, and before I knew it, I had fallen asleep as well, with Kat securely nestled against my chest.

Twenty-Three

Journal of Truths

Article Three:

In the time before the siphon, humanity, sorcery, and creatures lived in peaceful unity, creating a world filled with tranquility. Yet, not every mortal was deemed worthy of the mystic arts, and indeed, some lost that merit. In the grand tapestry of existence, there remained a duality—a mix of good and evil even within harmony. The source of strife is not found exclusively in the hands of malice; rather, it lies within the very channels through which that darkness flows. When darkness is wielded in excess, it ultimately engulfs its master. We, the eternal witnesses, observed as darkness overwhelmed the land, surrendering it to unbounded chaos. The relentless hunger of the abyss caused it to become entrenched, never finding a reason to leave.

Its purpose wasn't mere destruction, but the gradual absorption of malevolence, which rendered it incapable of halting its own advance. With clear foresight, we saw the growing imbalance that fulfilled the prophecy: magic dwindled from the realm, majestic beasts were reduced to vermin, and humanity—driven by a thirst for power—turned its weapons against its own kin. In anticipation of the looming catastrophe, measures were put in place, activated only when balance teetered on the edge of obliteration. Thus, the Tribunal was established, gathering leaders from every race and sheltering them in a liminal realm until the moment of need. A mortal was chosen as the channel for the future, selflessly giving up his very essence for the greater good, and in doing so, becoming an ethereal shadow of his former self.

Within our care lies the compendium of lore, destined to empower the chosen among humanity for the impending conflict, to be revealed only in times of dire need. This individual will serve merely as a guide. Additional safeguards lie dormant, ready to activate only in the face of total ruin— severing the bonds between our realms and confining the Tribunal within this domain as the earthly world falls apart. By decree, the Tribunal is bound to a selected vessel, refraining from intervention until the appointed moment for teaching arrives. The conduit, tasked with passing on wisdom, must verify that every recipient is capable of shouldering newfound power. Those who falter under its weight will face the ultimate consequence—their lives brought to an end.

Only after completing their training and demonstrating true strength may the unified power of the Tribunal be bestowed upon the chosen individual—a union that is a rare blessing, granted only to a select few among mankind.

Twenty-Four

Aria

In the sketchy motel room, I fell asleep with ease, surprisingly. Though I secretly longed to snuggle up to Vega, I knew a fleeting connection after our ordeal wasn't enough reason to seek comfort in his arms, especially with the rest of the group sharing the same bed. During the night, we all slipped into a shared dream, finally gaining clarity for our quest. We awaken, if that's what you want to call it, back in a field, gazing at the majestic golden elephant, Argus. The atmosphere is serene, yet the other tribunal members are absent.

"You and a select few have been chosen. While you've been informed of this, it's now time to learn more. You've all shown your worth, and as a reward, I will share

knowledge with you," he says. "I have existed since the dawn of time. I witnessed your creation and your development. For countless ages, humans and magic coexisted harmoniously. Animals were majestic creatures that roamed the earth, enhancing human magical abilities. When the Siphon attached itself to this world, the elders, including myself, foresaw the future. Gaining this vision cost us dearly, taking the life of one of our number. We watched as the prophecy unfolded and followed the elders' plan. We established the Tribunal, composed of leaders from the various magical species. We sealed the divide between realms to protect it. Your connections are with those same creatures. Some humans were involved in the project, but we couldn't fully preserve them in our realm. We created a conduit, with a mage named Baren volunteering for the role. His earthly life ended, but his mind lives on in the conduit to teach future chosen ones like you the art of magic. He has a human form but does not live and breathe as you do," Argus pauses. "The siphon is aware of your assembly and perceives you as a *threat. He will continue to pursue you, as recent events have shown. It's time for your training to begin. The Tribunal and I have created a safe place for this purpose, where you'll meet Baren. There is an entry point from your realm into our pocket realm, but it is not as simple as walking through a door. You need to concentrate because time is crucial. Once your training is complete, the battle will commence. We are already behind schedule, so use your time wisely. Trust your instincts to guide you to the right place. Now, WAKE UP."*

Suddenly, we're all awake, glancing at one another to confirm we'd all shared the same dream. I check my phone and inform the group that it's 6 a.m. Everyone begins hurriedly gathering their things, getting ready to leave. After yesterday's incident, we agreed no one should go anywhere alone, so when Jaliah suggests fetching coffee for everyone from the lobby, Archer and Kat decide to join her. I mention I'll load the vehicle, and Jaliah insists that Vega stays with me. Once they exit the room, an awkward silence settles in, making it hard for me to move.

"Did you sleep well?" Vega asks.

"I did, how about you?" I reply, feeling my nerves, which only seem to increase knowing he notices them.

"I did, but I woke up a few times to check on you. Yesterday was kind of scary for me; I can only imagine how it was for you," he says while picking up the bags to carry to the Jeep. I follow his lead, grabbing the remaining items and loading them into the back. "Do you want me to take the first turn driving this morning?" he asks me "If you want to, I can try to figure out on the map where we are headed" I reply as I hand him the keys and head to the passenger side.

He beats me to the passenger door, opening it for me. He stands in the way for a moment, reaching out and grazing my cheek with the back of his hand. I can't move, I am paralyzed by nerves. "Are you OK? And by OK, I don't mean because of the Siphon yesterday. I feel like I took advantage of you in a moment where you were -" he pauses for a moment before I cut in. "You didn't take advantage of me. You helped me, and if you hadn't, I am not sure where I would be right now, and as far as kissing me, I kissed you first, you were just being there for me" I say. "You only kissed me first because you beat me to it," he says with a half-cocked smile, "Now load up, we have places to be!" he winks at me and closes my door behind me.

I'm unsure whether his joking about the situation is good or bad. I shouldn't be concerned, especially since an end-of-the-world scenario isn't exactly the ideal moment to start a romance. Besides, I'm not even sure if he's the romantic type. I feel a twinge of guilt towards Archer, sensing there might be something between us, but I'm not playing mind games. I've never been in a situation where I have to choose between two men, which makes this as unfamiliar as the journey we're on. Secretly, I think I have already made my choice, at least my actions have, so I don't know why the thought of it is still lingering.

We arrive at the front entrance, and the rest of the group joins us in the vehicle. Kat hands me a steaming cup of coffee, while Jaliah gives one to Vega. We decide to stop and restock our supplies—and grab breakfast —at the next grocery store. A particular spot on the map catches my eye: a lake nestled within a national park bordering the Atlantic Ocean. Something about me pulls towards it, just like before, it has to be our destination — I can literally feel it. It's about a 12-hour drive, but if we take turns driving, we can make it straight through. I don't want to rely solely on my own instincts — or intuition, so I pass the map around to see the others' opinions. Everyone gravitates toward the same destination: Echo Lake in Acadia National Park. I select "drive" on the map and sync it with the car's dashboard display. I offer to drive the second segment, with Archer taking the third. We decide on 4-hour driving shifts to avoid fatigue. We postpone breakfast for a couple of hours, combining that stop with a bathroom and stretching break.

If we do have to stop overnight there are plenty of parks we can camp in and use the shower houses along the way. Even if we only get a few hours of sleep out of the car, at least it's a break. Looking into the back seat I wish now that I had gotten a vehicle with more space. Thankfully Kat is small, but the three of them back there are still squished. The only bright side is, eventually I will end up squished back there with Vega.

Twenty-Five

Vega

I'm trying hard not to glance at her sitting in the passenger seat. Usually, you'd find me driving a sports car with a tall blonde beside me, dressed in an expensive, skimpy outfit, with perfectly styled hair and makeup ready for the runway. Anything less would seem out of place for me. Those women often paid for every aspect of their appearance—eyelashes, breasts, rear, stomachs, lips, noses. I even dated a girl once who had bicep implants. In my circle, this was the norm, so much so that natural beauty seemed almost nonexistent. But she's different. Her beauty is genuine and unrefined, making me question why I ever spent time with those other women. I suppose once one woman starts with enhancements, they all feel the need to follow suit. If one gets fake lips, then the rest feel compelled to do the same. For us men used to being around such women, we stop noticing. The more they alter themselves, the more they lose their true essence, as if they need artificial parts to fill the gaps. I am not hating on them, obviously, I went for it often, I just don't think I ever thought much of it. I can understand if a person has a flaw and it hurts their confidence, but I realize now that those very flaws they hate may be the thing someone else is attracted to. Aria doesn't need any of that. Even if she felt she was lacking physically, which she isn't, her intelligence more than compensates.

For the first time in my life, I'm realizing how incredibly attractive it is for a woman to nurture her intellect rather than focus solely on her appearance. It's truly captivating. Today, her hair is down, messy yet perfect. She's got her bare feet up on the dashboard while she jots down notes in a journal, occasionally pausing to chew on her pen. She's wearing an oversized black T-shirt and leggings, nothing extravagant, but — wow. We've only been on the road for a couple of hours, and I'm already unsure how I'll keep it together in this car for another ten hours. I find myself craving more moments alone with her, yet I don't want to come on too strong and scare her away. There's something going on between her and Archer, and to be honest, he's probably the better choice for her, but I can't just step aside. To me, she's as close as I'll get to Pandora's box. I also don't want to create unnecessary distractions, especially since we all have a lot going on right now.

Kat is squeezed between Archer and Jaliah in the backseat. Fortunately, she's petite, and we can almost fit her anywhere. Even though we've only known her for a short time, she seems to blend in perfectly. It feels like she's been through a tough period. I recognize that look; I carried it myself for a long time. The difference is, I'm better at pretending than she is. Pretending helped prevent me from sinking deeper into darkness. Not that my coping mechanism is superior—it leads to emotional numbness—but her approach seemed like it could have been her undoing. I might be entirely wrong. Yet, I can sense when someone is grateful for being rescued, and she looks at us like we did more than just save her physically. I suspect there might be something brewing between her and Archer. It could just be my imagination, but if the two of them do connect, it would clear the way for me regarding Aria. Jaliah remains a mystery to me. I can't quite tell if she's had a tough life, but she doesn't view us as her saviors. Instead, she regards us as a new challenge or adventure. This journey opens up numerous possibilities for her. Perhaps her life was dull or routine, and this trip is the most excitement she's had in a while.

Most of the routes we've charted are back roads. They aren't the quickest, but for some reason, we all agreed they felt safer. Our instincts guided us in that direction. I had an odd sensation last night in the motel lobby. A man was checking in before me, and it was as if malevolence radiated from him; I could sense it, almost taste and smell it. I felt something similar when looking at the map. The major highways and interstates felt wrong, much like that man did.

"Want some music on?" Aria's voice cuts through my thoughts.

"Sure! Might help with the awkward silence," I reply with a wink.

She turns on the radio, and for some reason, her music choice feels significant, like it will reveal a bit more about her. I tried to guess her selection before she hit the power button. I was wrong; I expected it to be pop, but it wasn't. It was a blend of blues, soul, and reggae—not what I anticipated. I've never heard this song before, indicating she enjoys music that's not mainstream. It's good to know. People who prefer non-mainstream things often think more independently than those who simply follow trends dictated by others. She's chewing on the pen again, tapping her feet to the beat of the music. I have to force myself to turn my head back to the road. The never-ending road covered in trees that we are stuck on for ten. More. Hours. The gas light dings, breaking the concentration I just worked so hard to obtain, however, perfect timing for a distraction. Aria instantly grabs the map to type in the closest gas station. "10 minutes away — usually when the light comes on there's about 20 miles left," she says.

"Is that a thing every woman does?" I ask

"What?" she questions back.

"Ride on 'E' so often that you know how long the gas light lasts" I reply laughing.

She just rolls her eyes and smiles back, like she wants to be sarcastic, but she knows it's true. 10 minutes go by pretty quickly, and I can now see a sign signaling the gas station ahead. I pull in, put the car in park, and jump out to turn the pump on. I'm not sure where the others are at financially, but I have plenty, so they shouldn't have to worry. Aria comes around the vehicle and lets me know she could have gotten it. We come to a middle ground when we agree that she will grab us something to drink instead. Moments later Jaliah jumps out, pulling a tin from her bag. The moment it is open I can instantly tell what is inside, as the pungent odors floats my way. I turn to look at her as she flicks the lighter at the end of the small joint.

"Don't get all judgy, the backseat is uncomfortable, this is for my back" she says when she notices I am looking at her.

"No judgment! You do what you gotta do, just maybe not so close to the pump thats literally full of flamable liquid." I say. Moments later we're all back in the car, and back on the road we go.

Twenty-Six

Katerina

In just twenty-four hours, everything can change, sometimes even in less time. I found a friend in magic, wholeheartedly trusting its essence. I let it into my life, allowing it to guide me in ways I never experienced before. One moment, I was standing on the metaphorical edge, seriously considering ending it all, and the next, I was in a vehicle, squeezed between people I trust more than anyone else in my past, feeling completely safe. We've been given a mission, and for the first time, I feel like I matter. In the bigger picture, I used to be a nobody. I didn't truly matter. If I had died, the world would have continued spinning without a hitch. Now, I'm an essential part of keeping the world turning. I live for more than just myself now. We started our journey early this morning, and we've made significant progress. Vega drove for the first four hours, but now he's curled up by the back door, catching some sleep. Aria is driving now, with about an hour left before she swaps with Archer. I volunteered to go after Archer, mainly so I could sit up front while he drives. He thinks I was asleep last night, but I felt him comfort me. Nightmares are a common occurrence for me, but it's the first time since childhood that someone has tried to soothe them.

It's funny how something so small can create such a strong connection. It doesn't hurt that he's absolutely stunning. There's a good chance he doesn't see me in that way—I'm pretty sure he's interested in Aria, and so is Vega. But honestly, I don't mind; there's no rule against having a secret crush. Plus, it adds a little thrill to my days. I've had enough therapy to recognize transference, and maybe a part of me is projecting the "magic saved me" feeling onto him, but he's shown me his caring nature, and I'm definitely drawn to that. The day is already halfway over, and we're planning to drive partway through the night. We don't want to arrive at our destination in the middle of the night, so we'll look for a campground nearby when we get close. I'm using my time to check the map for a campground with a shower house and a spot to restock our supplies. Who knows how long we'll be with the conduit for training, so it's wise to pack some extra provisions for that as well.

I found a campground and luckily its only about 15 minutes off our route, which will leave us with an hour's drive tomorrow morning to reach our destination. Additionally, I located a Walmart a few hours from where we are now, perfect for restocking supplies and stretching our legs. I send the details of both locations to Archer's phone so he can update our map with the stops. At our next fuel stop, Archer will take over the driving, and I'll finally be free from being wedged between two sleeping giants. I close my eyes to catch a short nap during the next hour of our journey. When I wake, we're pulling into a gas station—one of the good ones with a variety of snacks and drinks. Up until now, we've only come across small country stations with barely a working cooler. I'm craving a fountain drink. I slip my boots back on and hurry inside to grab one, with Archer trailing behind me. He jokes about me needing to stop for a bathroom break if I gulp down that fountain drink, but I'm willing to stop on the roadside if necessary—it's a small price to pay.

When we are back in the car, I am comfortably up front while Archer is in the driver's seat. I notice as Aria slides into the middle of the back seat that Vega is quick to claim the seat next to her. I also notice the little looks they share with each other, the kind that screams "We have a secret". It is cute actually, plus, once again, that takes Aria out of the game for Archer. Archer flashes me a smile as he puts the Jeep into drive to pull off, asking me if I am happy now that I have my drink. His smile is perfect, but

I am holding my facial expressions back, so he can't tell that I think that. Shortly after we set off, raindrops begin to hit the windshield. I gaze out at the sky as the clouds above us darken. I've always found bad weather comforting—perhaps it mirrored the gloom I once felt inside. Even though I've managed that darkness now, I still adore the rain. The thunder reverberates through my chest as it rumbles across the sky. I sense Archer's gaze on me, but I keep my focus on the storm.

"You know, it might be wise for everyone to touch base with family or whoever before we arrive," I suggest to him.

"Why do you think that?" he asks.

"Well, we don't know how long we'll be gone. What if someone notices we're missing and panics?" I explain.

"Yeah, good point. My family isn't used to hearing from me often, but it might be smart to check in," he agrees.

"We should all decide what we're going to say. Not that our friends or family know each other enough to compare stories, but just in case something happens, we can stay consistent with our story," I propose.

"True, I suppose saying we're off to the woods to learn magic isn't the best idea," he chuckles.

"Maybe we should just tell everyone we're going on a cruise. That would explain why we're out of contact for a while. Or say we're on some retreat that doesn't allow cell phones. Not that we won't have them, but there's a good chance we won't have service, woods and all ya know." I suggest.

"True, maybe the retreat is the best bet. No one judges someone for disappearing for a retreat, everyone has reason for that" He says. He is right, there are a million reasons a person might leave for a retreat of some kind.

Talking with him feels effortless. Unlike many others, he doesn't dismiss me or treat me like a child. Due to my small stature, people often assume I'm much younger, leading them to overlook me. Not that ignoring a child is acceptable, but it happens. During the next part of our journey, time seems to fly by. Archer and I chat about various topics, nothing deeply personal—just music, hobbies, and lighthearted jokes about using magic to avoid working for money. The storm trails us as if moving in the same direction, which suits me perfectly. About ten minutes from reaching Walmart, the rain intensifies, obscuring our view of the road, forcing us to crawl along at twenty miles per hour. The downpour is so loud against the Jeep's soft top that it rouses everyone in the backseat. Arriving at the parking lot, we quickly decide to dash inside to avoid getting drenched. Archer drops us at the entrance, and we wait just inside the doors for him to park and join us. We stick together, ensuring no one is left behind. Once we're all safely inside the store, we split into two groups to tackle the shopping list more efficiently.

Fifteen minutes later, we all gather at the front of the store, ready to check out. It was the quickest shopping trip ever. We pay and head towards the exit, prepared to dash to the car, but to our surprise, it's completely dry outside. It seems the rain had unleashed everything it had at once and now had nothing left. We leisurely load the Jeep, as everyone seems tired of being cramped inside and reluctant to get back in. I inform them that I found a nearby campground, so we won't be confined much longer. We pile back into the vehicle and set off, this time fully awake, singing along to the music and making the most of the seemingly endless drive. We arrive just before sunset, with just enough light to set up camp. Everyone immediately starts grabbing gear as if they have designated roles I wasn't aware of. I decide to choose a task and join in, so they don't think I'm slacking off—firewood it is. I search the woods near the site, careful not to wander too far, staying within sight of the group. I carefully stack the wood into a teepee shape in the center of a rock circle and place some small sticks inside. I look through the bags for a lighter but don't want to interrupt anyone since they're all busy.

Something inside me suggests I don't need a lighter to ignite the fire, like a intuition or something. I walk back to my pile of sticks, extending my hands toward them. They had told me about testing out thier magic skills and that they used intention to manipulate it. I draw on something within and will the fire to start. A warmth spreads through my body, beginning at my feet and moving through my core, up my arms, and out through my hands. Red bands of glowing light emerge from my palms, with tiny embers of bright orange flickering around them. In moments, the fire is blazing with red flames tipped in blue. I am bursting with pride, smiling at my creation. I did that! With my hands! Archer walks over, nudging me in the ribs and telling me I got that done quickly. I am giggling with excitement telling him I did that with my magic. He gives me a smirk, letting me know he is impressed. This was my first real go at using magic, and I did it!

One by one, they gather around the fire, each of us lost in silent contemplation. We're uncertain about what tomorrow holds—whether it will bring fear or excitement. We don't know if it will be a physical or mental challenge, or if it will grant us a bit more freedom. But for now, we are safe, happy, and not alone. Aria and Jaliah distribute dinner, advising us to have a good meal before bed. We eat our fill and laugh about what seemed important just a week ago. When tough times come, I want to remember this moment. This moment, along with Archer's kindness last night, will help me through the challenges ahead. We decide to get a good night's rest since we're unsure how much sleep we'll get after tonight. We reach out to our connected, calling them as a team. They join us promptly, standing united across from us.

"We called you to ask if you could place a protective boundary around our camp like before?" Archer inquires.

"Unfortunately, right now only certain locations on earth can be protected this way, but unlike you, we don't need sleep tonight. We will watch over your camp and awaken you if danger arises," Ophelian replies.

"Any idea what we should expect tomorrow?" Aria questions.

"You will learn, observe, and practice. It's not a vacation or summer camp. Your goal is not merely to survive, but to grow your power and thrive," Atticus explains.

"You've impressed us so far, supporting each other, expressing emotion, and becoming a team without realizing it. We are proud," Lexora comments.

"Rest now, we'll be here keeping watch," Nyterian concludes.

We crawl into the tent and slip into our sleeping bags, each of us feeling a shared sense of unease. Our closeness is evident as we choose to sleep within arm's reach of one another, providing comfort in proximity. I find myself unintentionally positioned between Vega, whose back is turned to me, and Archer. I roll onto my side to face Archer, who is also facing me. In a hushed tone, I confess, "I've had nightmares ever since I was a child, they stopped for a moment when I met Nyterian, but occasionally one slips through." Despite knowing he's aware, I felt the need to voice it.

"I know," he softly replies, "You had one last night. Don't be embarrassed; it's just a dream, and you're not alone. I'm right here." His fingers intertwine with mine as he reassures me.

"Goodnight, Archer, and... thank you," I whisper, closing my eyes and quickly drifting off to sleep.

Twenty-Seven

Aria

Morning arrives quickly, making it feel as though we had only just fallen asleep. I missed witnessing the sunrise today, but I suppose I needed the extra rest. The tent is so silent that I hesitate to move, not wanting to disturb anyone else. Vega's arm is outside his sleeping bag, his hand resting beneath my hip. Hopefully, the others didn't wake up and notice, but if they did, maybe they assumed it was accidental. I carefully unzip my sleeping bag, moving as slowly as possible to avoid waking the others, and step over the sleeping bodies between me and the door. I'm trying to quietly unzip the door when I hear Archer stirring, getting out of his sleeping bag. I slip outside, with him following, zipping the door just enough to keep it closed but not completely. I gather the coffee supplies, fill the percolator, and place it on the grate over the now extinguished fire. I attempt to light it using my magic, like Kat did last night, but I can only manage a small flame. Archer joins me, but even together, we can't ignite it as Kat did. I end up tossing some small sticks and logs under the grate and use a lighter to get the fire going. It didn't take long for the fire to make the coffee maker rattle around while it boiled the heavenly nectar. The smell of coffee fills the air, making my senses wake up just a little bit.

"I'm glad you took the plunge to get out of the tent," Archer says

"What do you mean?" I ask

"I have been awake a while but didn't want to move around and wake the others, so when you started out of the tent I decided to take the window before it was quiet again" he answered.

"I can't believe I slept past the sunrise, I guess the drive made me more tired than I thought," I say

"I think the only reason I was awake so early was because of the anticipation. I don't know if I should be scared or excited for today, but I do know it at least feels like progress" He says

"How are your lungs doing? Still all healed and feeling good?" I ask

"Honestly, it feels like I was never even sick. This trip feels like we have been doing this for ages, I have to actually force myself to remember that just a week ago I was basically on my deathbed at the mercy of someone else's death to make a transplant available. It's crazy you know, to remember where we were and look at where we are. Like how was that even our real lives?" He says in a very philosophic demeanor.

"It's been a wild ride, and I am pretty sure next week we will look back in even more shock and awe" I laugh in reply

The tent's zipper slides open, and Jaliah pokes her head out, her messy curls wrapped in satin. She glances at us with a mock look of disgust, realizing we're wide awake when she'd rather still be asleep. "Good morning bitches" she says as she yawns and stratches. Vega and Kat emerge after her, suggesting our attempts at stealth were less effective than we thought. I pour coffee for everyone and hand out the cups to the eager hands before me. There aren't many verbal "Thanks," mostly just grunts that serve as gratitude.

"I plan to head over to the shower house for a quick rinse before we hit the road. Does anyone else need one before we leave?" I ask the group.

"I want to rinse off too, but I'll take down the tent first. Maybe we should go in groups to avoid delaying our departure and because it's safer if no one goes alone," Jaliah suggests.

"Alright, I'll gather my stuff. I think each shower is in a separate room, so if anyone else wants to go, I might be able to save the one next to mine," I respond. Everyone is so exhausted that no one is really paying attention, nor do they look ready for a shower. I head to the back of the Jeep to grab my shower bag and a change of clothes. As I turn around, I accidentally bump into Vega's chest.

"Whoa! Sorry! I didn't even hear you come up!" I exclaim, startled and a bit embarrassed, feeling the heat rise in my cheeks.

"No, I'm sorry! I didn't mean to sneak up, I was just going to grab some clothes and go rinse off too, none of the others are alive enough, and you don't need to go alone" He says, completely aware of my red cheeks but covering it up for me.

I watch him as he grabs his t-shirt, jeans, and a towel and heads in my direction. We make our way to the shower house in silence. There are a lot of unspoken words floating in the air that neither of us speaks. God, he is so hot, even first thing in the morning, without even trying. He is scary hot — like I should run hot. But of course, I don't, I just keep walking towards the showers, trying my best not to picture him naked in that shower.

When we get there, we find only one shower room available, with two stalls inside. This actually works out better for safety reasons, but my mind races with thoughts of him showering—naked—in the stall next to mine. He politely offers to let me go first, saying he'll keep watch at the door. I assure him it's fine, and he can use the other stall. We enter the shower room and secure the door, ensuring no one or nothing can come in after us.

I pull the curtain closed in my stall and hang my clean clothes high on a peg to keep them dry. Campground showers always seem to have water splashing everywhere. I turn on the faucet, hoping for hot water—ideally, scalding—to kickstart my morning. Thankfully, it's perfect! I strip off my dirty clothes and step into the stream, letting it pour over my head and body. As I lather up my washcloth and begin scrubbing my arms, I hear the sound of my curtain rings scraping against the metal rod. Suddenly, familiar arms wrap around me. I freeze as my heart feels like it's about to burst from my chest. I know these are Vega's arms, having memorized them in a non-creepy way, and besides, the door is locked. I force myself to relax so I don't scare him off, thinking he's crossed a line. I want this, even if it's just a temporary distraction for both of us, and though it's not typical for me, I still want it.

For a fleeting moment, he stands motionless beneath the cascading water, its warm current wrapping us in an intimate, liquid veil. In that suspended second, his hesitation flutters like a whispered secret—as if he teeters on the edge of an unspoken boundary. In response, I sink deeper into his embrace, silently assuring him that his nearness is not only welcome but deeply craved, dissolving any remaining distance between our souls. Encouraged by this unspoken communication, his stance relaxes while his hold grows surer, and he plants tender, lingering kisses along the nape of my neck. As I tilt my head ever so slightly, inviting his passion to trace each curve, I can physically feel his arousal. With his left arm securely entwined around my waist, grounding me in our shared world, his right hand embarks on a voyage of discovery. Though I strive to remain composed, the exquisite sensation of his touch on my nipple sends ripples of delight through me, stirring emotions that threaten to overwhelm my restraint.

I shift within his arms, turning to face him as my touch beckons him closer. With a possessive grip around his neck, I pull him nearer, closing the gap with a yearning too profound for words. As warm steam swirls around us, thickening the atmosphere and softening every breath, he clutches my hips and effortlessly lifts me. My legs instinctively wrap around his waist, heightening the intimacy until our kiss becomes a fiery frenzy, consuming every ounce of restraint. In a dizzying turn, I feel the cool press of a tiled wall behind me as he gently guides me against it, his lips mapping a trail downward to my breast. Each caress kindles new shivers throughout my body until the intensity is nearly palpable. he pulls back, looking at me as if he is worried, "Are you ok with this?" in a tender whisper. I nod, my answer unspoken yet unmistakable, before pressing my lips to his once more—and then, in a surge of passion, he enters me, a consummation of desire and profound connection that sends ecstatic waves reverberating through every fiber of my being.

He begins with a delicate cadence, each measured thrust unleashing a cascade of tingles that ripple through me. A spontaneous moan escapes my lips, a momentary echo of vulnerability that I quickly banish, choosing instead to surrender fully to the intensity of our union. As his rhythm shifts from gentle to fervent, his arm secures me against the wall, ensuring that I remain anchored in our shared heat. With every thrust, a wildfire of sensation ignites between us, pushing me ever closer to the edge. Amid the swelling pleasure, our eyes meet—his gaze mirroring the storm of desire brewing within me. I see in his eyes the silent struggle to maintain control, the bottom lip caught between teeth in a breathless battle against surrender. Witnessing his equally conflicted yet unabashed desire shatters my resistance; a flood of ecstasy courses through me, compelling uncontrollable expressions of bliss as my shoulders press against the cold tile and my center arches against him. A primal growl escapes him, deep and resonant, harmonizing with our shared release until my limbs soften and I collapse into a state of sweet, exhausted rapture.

After tenderly placing me down, he turns me until I face the wall, and the charged tension between us solidifies into a nearly palpable current. His determination intensifies, driven by the certainty that he has completely unveiled every layer of my being. My fingers splay against the cool tile for support as his hands possessively cradle my hips, thrusting into me with deliberate force. One hand snakes from behind, wrapping around my throat—not to constrict, but to draw my upper body closer, his teeth sinking softly into my shoulder, sending shivers down my spine as he rhythmically moves within me. His hand glides with purpose from my throat, pausing to appreciate the fullness of my breast before journeying down to my clit. With practiced precision, he circles and flicks in perfect harmony with his thrusts until restraint is no longer an option. In that exquisite moment, I recognize that my supposed self-control was nothing more than an illusion; as my climax washes over me with overwhelming force, it grips him with equal intensity. Our shared release reverberates like an intricate symphony, our souls interwoven in a magnificent crescendo of raw passion and absolute surrender.

Then, with a gentle shift, he pulls me close once more, turning me to face him and encircling me in his arms as he presses me against the wall and leans in to bestow upon me a new series of slow, tender kisses filled with raw, unspoken emotion. After a few moments of whispered intimacy, he tenderly releases me and turns me away, leaving the lingering taste of his affection in the air. The soft snap of a shampoo lid interrupts our sensual haze, and I feel the stirring anticipation of further intimate care. His fingers deftly weave through my hair—a sensation both electrifying and soothing. With a deliberate tenderness, he rinses the shampoo from my strands and follows with the same meticulous attention while applying the conditioner. In that intimate act, I discover a hidden passion in the simple art of care—a realization that having a man wash my hair can be an exquisitely erotic experience. And his actions do not cease there; once my hair is gently cleansed, he retrieves a bar of soap and, with slow, circular motions, caresses every inch of my skin.

I stand in awe, surrendering to the spectacle of him worshipping my body with reverence. In that unguarded moment, there is no room for shyness—only the raw, unfilteredness of our connection. In return, I offer the same indulgence, letting my fingers trace the flawless contours of his sculpted physique—a body that seems designed for both forbidden magazines and whispered admiration. Together, we rinse away the remnants of passion in the now warm, languid water as he continues to paint fleeting kisses along my forehead and down my neck. And in that surreal, unyielding moment, I revel in the delicious clarity that I am unequivocally awake, living a dream crafted entirely of raw desire, but also — tender intimacy.

We dry off and dress in silence—not out of awkwardness, but because everything that needed to be communicated was already said in that shower without a single explicit word. The way he kissed me didn't hint at a casual fling; it declared his desire, as if he not only wanted me, but needed me. Rather than simply finishing with me and leaving me to tidy up on my own, he even washed my hair. That simple act felt like one of the most romantically charged encounters I've ever experienced. I do my best to towel dry my hair and run a hairbrush through it, eventually handing the brush over to him when I'm done. As I grab my toothbrush and begin brushing my teeth, I glance over and see him doing the same, and I can't help but giggle at the sight.

"What?!" he exclaims, the first real words spoken aloud beyond whispers or moans since we came into this room.

"Nothing," I reply. "With everything happening and—well, you know—other things, here we are, just casually brushing our teeth together."

"Oh, darlin', there isn't a thing casual about it," he says, managing to sound irresistible even with a toothbrush in his mouth.

We finish up and leave the shower house for the camp, exchanging lighthearted jokes as we regain our composure. I pause, turning to him, "Okay, this might sound really stupid, but I have to ask," I blurt out.

"Alright, shoot," he says.

"On our first night in the tent...I mean, I think I dreamt about us... actually, it's harder to say than I thought. Fuck..Umm.. Did we mess around?" I ask, hesitating.

"If we had, I'd hope you wouldn't be left wondering if it was all just a dream," he replies with a wink. "To answer, no, we didn't.

I thought about it—a lot—but didn't want to ruin things before they even began."

"Okay… Well, damn. I guess it was just a really vivid, realistic dream," I say, laughing off the awkward feeling.

As we head back to camp, Archer and Kat have gathered their things and are ready to head to the showers themselves. I mention that only one shower house is open and that we have to take turns, omitting the detail that the turns come in the form of orgasms rather than showers. It isn't long before they return. Jaliah had rushed down when another shower became available, quickly rinsed off, and rejoined them. By the time they got back, we'd already finished loading the Jeep and tidying the campsite. They tossed the remainder of their gear into the back, and we set off, letting Vega handle the drive for the next hour toward the forest entrance marked on our map.

Twenty-Eight

Vega

We have just an hour left until we reach our destination, yet I can't shake off thoughts of this morning. I need to be careful about fixating on it, or everyone in this car might catch on. This morning made all my past encounters seem trivial. It's not that I haven't had great experiences before—I certainly have—but nothing ever felt like this. What happened earlier wasn't just incredible in sex; it was an intense combination of raw emotion and flawless connection. It set a standard that seems unattainable for anyone else. She's up front again, her bare feet perched on the dashboard, chewing a pen. Why does that drive me crazy? If we were alone, I'd be tempted to stop the car just to kiss her. I don't need anything more; the kiss itself would be enough. Her eclectic music is playing again, and she's singing along as if no one is listening. On our first night at camp, she accidentally accessed her magic, making us all feel what she was experiencing. That thought lingers. I briefly wondered if that's what draws me to her, but I felt this pull even before we dove into our magical abilities.

That night in the tent, she dreamt about me. If she'd made us all feel what she was experiencing, the tent would have been uncomfortable the next morning. Her dreaming of me meant she desired me just as much as I did her. I'm accustomed to women wanting me, but I've never longed for their desire like I do for hers. Truthfully, now that I know she desires me, I can't imagine wanting anyone else's attention. The parking spot our instincts led us to is a small grassy area in the national park, marked by a wooden sign with a built-in map. Only those planning to stay overnight would park here, as none of the trails are day hike loops, leaving the lot entirely empty. I shift the vehicle into park and turn off the ignition. We sit silently for a moment, as if we're all pondering the next step.

"Should we get out?" I whisper, as if someone might overhear who shouldn't. Without a word, everyone begins unbuckling and exiting the Jeep. I walk over to the wooden sign with the trail map to understand what lies ahead when I hear the sound of wings landing behind me. Turning around, I see Atticus and Ophelian touching down in the parking lot. Moments later, Lexora, Kobin, and Nyterian emerge from the woods into the clearing. "Glad you all found your way," Atticus remarks with a neutral tone.

"I know you have questions, and we're here to assist. You need to bring everything you can carry because you won't be returning for supplies during your training. Whatever you don't pack, you'll have to find a way to procure. The forest provides nearly everything you need, but not everything you want. Enter at the trailhead and follow the path. You'll instinctively know where to go, without a map or further instructions," Ophelian explains.

"Stay alert and stick together," Lexora advises. "You'll encounter things that aren't what they appear to be, and some you might not comprehend initially. The conduit lies in a protected zone, a space between two realms, meaning you'll be crossing through the time barrier. Observe everything, as each element tells a story, and every story holds knowledge to gather." The Tribunal turns away from us, heading into the woods at the trailhead entrance and vanishing into the shadows. We grab our packs and load them with as much as possible. We swap out some basic food for other supplies, as food can be gathered, but not the other essentials. The packs are heavy, but once strapped on, the weight is manageable.

Archer and I have a brief discussion and agree that it's best for us to take charge of the group's front and back—one leading and one guarding the rear. It's not about power;

it's about safeguarding the group and keeping us unified. I offer to take the rear if he wants to lead. We're unsure of what lies ahead or what might follow us, so both positions pose risks. With everything ready and the Jeep securely locked, we head to the trailhead, each taking a deep breath as we step across the threshold. The trail is well-marked with red triangles nailed to trees for direction in case the path becomes unclear, but it's currently well blazed. The woods are stunning, with towering trees reaching out as if in a friendly embrace. The vibrant colors and earthy scents are inviting and warm.

Occasionally, wild animals cross our trail and pause to observe us, not out of fear, but with curiosity. Squirrels and chipmunks scamper among the trees, perching on branches as our watchers. It feels as though even the forest creatures are cheering us on. We hike throughout the day and set up camp at night, falling asleep instantly once everything is set up. Our plan is to continue in the morning, even though our destination remains uncertain. This routine repeats the next day, but by the third day, it feels like we're finally making progress. After about an hour of hiking, we begin to hear a faint ticking sound, kind of like a clock, somewhere in the distance. With each step, the sound becomes clearer. As it grows louder, more forest animals gather to watch us, turning our journey into a parade with them as the onlookers. As we approach, the rhythmic ticking intensifies, leading us to the core of the trail. There, a magnificently massive wooden clock tower emerges, commanding attention with its grandeur. Intricate gold details embellish its structure, creating an elegant tapestry within the woodwork. The clock face, made of solid gold, shines with a timeless allure, while tiny wheels inside the tower spin with each measured tick.

Massive golden gears affixed to the clock's face turn in perfect unison, projecting hypnotic patterns of light and shadow. The steady tick-tock fills the air, drawing us in with its rhythm as we draw near as a group, entranced by the complex splendor of this venerable timekeeper. We approach the clock tower with a mix of caution and certainty, knowing all too well that this is our destined spot. As we align ourselves side by side, eyes fixed on the clock, the ticking abruptly ceases. An eerie silence falls—no ambient noise from nature, no whisper of wind, no hum of life, not even a beat of our hearts dares to break the hush. For a few lingering moments, time seems to hang in a silence so profound it almost shouts. Then, without warning, the clock roars back to life, startling us all. Its ticking quickens, each pulse accelerating time until the world blurs into a wild, dizzying dance.

In the blink of an eye, rapid flashes of history burst around us in vivid detail, as if we are living in the moments long past. The scenes play out around us, like recordings being projected all around us. We remain rooted to the spot, swept up in the relentless flow of history surging about the ancient clock tower. Knowledge floods us in the way the

Tribunal had promised. Right before our eyes, every fairy tale and superhero archetype we once knew from stories spring into life. They seem different than the legends we remember, yet their existence is unmistakably real—Snow White mingling with woodland creatures, Cinderella clad in her elegant gown and iconic glass slippers, and Belle standing alongside a misunderstood beast of a man. They inhabit a realm where magic intertwines with the everyday, casting enchantments under the shadow of an ancient castle.

Goldilocks plays in the forest with a family of bears, while a soaring figure reminiscent of Superman swoops in to rescue those in peril. Each unfolding scene is rendered with such clarity that it defies belief, revealing these iconic figures not as mere fictions but as historical personalities whose adventures were once dismissed as children's stories. It gradually becomes clear—the truth long hidden beneath layers of myth. These are not simply fanciful tales, but remnants of events that once shaped our course, deliberately obscured to diminish their importance. Surrounded by the living embodiments of legend, all the pieces of our narrative fall into place, transforming the discarded fantasies of our youth into a profound, undeniable reality. Everything we thought we knew was wrong, and everything we thought was made up, was real.

Amid these fantastical projections, we catch sight of an earlier age—a time when humans lived in reverence with nature, nourishing the very earth that sustains us. Fleeting images recall ancient civilizations: the fabled city of Atlantis, and the enduring myths of Greek gods and goddesses. Here, divine figures, once worshipped as incarnations of power, are unveiled as flesh-and-blood beings who walked among mortals and steered the flow of human events. Man and beast exist side by side in a seamless tapestry, each drawing life and energy from the fertile earth and its creatures. These ancient scenes offer a glimpse into a world where humanity's bond with nature was sacred, where the line between mortal and divine blurred, and where life's rhythms danced in step with the heartbeat of the land. In this merging of myth and fact, we are reminded of the archaic wisdom that once guided our forebears—a wisdom now calling us to rediscover our rightful place in the intricate web of existence.

As the clock's pace quickens, the vivid images meld into a frenzied cascade, as if our minds are absorbing knowledge at an overwhelming rate. Everything we once believed unravels before us, revealing both deception and truth. It is so much information uploaded that my head starts to ache at the temples. We witness the collapse of balance as humanity succumbs to the allure of power and greed—wars shatter lands and great civilizations crumble under ambition's weight. The hallowed texts of history are contorted into mere fables, their truths hidden by the relentless march of time. Politicians we once trusted are exposed as masters of deceit, masking harsh realities that lurk beneath the surface. The world, once nourished by nature's bounty, is now devoured by the unceasing quest for artificial riches, a plague consuming existence itself. In this unstoppable flood of revelations, we see the very foundations of humanity erode. As the clock's tick becomes ever more rapid, we are forced to face the consequences of our choices and the future path of our world.

Then, the images coalesce into a single, dazzling blur of radiant magic, so intense that we shield our eyes. The clock and its surroundings start to dissolve as we plummet into a boundless, brilliant light. And then... Everything comes to a halt. Darkness surrounds us. No sounds, no scents—only a void. Words fail to escape me no matter how hard I try. I feel the cool, damp earth beneath, blanketed by soft moss. Gradually, a faint aroma returns, flooding my senses with the rich scent of an earthy woodland. Light begins to break through, gentle as a distant sunrise spilling its glow over everything. I find myself in a forest—a forest that seems to embody all types of geographical forests. It is the place where I once awoke in my dreams, before understanding what was truly happening. The only difference now is that I can move; this is no longer a dream, but reality.

Twenty-Nine

Aria

Everything I believed to be true has turned out to be false — well, 'false-ish'. So many truths have been concealed that we, as humans, can no longer tell what is genuine. The figures I grew up admiring were real people in history, but in our reality, they've been transformed into fictional characters to hide the truth from us. This isn't a recent development; deception has been part of human history for so long that we've created an entirely new narrative. My mind is completely overwhelmed. It feels like my brain has been connected to a supercomputer and refreshed with new information. When I opened my eyes, I found myself in a place that was both familiar and unfamiliar. It was the forest from my dreams. The scent, the atmosphere, the appearance—

everything matched my dreams perfectly, except this time, I'm truly here, not dreaming. I take a moment to look around, letting my mind process the situation. The entire group is present, all of us sharing the same bewilderment. I suspect that the moment we experienced the clock and the uploaded history session was when we were transported to this place.

I pull my phone from my back pocket and notice the small SOS symbol at the top. No cell service, which is expected. Thankfully, we all made sure to inform anyone who might worry about us that we were heading on a retreat. My job wasn't thrilled about it, but they'll have to deal with it. If we don't succeed here, it won't matter anyway. As I stand up, a wave of nausea hits me, a metallic taste fills my mouth, and the world spins briefly before settling. Perhaps it was a surge of magic—it's not like our bodies are accustomed to traveling through magical portals. The forest is a vibrant green, with various trees thriving. Its colors are more vivid than any forest I've encountered before. The ground is carpeted with flowers, scattering blues, yellows, and purples like confetti. To our left, a path awaits us, lined with small wooden lanterns, each holding a flickering flame. As we approach the path, we exchange a look of excitement, acknowledging the adventure ahead. Tiny golden and blue sparks dance across the forest floor, adding a magical touch as we step onto the trail. As we walk, I'm captivated by the lush vegetation, feeling ferns brushing against our legs, their touch enhancing the enchantment of the forest.

After a short while on the trail, a small cottage appears in the distance, like an enchanted forest home you would see in a movie. Its moss-covered roof merges seamlessly with the surrounding greenery. The cottage's whimsical curves and fairytale design evoke a storybook scene, I can literally picture Snow White singing with birds here. Soft, inviting glimmers peek through the cracks of the wooden shutters on the windows, hinting at the warmth and coziness inside. A gentle stream of smoke gracefully rises from the chimney, adding a rustic charm to the picturesque view. As we approach, the small cottage appears larger, its charm enhanced by the details around it. Wind chimes sway from the low branches of the massive oak trees encircling the cottage, their tones whispering magic in the air. Small glass bottles of various colors hang from the branches, each holding a flickering candle that casts a warm glow. The flower gardens grow more vibrant as we near, their blossoms creating a colorful carpet on the walkway to the doorstep. .

A small creek with crystal-clear blue waters cuts across the path, where a charming bridge calls us forward. I step onto the bridge and gaze down into the creek, entranced by the view. Vibrant fish glide elegantly beneath the surface, their scales shimmering with golden highlights in the sunlight filtering through the canopy. Along the creek's edge, beneath the ferns, a family of ducks takes shelter. Their feathers glisten with golden hues as they nestle among the greenery, and the creek's gentle murmur becomes a soothing melody. After crossing the bridge, we reach the cottage's gated entrance. The wrought iron twists into intricate patterns, adding a touch of elegance. Lanterns on either side of the gate, with golden flames, cast a warm glow on the path ahead. Vega's hand hovers over the gate, pausing as he glances back at us. His gesture silently seeks our agreement to proceed. The air is thick with anticipation and curiosity as we stand on the verge of discovery. "I am going to this is where we're meant to be, and there won't be any witches cooking us for dinner, I mean… we did just learn the whole fairytales are real thing," Jaliah jokes.

"Well, I don't see another path, so let's just go. If there's a witch, let's hope they choose Vega first," Archer jokes back. "What?! I only mean because he's the strongest!" he laughs as Vega gives him a look. With determination,

Vega pushes the gate open, which creaks as it swings wide. A breeze swirls around us, infused with gold and blue hues, welcoming us through. We step through, feeling the warmth engulf us like a comforting embrace. As the last of us crosses into the sanctuary, the gate gently closes behind us, not as a barrier, but as a gesture of belonging. Suddenly, a majestic deer emerges from the shadows, its towering form radiant in white, with antlers gleaming in gold. We recognize it immediately as a member of the Tribunal, at least we assume it is since it matches how our connected look, its body adorned with the same golden filigree. In its noble gaze, we sense not only authority but also a profound sense of welcome.

"My name is Ethos. I am a member of the Tribunal and the connected of your teacher, Beren. He has asked me to welcome you all, as we have been anticipating your arrival for quite some time. Your rooms are prepared with nearly everything you will need. Please go ahead, unpack, and then join us at the back of the cottage for a meal and some instruction," he tells us, his voice resonating with strength and intelligence. Following Ethos's directions, we enter the cottage and are immediately struck by the contrast between its modest exterior and the lavish grandeur inside. What looked small from the outside now unfolds into a grand mansion of regal proportions. Beneath our feet lies a grey marble floor, each stone embellished with swirling black patterns that seem to dance vibrantly. In the center, a grand staircase rises with elegance, its banister seemingly carved from raw gold, shimmering with an otherworldly glow. Our eyes drift to the walls, where the interior resembles the heart of a geode. Rich purples and turquoises intermingle with veins of gold, creating a mesmerizing tapestry of color and light that fills the room with a celestial aura. It feels as though we have stepped into a place where the essence of nature intertwines with the splendor of the unknown.

As we climb the staircase with deliberate care, the room's very nature appears fragile, as if each step might disturb its otherworldly charm. In the corners, trees seem to sprout from the floor, their branches ascending to form elaborate supports for the ceiling. This ceiling, a stunning stained glass wonder, fills the space with a vibrant array of colors, sending prismatic light dancing around the room. At the top, a long corridor unfolds before us, stirring our curiosity. Doors that resemble leaves line the walls, each labeled with a name. We find our own names among them, but some we don't recognize.

"Well, I guess this is my room," Kat remarks, approaching the door bearing her name and an intricately carved fox. I spot mine too, marked with an owl. As everyone else finds their room, I can't help but admire the detailed carvings on each door. Stepping into my room, I set down my pack and take in the space, struck by how much it mirrors my dreams. The room feels oddly recognizable, as though it were plucked straight from my imagination. My gaze settles on the bed. Delicate curtains in an array of beautiful hues, accented with gold stitching, hang gracefully from the ceiling around the bed. Every fiber of my being longs to sink into those sumptuous linens, to be swallowed up by their softness, and succumb to the tranquility of the room. Standing at the threshold of this enchanting space, I feel profound gratitude for the opportunity to experience such beauty and comfort.

When I open the wardrobe tucked in the room's corner, expecting a simple closet, I'm astonished to discover much more. It unfolds into a spacious dressing area, its shelves and racks adorned with garments for every occasion. My eyes drink in the sight before me, lingering on elegant pieces that hang with regal poise. Neat rows of exquisite shoes await their turn to add a touch of glamour, while silken gowns, delicate and luxurious, fall casually from their hangers. Among the finery, I also spot attire fit for training—sleek and impeccably tailored, designed for easy movement. Yet interwoven with the practical garb, flowing robes offer a gentle allure, their silken fabrics whispering of leisure and relaxation. With a sense of appreciation, since honestly, everything I have with me has already been worn and stinks, I stow my pack in the corner of the closet and draw a robe whose cool, smooth fabric caresses my skin. "This will work for dinner!" I muse.

Once changed, I venture back into the hallway only to see the rest of the group embracing the same transformation. Everyone seems to have donned what looks like luxurious loungewear—I haven't felt this comfortable in days! I laugh to myself, we told our jobs and families we were going on a retreat, and right now — we look just like the rich people who go on 'spiritual' retreats just to check out of reality for a bit. We are definitely checked out of what we thought was reality. We all head down the stairs, making our way toward the back of the cottage. The back opens into an immense sunroom where tropical plants flourish in every nook. At the very center, a table large enough to seat about twenty people stands, seemingly hewn directly from a colossal redwood tree and placed before the walls were even built. Across the room, a man in a white robe stands by a giant window. I suspect it's Baren, though my attention is immediately captivated by the view. It feels as if the cottage has been carved into the side of a waterfall—green moss clinging to the rock bordering the window while water cascades gracefully down the vertical face above us.

The man turns to greet us, his stature towering above us in his long white robe. His long, white hair and beard frame eyes that seem to hold all the world's wisdom. In moments, memories flood back from the clocktower—the realization that many of our childhood tales were actually inspired by real individuals. My inner child overflows with excitement, knowing that although those stories were fictionalized, they still captured the essence of the people they were based on. He looks just like….. Sensing the thoughts racing through me, Baren fixes his knowing gaze on me and speaks, his voice laden with timeless wisdom and familiarity. "Yes, my dear child," he begins. "While Albus is not my name as the stories use, it reflects the essence woven through generations of stories. I do, however, have vast knowledge, and I am here to guide you, not as a 'wizard professor' but… a teacher nonetheless. The Tribunal has worked diligently to preserve fragments of magic in your realm— sometimes these sparks were kindled by inspiring tales." With a playful tone, he adds, "I quite enjoyed that tale myself—perhaps not entirely accurate, but imbued with the essence of guidance that I now bring to you."

I am utterly amazed, looking around to see if the others are as taken aback as I am—each of our faces mirroring the same expression. He then invites us all to sit and dine, explaining that proper nourishment is essential if we are to make the most of the limited time we have. Naturally, we follow his suggestion. Who wouldn't? I'm certain the child inside me would never allow my adult self to let down one of its all-time heroes and favorite storytellers.

Thirty

Aria

We gathered around the table, soaking up the surroundings while listening intently to every word from Baren. He has a remarkable gift: even the simplest sentence from him carries a depth of meaning that you can ponder for hours. The food was exceptional—gourmet to the extreme, completely absent of the processed, preservative-laden fare I was used to. If we were not eventually being called back to the real world to save it, I would choose to remain here forever. We were served wine in heavy, golden goblets, each glass elegantly garnished with delicate orange slices. This wine was unlike any from Earth; it possessed a sense of completeness, its sweetness laced with the flavors of nearly all of my favorite fruits. As the meal concluded, Baren informed us that we would be moving to the back patio with him. It was time to explore the fundamentals—the origins of our magic and the basic techniques to harness it. We got up to clear the table just as two stunning women, their hair flowing down to their knees, entered and offered a graceful bow. They began gathering items from the table, and soon after, two more arrived to wipe and tidy everything up.

We exchanged knowing glances, silently acknowledging that we had stepped into a realm of luxury. Stepping onto the back patio, we were immediately captivated by its surreal beauty. To our left, a magnificent waterfall cascaded down, blending effortlessly with the sunroom's architecture. Crystal-clear water filled a nearby pool, begging us to take a dip via steps leading directly from the patio. Straight ahead, the patio descended onto a lower deck bordered by two majestic oak trees, whose intertwined branches formed a natural canopy overhead. Oversized swings, large enough to serve as daybeds, hung from the sturdy oak branches on either side, providing perfect spots to relax. Tiny, magical lanterns floated in the air, casting a soft glow that danced among the branches and heightened the enchanting atmosphere. To the right, a cozy sitting area awaited, with stone chairs arranged in a circle. As we approached, our attention was drawn to another woman with flowing locks, standing beside a stone basin filled with water and adorned with floating water lilies. With a gentle gesture, she invited us closer and proceeded to cleanse our hands with meticulous care.

We took our seats, filled with eager anticipation of what was about to unfold. In the center of the circle, sparks of every hue began to swirl, creating a mesmerizing display of glowing colors that danced and intertwined, sparking our curiosity and wonder. Baren stepped into the circle and traced a circular motion with his finger, indicating that he was the source of the luminous sparks. In a matter of moments, the sparks coalesced to form the silhouette of a plant; stems shot upward, and flowers unfurled as the sparks wove themselves into a living form. As the sparks disperse and meld into the plant, a living hibiscus bush materializes before our eyes. Baren glances at us, anticipation evident as he observes our reactions. With a determined motion, he swirls his finger in the opposite direction, conjuring a small rain cloud above the plant. Droplets cascade from the cloud, gently caressing the leaves before trickling down to nourish the soil in the clay pot cradling the newly formed plant.

"This is basic magic, a gift once inherent to all humans," Baren explains solemnly. "Tending to the earth was once a shared responsibility among mankind. The earth, resilient as it is, struggles to withstand the onslaught of humanity's unchecked expansion and diminishing connection to magic. We deplete its resources faster than it can replenish itself, and with this degradation comes sickness to all aspects of the natural world—plants, animals, soil, water, and even humanity itself." He pauses. "You have the capacity to do this as well, and today we will evaluate your abilities," Baren asserts. "Mastering the art of growing a plant is the foundation upon which all other aspects of nature magic rest. Defeating chaos is but one facet of our mission; the healing of the earth is equally crucial. Humanity has grown complacent, exploiting resources to create disposable conveniences that serve only to ease our short-term existence. We consume without replenishing, disrupting the delicate balance of nature. Even if chaos were eradicated today and the Siphon terminated, humanity would continue to ravage the earth at the same unsustainable pace—they know no better. It falls upon us to initiate a restructuring of this balance."

"With that in mind, it's important to recognize that each of you possesses a unique strength in nature magic," Baren continues. "Some of you will excel in the art of growth, nurturing seeds into flourishing plants. Others will find their strength lies in the healing of what has already grown, restoring vitality to wilted leaves and fading blooms. While all of you have the capability to perform both tasks, you will naturally gravitate towards one or the other, honing your abilities to their fullest potential. Other elemental magic will be determined later."

"So, who can guess where we start?" Baren prompts the group.

"Um, so far pulling from emotion or intuition has helped with the little bit we played with before," Archer suggests tentatively.

"That is basically correct," Baren confirms. "You will reach inside your soul and summon the magic from within, coaxing it to flow through your body and out through your hands. It's not critical what you do with your hands, but for basic magic, they act as the portal. Visualize your intention and direct the magic where you want it to go," he explains.

"Archer, you'll go first," Baren directs. Archer stands up, shaking off his nervous energy as he stretches his hands toward the center of the circle. Unlike Baren's own demonstration, only blue sparks converge in the middle. The swirling sparks intensify and gradually take shape—smaller than Baren's creation, yet clearly resembling a plant. Thin green tendrils sprout from a clay pot filled with soil, unfurling into longer strands. It is a fern, coming to life right before our eyes. Archer beams at his success as Baren offers him an approving nod. The long-haired woman steps into the circle, gently picks up the pot, and places it along the patio banister to clear the space for the next demonstration.

"Your skill will grow with every practice. Soon, you'll be able to conjure even larger plants. Well done, Archer," Baren commends. "Katerina, it's your turn now." Kat rises, her anticipation evident in her smile. With measured intent, she positions her hands at her sides, spreading her fingers as though directing the very air toward the center.

Flame-colored sparks burst around her, swirling vividly. A sprout bursts from the soil, rapidly stretching into a robust stalk adorned with fuzzy tendrils and light green leaves. At its peak, a flower bud slowly opens to reveal a striking black sunflower—a perfect reflection of Kat's personality: enchanting yet tinged with darkness. Baren nods approvingly as Jaliah steps forward. Her magic swirls into the center of the circle, deep purple sparks dancing around it. From these sparks, a beautiful orchid blooms, its purple and white petals staging a stunning display. I marvel at the unexpected beauty, surprised by her choice, as Jaliah smiles with quiet satisfaction.

After Jaliah's orchid is carefully removed, Vega stands up for his turn. Stretching out his hands, green sparks escape his fingertips, coalescing in the middle with an unusual, fog-like aura. The sparks whirl faster than anyone else's, effortlessly capturing our attention. Rather than a plant, the pot fills with tiny white buttons. As the sparks settle into the soil, they nourish it, and soon white, trumpet-shaped mushrooms blossom, their undersides glowing with an eerie green luminescence like something off a movie. "Interesting choice," Baren remarks with a nod, acknowledging Vega's unique creation. He explains that the green glow is actually bioluminescence—a phenomenon usually visible only in complete darkness. Yet, with the magical abilities we possess, we have the remarkable capacity to see what ordinary eyes cannot.

Nervously, I rise for my turn, feeling the weight of everyone else's successes. What if I'm the only one who can't perform? Setting those doubts aside, I extend my hands and dive deep into my soul to summon my magic. Thoughts of healing the earth and helping others bolster my resolve as a surge of magic emits from my fingertips. When I open my eyes, I see sparks of deep red and fuchsia swirling above the clay pot. Taking a deliberate step forward, I concentrate on forming a small cloud overhead to drizzle water onto the soil as I nurture my plant. Inspired by the jars of herbs back home, I decide to infuse the pot with some of my favorite botanicals. Minutes later, delicate purple blooms adorn lavender stalks while yellow dandelion buds open to reveal themselves. Citrus scents fill the air as a lemon balm flower blossoms. A profound sense of accomplishment washes over me— I've done it. Not to mention, I can grow my own medicine now... I have never been good at growing anything!

Exchanging smiles, we all recognize that we have successfully completed our first lesson in magic, each of us now able to grow a plant from nothing. Baren congratulates us before explaining that if our plants wither over the next few days, we will have failed the lesson —always a catch. He informs us that we have some free time to get acquainted with the cottage until supper, reminding us that he's always available should we have any questions. He also reminds us that this is only the easy part, so we must enjoy these moments of downtime while we can. Jaliah heads inside, mentioning that she's off to enjoy the perfect bed in her room and catch a nap, while Kat and Archer decide to go swimming and savor the refreshing water. I choose to head indoors, assuming that a mansion as grand as this must have a library —and I intend to take full advantage of it.

As I wander through the hallways, I stumble upon a room with the tallest ceilings I've ever seen. I knew there would be a library; how could a place managed by a repository of knowledge like Baren not have one? Shelves stretch from floor to ceiling, filled neatly with books arranged in an aesthetically pleasing manner. In one corner, a plush couch as large as a king-size bed sits near a gigantic circular window that looks like a gateway to the forest outside—the perfect reading spot. I roam the room, my hand gliding over the spines of the books, silently waiting for one to call to me. Across the room, my gaze lands on a dark red book with gold lettering on its binding. That's the one. I move over, pull it from the shelf, and read its title: Atlantis. I settle down on the couch just as I hear the door open softly. Another long-haired woman enters, carrying a tray with a small tea kettle and teacup. Smiling warmly, she places the tray on a small table beside the couch. "It's lavender tea, ma'am. We thought you might enjoy it. If you need anything, just say my name—Alana—and I'll be here," she says with a nod before exiting the room.

I choose a blanket from a woven basket beside the couch, and soon the door opens once more. This time, it's Vega.

"I thought I might find you here. Mind if I stay? I promise I'll be quiet," he says, smiling at me with his "oh so sexy" perfect smile.

"Sure, there's plenty of room," I reply, gesturing toward the couch.

He climbs up, rearranging the pillows and making space by patting the area between them. I join him, leaning my back against his chest as I pull the blanket over my lap. Vega reaches over and pours some tea into the cup, adds a small teaspoonful of honey from a nearby jar, stirs it, and then hands it to me. On the opposite side of the window, a modest pot-belly stove serves as a fireplace. The soft crackle of embers, together with the gentle chirping of birds outside, fills the room with a soothing ambiance. Vega's arm wraps around my waist, drawing me closer as his chin rests tenderly on my shoulder. Just a week ago, romance was hardly a thought, and magic was even less; today, everything has changed. Here I am, nestled in a room buzzing with magic and the warmth of a newfound romance. I try to stifle the fluttering butterflies in my chest and the tingling in my belly as I turn my head, brush my lips gently against his, then open my book.

Thirty-One

Atlantis

Atlantis, the jeweled realm of legend, emerges from the crystalline embrace of the Adriatic—a city where resplendent towers of crushed pearls stretch into the sky, then vanish into the mystic blue depths of the sea. In this enchanted sanctuary, its inhabitants exist in harmonious symphony with the creatures of the deep. Unlike mortal souls tethered to earthly limits, these seafaring sages possess the wondrous magic to breathe beneath the water's surface for endless moments, their lives an endless dance with the ocean's heartbeat.

Beneath the vibrant, iridescent tides—where colors burst in a riot of life far more brilliant than the muted shades of the land—ancient waters swirled with purity and veneration. In *those ages, marine beings roamed wild and free, unafraid of humankind, and humanity, in turn, cast aside dread for the denizens beneath the waves. Offspring born of these mystic waters were forever entwined with the secrets of the deep, their destinies knitted with the creatures of the abyss. Yet even those who sprang from the earth could find their spirits kindred to the mysterious life of the ocean floor.*

Once, Atlantis had flung wide its opulent gates to embrace all of humankind, inviting travelers to drink in its unparalleled wonder. When chaos reigned over the world above, this resplendent haven stood as the last gleaming fortress, immune to the storms of mortal disorder. But as greed began to coil around men's hearts, poisoning pure intentions, Atlantis was forced to retreat behind enchanted barriers, welcoming only those souls whose spirits sang in tune with the ancient swells of the sea.

As cataclysm heralded the fall of magical civilization, the citizens of Atlantis dispersed, blending into neighboring worlds to protect their sacred sanctuary. United, a mystical Tribunal gathered, weaving spells of concealment and sealing their hidden city from the prying eyes of an unraveling world. With a final, awe-inspiring act of preservation, they summoned their combined powers to shroud Atlantis deep within the ocean's forbidden abysses—a secret realm guarded from the pestilence of corruption. There, beneath the weight of time and tide, Atlantis slumbers in enchanted seclusion, awaiting the moment when the scourge of the surface world is banished and she may once again rise, resplendent, into the radiant light.

Thirty-Two

Archer

While everyone else had already tucked into sleep or a good book after our first lesson, Kat and I set out for a spontaneous dip in the swimming hole. I held a small thought that the others might join us, but soon it was just the two of us. The initial excitement quickly gave way to an awkward tension. While I was changing into my simple white swimming shorts, a sliver of doubt made me consider backing out entirely. I could feel a spark growing between us, yet I wasn't certain if I was ready to follow that path. Besides, I suspected I might be using her as a mere distraction since Aria seemed completely charmed by that notorious playboy, Vega. Kat's beauty was undeniable, and it felt like this magical journey was renewing her spirit—a transformation I could relate to all too well, even if it left me torn between wanting to be drawn to her romantically and wanting to protect her like a sibling. She had that way of clinging to anyone who offered even a small kindness, and I worried she might latch onto me before I truly knew what I desired.

After changing, I stepped out of my room and immediately bumped into Jaliah. Today, she was wearing the tiniest white silk sleeping gown I had ever seen—its material barely held itself together to cover what it needed to—and the matching ribbon securing her hair only added to the seductive, careless vibe she exuded. "Whoa, you in a hurry? Watch where you're going!" she called out, regaining her balance after our near collision.

"Sorry, didn't see you there! Kat and I are headed for a swim—want to join?" I replied.

"Nope. I'm off for a siesta, completely wiped out from all that magical plant growing. Plus,

Im not a cock block bruh. I'm really just headed to grab something to drink from the kitchen… Speaking of which, any idea where it might be?" she inquired. "They probably don't have a proper kitchen—more like something whipped up by magic, like where the teapot has a name and talks in an English accent," I joked.

"You're no help. Have fun splashing around… or maybe wooing dear Kat," she teased. "That's not…" I began, but she quickly waved me off, adding a snarky, "Yeah yeah, tell someone else."

Leaving her behind, I walked down the long hallway toward the stairs. Then something outside the giant front windows caught my eye. Baren was there, just past the gates, with another group of individuals who, though roughly our age, seemed to be more versed to this realm. Their attire—a kind of training clothes eerily similar to what we found in our closets—hinted that they'd made it here before us. The Tribunal had mentioned the existence of others like us, but seeing them now confirmed it. I watched for a moment, curious to see what they were up to, but then realized Kat might be waiting. I tore myself away from the window and headed out to the patio, grabbing towels from the cabinet as the long-haired lady had shown me. I slipped off my shoes and dipped my toe in; the water felt perfectly tempered, as though someone had intuitively set it just right.

Before I could fully appreciate the feel of the water, Kat appeared behind me. With barely a moment's notice, she gave me a hearty shove that sent me flying into the water. As I spluttered and resurfaced, she stood there laughing uncontrollably. Seizing my chance while she was distracted, I leaped out and wrapped an arm around her waist, dragging her back into the cool water. Serves her right. Not willing to let the playful war end so soon, she retaliated by splashing water in my face. "No fair! Cheating! You can't use magic in a water fight!" she hollered between bouts of laughter, even as I conjured a small sphere of water with my magic and draped it over her head.

After our spirited bout, we relaxed and explored the swimming hole together. Unlike a regular pool, this spot was alive with vibrant, multi-colored fish darting about near the edges. They resembled goldfish, though I was amazed to see one with a striking purple hue and yellow dapples. While the water was only about waist-deep near the steps, it soon plunged into a mysterious deep hole. Mossy rocks rimmed the back edge, leading up to a waterfall where small trickles cascaded down. A gentle current stirred in the center, hinting that this was a natural spring. The rocky walls below, covered with thriving algae, were decorated further by what looked like coral and sea fans, swaying with the water's gentle motion. It struck me as odd—coral and sea fans typically belong in saltwater, not a freshwater spring. Even tiny fish peeked out from their hideaways in the coral, as if curious about our presence. At one point, a particularly bold fish crept out of the crevices to gently nibble at Kat's feet, sending her into another fit of laughter. I couldn't help but notice that when she laughed, a soft glow seemed to emanate from the fish, as though they were in on the shared merriment—a moment of simple, breathtaking beauty.

After an hour of playful exploration, we decided it was time to head back. Baren had reminded us earlier that when it came to supper away from the field, we were to don the formal attire kept in our closets. Once back in our room, I took full advantage of the private shower, soaking in steaming water before getting dressed. The formal clothes here weren't exactly what we'd consider formal back home—at least, the men's wear was closer to smart business casual—but they had a certain charm. I selected an outfit hanging neatly from a fancy hanger; as soon as I slipped it on, it felt like it was made just for me. The off-white silk shirt was soft and smooth, tailored perfectly to my shape, and the matching pants hugged me in all the right places. I completed the look with brown loafers and ran my hand through my hair, feeling unexpectedly confident as I headed downstairs.

At the bottom of the stairs, I encountered Jaliah again, this time in a stunning floor-length dress made of the same material—a rich dark red that seemed painted onto her skin, accentuating every curve. As I caught up with her before entering the dining hall, I remarked that she looked lovely. Her playful response—a "Well duh, I am a fucking dish — you don't look too bad yourself" accompanied by a toss of her hair and a cheeky eye roll—made me smile.

Inside the dining room, we soon discovered we weren't alone. The group I'd seen earlier through the window had arrived as well. As our group gathered, Baren informed us that this other group had come a couple of days ago. "You are all the test group," he explained, "and if you pass this trial, it will set the tone for future groups. Tomorrow, you will all train together as one cohesive unit—you must bond as one to succeed." He carefully introduced each member of our group to the newcomers. The first to be presented was Riya—a young woman of about twenty-two with a chic blonde pixie cut. Dressed in a sleek dark blue gown that clung elegantly to her slender figure, she was noted as "connected to the wolf we call Zuri." With a warm smile and nod, she took her seat.

Next came Talon, a tall redhead whose build echoed that of Vega's. "Talon is affiliated with the ape we refer to as Silas," Baren announced. Talon offered a playful smirk and even shot an eyebrow toward Jaliah before finding his seat. Baren then introduced Callen—a man whose towering presence and chiseled features were reminiscent of a young Dwayne Johnson. "Callen is linked to the python we call Kyson," he explained. Following that, a woman who bore a striking resemblance to Gal Gadot during her Wonder

Woman era stood up. Draped in a strapless silk gown that shimmered like liquid gold, she was introduced as, "Annalise, connected with the spotted leopard we call Cassius." She gave a fierce yet graceful smile before resuming her seat.

Finally, a tall, athletic blonde man with a distinctly military bearing rose for his introduction. "Last but not least, Greyson, bonded with the eagle we know as Isador." With that introduction, Baren clapped his hands. "Now, let's eat! You'll need your energy tonight—tomorrow will be nothing short of exhausting."

We savored a hearty meal prepared for us, all the while carefully moderating both the sumptuous food and the freely poured wine. I later discovered that the other group's rooms were intermingled with ours—a detail that made sense now as I recalled some unfamiliar names mentioned earlier in the day. Back in my room, I'm still convinced that the bed I climbed into was enchanted because the moment I lay down, I was carried away into a deep, unbroken sleep.

Thirty-Three

Journal of Truths

In the days lost, each creature that wandered this vast realm bore within it a spark of enchantment. Such magic, bestowed by divine decree, also graced the souls of worthy mortals. Upon the birth of a child, the Elders of the realm would scrutinize their hearts and peer into the veil of destiny. Should the child prove deserving, a bond would be forged connecting them to their animal. As the child matured and embraced their birthright, their mystical prowess would burgeon in tandem. Though all beings, human and creature alike, harbored the rudiments of sorcery, the connection between human and beast heralded a higher realm of enchantment.

The wise elders, custodians of myriad mystical arts, organized magic into four sacred clans. The Vayu lineage wielded mastery over the airs, enabling them to soar the heavens, shape tempests, and command the very essence of wind. The Agni bloodline, blessed with the flames of divinity, kindled fires of myriad forms and manifestations. The Jala clan, stewards of the aqueous realm, held dominion over the waters, breathing beneath waves and bending currents to their will. The Prithvi drew sustenance from the bosom of the earth, nurturing it, shaping it, and harnessing its boundless energies.

Though each clan held its own mysteries, they were never islands unto themselves. United in purpose, they wove their magics together, enriching and completing each other's craft. Thus, they studied within their respective lineages yet also communed in shared wisdom, ensuring the harmony and continuity of their enchanted world.

Thirty-Four

Vega

Last night, as soon as I got into bed, an overwhelming wave of sleep swept over me. I tried to linger in wakefulness, attempting to recall everything that had happened during the day, but it was futile—I had succumbed to sleep within minutes. This morning, when I opened my eyes, I noticed that it was still mostly dark outside, with slivers of sunlight timidly pushing through the twilight sky. I leapt out of bed, slid my feet into my slippers, and headed for the door. Sunrise is her favorite time of day, so if Aria is awake, she'll be somewhere watching it. It might be the only quiet moment I get with her today. Our group has grown in size since yesterday. While being introduced to the new members last night, I experienced an unusual feeling—jealousy. Though nothing specific warranted it, I couldn't help but notice that all the men in the group were attractive. I could easily imagine some of them vying for her attention, and I'm uncertain about our current standing or even what our relationship really is now. One thing, however, is clear: I don't want someone else to take her.

I jogged down the stairs, skipping every other one to speed my descent, and took a quick peek out the front door. I doubted she would be there since the sunrise appears to emerge at the back of the cottage, but I still checked. Finding her absent from the front, I made my way to the back patio. As expected, there she was—lounging on one of the swings, as large as a bed, gazing through the tree branches in eager anticipation of the coming light. I then scanned the area and spotted the kitchen at the end of the hallway, opposite the dining room. I rummaged around until I found the giant pot of freshly brewed coffee, which smelled even more enchanting than the coffee back home. With two fresh cups in hand, I headed out the back door. Yesterday, we were so captivated by the waterfall and the swimming hole that we hadn't even noticed the spiral staircase off to the side. I looked up at it and saw what appeared to be a small balcony-like patio above. How perfect. I whistle briefly in her direction, catching her slightly off guard. She responds with a yawn and a stretch as she rises to join me.

"Good Morning," she greets me with a sleepy smile.

"Morning, check that out," I say, nodding toward the stairs while handing her a cup of coffee.

"Perfect," she replies.

We walk quietly upstairs to a wooden patio where lounge chairs are set up high enough to overlook the treetops and the waterfall. I turn two of the chairs to face the sunrise and notice a cabinet at the corner filled with blankets. She takes a seat as I fetch two blankets, draping one over her lap and wrapping the other around myself. We watch in silence. The night sky is alive with flickering starlight, interspersed with deep purple ribbons dancing like the aurora of the northern skies back home. The view is so mesmerizing that words seem unnecessary, yet I still feel the urge to speak to her. Overwhelmed by unfamiliar emotions, I worry that if I don't express them, they might get lost in the chaos of our new life.

"Aria," I say softly.

"Vega," she teases in response.

"So…" I hesitate before continuing, "I feel like I need to say something, and honestly, I'm not expecting a reply—I just have to get it out."

"Okay, what's up? Is something wrong?" she asks, her tone shifting from playful to concerned.

"No—nothing's wrong. I'm just going to say it, and then we can change the subject. Deal?" I reply.

"Deal," she agrees.

"I think...I mean, I know I have feelings for you. They don't quite have a name yet, but it's not something I've ever felt strongly before. Love and romance have never really been my thing. Dating is okay, fun is okay, even sex is fine—but anything more just complicates things. Love often leads to heartbreak, greed, anger, and resentment—in my work, I've seen it all too often. So, I've always steered clear of it. But this is different. It's a feeling I actually enjoy, and I want to give it a name..." I pause, studying her reaction. "I've spent so long avoiding pain that I forgot how to truly feel. Then you came along, and for the first time in as long as I can remember, I feel something real. I'm scared to admit it, but I'm even more afraid of never saying it at all." I let out a breath I hadn't realized I was holding, waiting for the world around us to shift.

"OK," she says simply. It isn't exactly agreement, but at least she doesn't run off. Her eyes meet mine as a slight smile plays at the corner of her lips, a faint blush appearing on her cheeks before she looks away. We sit in silence for a few minutes, taking in the view, until she speaks again. "Thank you for the coffee—how did you know where to find me?"

"The sunrise; it's your favorite," I respond.

The sun breaks through, conquering the night as its orange glow mixes with purple tones across the sky. Birds begin to sing joyfully as light spills over us, pushing the darkness aside and revealing a new vista from our balcony. Below lies a varied landscape of valleys and peaks. Behind the house, jungle-like terrain merges with forests; to the left, miles of land evoke memories of the Sahara; and to the right, towering mountains surround a vast lake. In silent agreement, we turn our gaze to the view in front of the house, where the jungle gives way to canyons painted in earthy tones. Everywhere we look, nature's diversity unfolds before us. I was struggling with expressing the emotions, and it felt like I was stuck in the dark and needed to shed light, I voice my emotions and moments later the most beautiful sunrise I have ever seen leaks into the sky. It has to be a sign right?

It isn't long before others emerge onto the patio, coffee cups in hand and yawns still echoing the remnants of last night's deep sleep. Jaliah and Riya are the first to notice us as they climb the stairs. Riya recounts their day from yesterday while waiting for our arrival—Baren had sent them into the forest to collect various plants for his apothecary. They wandered through parts of the forest unaware of the other diverse terrains surrounding us. She remarks that everything seems so close when seen from up here, yet once you're out there, it feels far away.

Jaliah says little, true to her disinterest in mornings, while Kat is the next to join us, climbing the stairs in obvious awe of the land around us. "I never want to go home—how could anyone after seeing this place?" she exclaims in amazement. We all silently agree. This realm feels unlike Earth: simple and beautiful. Even the cottage we're staying in blends naturally with the landscape, a stark contrast to the skyscraper condos that plague Earth. Humans have a knack for ruining things—we stand in admiration before a beautiful beach only to see it marred by tall structures that spoil the view. Our oceans are filled with garbage, our forests are cut down for paper that ends up in landfills; we humans are inherently messy. We seem to work against the earth instead of with it, having lost the ability to use its gifts for good. Anyone who wants to make a change is quickly labeled a "tree hugger" rather than recognized as a conservationist.

It's truly disheartening that we even have preserves in our realm—why must we designate an area as a preserve before we learn to treat it with respect?

I don't think I've ever taken a moment like this to see our realm in such a light. Witnessing this place has unlocked a wave of new emotions in me—a trend I've noticed lately. The Siphon did its work well; the best way to create chaos and devastate Earth was to let mankind do it on its own. The leadership here is different from that on Earth. Here, you're taught about the power within you and how working together can bring about positive change, while back on Earth, leaders manipulate you, encourage dependency on systems that fill their pockets, and pit their followers against one another in an invisible conflict. Most of the conflicts humans engage in stem from issues they have created themselves. This isn't to say these issues are unimportant, but they exist because humans have invented them. Concepts like racism, war, and poverty are all human constructs. Our preoccupation with these issues persists because our leaders perpetuate them. Here, none of those problems exist. It's refreshing to experience genuine peace, to coexist harmoniously with the land instead of opposing it. With magic in the world, perhaps one day we can restore that balance on Earth too.

Thirty-Five

Aria

I'm not entirely sure, but I think Vega just admitted his feelings for me. Whether it was love or not, it certainly sounded as if he was opening the door to that possibility. Ok, he *DID* admit them, I think I might be in shock a little. Honestly, I'm still uncertain about where I stand on the matter. I could imagine loving him, yet there are things I've learned about his past—pieces that paint him as the playboy he once was. I'd hate to get swept up only to discover he's still that person. If he were truly that man, why else would he reveal what he just did? I have emotions, though I haven't fully defined them yet, so I understand his implication. That doesn't mean I need to confirm them to him right away. Now that I've got a sense of his position, I can stop second-guessing and just go along with it—while keeping my own decisions private. That way, if he reverts to his old ways, at least I won't feel foolish for having let him know. It's not a game; it's about protecting myself.

But I must admit, every fiber of my being melted right there on that lounge chair as he spoke. Every blood cell in my body tingled, and all I wanted was to kiss him. I managed to remain strong and composed, though! Luckily, the sunrise interrupted our moment, and soon others arrived, unwittingly creating a buffer. Now we're all gathered in the dining hall for breakfast. Vega is seated directly across from me, and each time our eyes meet, I feel my cheeks heat up. It's nearly impossible not to let the blush show; every time I look at him, my heart flutters like a nervous schoolgirl.

"What's on the agenda this morning?" Callen asks Baren.

"You'll find out soon. Eat up—you'll need your energy! Today is going to be a long day for all of you," Baren instructs. We obey and fill our plates, probably a bit too much, because I soon find myself craving a nap. After breakfast, we head up to our rooms to change into the training clothes. I'm halfway into my room when I suddenly feel a hand slip between my fingers, gently pulling me back into the hallway. Before I can process it, Vega plants a swift kiss on my lips, then on my cheek, finishing with my forehead.

"I just didn't want to go all day without that, and since it's going to be such a busy day, I seized the moment," he says, smiling.

I smile back, feeling an urge to let him know that it's perfectly fine for him to kiss me whenever he wants—though I'm certainly not going to spell it out. So instead, I reach for his cheek, pause for just a moment, then wrap my hand around the back of his head. Standing on my tiptoes to bridge the gap, I pull his lips to mine. That kiss conveyed everything I felt, silently telling him my truth, before I ended it with a quick peck.

"If you're going to seize the moment, make it count," I wink at him before ducking into my room to change. Fifteen minutes later, we're all dressed and gathered on the patio. Baren steps out, and without any prompting, we form a semi-circle around him.

"Today each of you will discover what lies within, the gifts you receive through your connection with your animal companions, who will be joining us," he explains. One by one, from the steps leading into the forest, our bonded animals approach the semicircle as Baren introduces them. Ophelian, Atticus, Lexora, Nyterian, and Kobin are presented. Even though we already know who they are, they never fail to take my breath away. Next comes Greyson's eagle, Isador—a massive, pristine white bird adorned with gold filigree reminiscent of our own creatures. After that, Annalise's leopard appears, also white with golden filigree; its dark spots seem to shift hues as it gracefully settles beside Lexora. Callen's python, Kyson, follows. Contrary to the image I had of a python, Kyson is midnight-dark with shifting gold markings, his eyes a kaleidoscope of colors, and his size more in line with the behemoth from the movie Anaconda.

Then up the stairs comes Talon's ape, Silas. This towering animal boasts a snowy white body decorated with familiar gold filigree. On the bare parts of his chest, intricate tattoos of vines and tree silhouettes shimmer in gold ink. The last to join is Riyas's wolf, Zuri, jet black like a shadow with a single golden diamond embedded in her forehead. Though she isn't as large as Kobin, her size is still remarkably impressive.

We all stand in silence, captivated by the creatures before us. They are mythical yet strangely familiar, unlike anything we've encountered, even in films. Baren concludes his introductions, and a woman with long hair steps into the middle of our now perfectly arranged circle, holding a golden box adorned with what seems to be Sanskrit on each side. I recognize the script from an anthropology class I took in college. The box sits on a rotating platform and begins to spin slowly as soon as she places it down. Although I can't translate it, I was always drawn to its beauty. "Stand beside your animal," Baren instructs. "This test will reveal your clan. All clans are equal and essential, each possessing a unique directional power. While everyone can wield magic, your clan will define your specialty. To succeed, clear your mind, emotions, and intentions. Your desires are irrelevant here and won't influence the test. With a clear mind, channel your power, draw from your animal's power, and direct it at the reliquary."

"This won't be as easy as the magic you've used before. It requires practice and might take several attempts. There's no hurry. We have all day, and what isn't accomplished today can be done tomorrow," he concludes. He instructs us to line up to the far right of the reliquary, away from the action. Callen is the first to try. Unsure of what to anticipate, we watch carefully as Callen and Kyson approach the box. Baren helps Callen clear his mind, identify the magic within, and grasp it. After a few attempts, and twenty minutes later, it finally works.

Callen's hands glowed with bands of white magic, while Kyson's radiated golden ones, intertwining effortlessly. Together, they channeled their spells toward the reliquary. With each rotation, the box spun faster until it became a blur. At its peak, an orb appeared above it. As the reliquary gradually stopped, so did the magical bands, leaving the orb hovering in the air. Inside its watery depths, the vast ocean came into view. The word   was inscribed upon it, shining with a brilliant blue before fading into darkness. Callen turned to Kyson, puzzled by the message. Suddenly, Baren's voice echoed inside him, proclaiming, "Callen, connected with Kyson, of the Jala Clan, your purpose is unveiled." As soon as Baren finished speaking, a vibrant tattoo, adorned with gold, spiraled up Callen's arm, displaying intricate ocean designs and its myriad creatures. Callen stepped back, gazing at his arm with awe and excitement.

Next up was Greyson, who took a bit longer than Callen, but eventually, the reliquary started spinning. When it stopped, a tornado appeared above it, and the engraving glowed white. "Greyson, bonded with Isador, of the Vayu Clan, your purpose is unveiled," Baren announced. Like Callen, Greyson's arm transformed into a masterpiece, depicting a mountaintop surrounded by clouds. We all stood, filled with renewed excitement! Archer was next, the first from our original group. It took him a bit longer than Callen, but not as long as Greyson. When the reliquary ceased spinning,   " illuminated in dark green, and a magical tree sprouted from the box, with golden sparkles dancing around it. "Archer, connected with Lexora, of the Prithvi Clan, your purpose is unveiled," Baren declared, and just like the others, his tattoo appeared. It was colorful and beautiful, with nature itself winding up his arms, faint tiger stripes hidden within the tree bark.

Kat steps onto the stage for her turn, and the bands form quickly around her. This time, instead of white bands, hers are dark shadows intertwined with Nyterian's golden ones. They're not the menacing shadows of a horror movie, but rather the gentle ones of a cool summer evening, when you're eager for the sun to set to relieve the day's heat. When the reliquary ceases its spinning, the engraving glows red, with a beautiful flame flickering from its top.

"Katerina, bonded to Nyterian of the Agni Clan, your purpose is revealed," Baren announces. Her tattoo shimmers with otherworldly energy, winding up her arm like a living flame released from a mystical forge. It illuminates her skin with vibrant hues that dance and flicker, each color embodying the wild spirit of fire. We each take our turns, one by one, until we are all assigned to a clan. We stand together, admiring our new tattoos, completely satisfied with the gift that has chosen us. Baren stands at the center of the large patio, beside one of the long-haired women holding a scroll. She unfurls the scroll before him, and he begins to officially announce the members of each clan. Golden bands of magic flow from him, inscribing our names onto the paper.

The Vayu Clan, revered as the custodians of the air and its boundless essence, extends its warm embrace to its newest delegates. With wings outstretched, they are welcomed into the fold, entrusted with the sacred duty of safeguarding the breath of life itself.

As members of the Vayu Clan, they inherit the legacy of the winds, mastering its currents and harnessing its might. From the gentle zephyrs that caress the land to the tempests that rage across the skies, they hold sway over the very essence of air and all its properties.

Bound by the whispers of the breeze and the whispers of ancient wisdom, they stand as stewards of harmony and balance in the ever-shifting tapestry of existence.

In the name of Vayu, and the legacy of generations past, let the new delegates of the Vayu Clan rise, their spirits soaring on wings of air, to embrace their noble calling with courage, wisdom, and grace. The Tribunal welcomes Aria, connected of Ophelia. Greyson, connected of Isador, and Vega, connected of Atticus.

We bow in acceptance of our new clan, smiling at each other with the thoughts of all the possibilities.

The Agni Clan, revered guardians of the flames and masters of its elemental force, warmly extends its embrace to its newest delegates. With hearts ablaze with the eternal fire of passion and purpose, they are welcomed into the fold, entrusted with the sacred duty of tending the hearth of creation itself.

As members of the Agni Clan, they inherit the legacy of the inferno, wielding its power with reverence and wisdom. From the gentle flicker of candlelight to the roaring conflagration that consumes all in its path, they command the very essence of fire and all its properties.

Bound by the searing heat of transformation and the enduring flame of enlightenment, they stand as beacons of strength and illumination in the ever-shifting tapestry of existence. May their journey be guided by the eternal flame of knowledge, as they navigate the trials and tribulations of the mortal realm.

In the name of Agni, and the lineage of ancestors past, let the new delegates of the Agni Clan rise, their spirits alight with the fervor of creation, to embrace their noble calling with courage, resilience, and unyielding resolve. The Tribunal welcomes Katerina, connected of Nyterian, and Riya, connected of Zuri.

The Jala Clan, esteemed commanders of the boundless oceans and the life-giving waters, joyously extends its embrace to its newest delegates. With hearts as vast as the endless sea and souls as deep as the ocean's abyss, they are welcomed into our sacred circle, entrusted with the solemn duty of safeguarding the ebb and flow of existence itself.

As members of the Jala Clan, they inherit the legacy of the tides, mastering its currents and nurturing its bounty. From the tranquil depths of lagoons to the tempestuous waves that crash upon distant shores, they command the very essence of water and all its realms.

Bound by the fluid grace of transformation and the enduring rhythm of renewal, they stand as stewards of harmony and balance in the ever-changing dance of creation. May their journey be guided by the gentle whispers of the sea, as they navigate the vast expanse of the watery realm.

In the name of Jala, and the wisdom of the ancient mariners, let the new delegates of the Jala Clan rise, their spirits buoyed by the currents of destiny, to embrace their noble calling with courage, compassion, and unwavering devotion. The Tribnal welcomes Callen, connected of Kyson and Jaliah, connected of Kobin.

पृथ्वी

The Prithvi Clan, revered menders of the earth and guardians of its natural balance, extends a heartfelt welcome to its newest delegates. With roots that run deep and spirits as steadfast as the mountains, they are embraced into our esteemed circle, entrusted with the sacred task of nurturing the land and preserving its sacred harmony.

As members of the Prithvi Clan, they inherit the legacy of the earth, tending to its soil and honoring its sacred cycles. From the fertile fields that yield life's sustenance to the towering peaks that touch the heavens, they hold the essence of the earth and all its wonders.

Bound by the timeless wisdom of nature and the enduring rhythm of creation, they stand as custodians of balance in the ever-changing tapestry of existence. May their journey be guided by the sturdy footing of the soil and the silent strength of the mountains, as they walk the path of stewardship and reverence.

In the name of Prithvi, and the ancient wisdom of the land, let the new delegates of the Prithvi Clan rise, their spirits grounded in the richness of the soil, to embrace their noble calling with humility, compassion, and unwavering dedication. The Tribunal welcomes Archer, connected of Lexora. Talon, connected of Silas, and Annalise, connected of Cassius.

Baren gives us the next few hours to have lunch and converse about our new revelations. We all inspect each other's new skin art and make friends with each other's connected. I don't know what I expected for all of this today, but this for sure wasn't it.

This goes beyond anything I could have ever imagined, and I am totally here for it.

Thirty-Six

Katerina

When dark shadows emerged from my hands, I was filled with fear. I hadn't entertained any dark thoughts since joining the group, yet here they were, showing up in my magic. I avoided making eye contact with anyone and tried hard to conceal my feelings. What if I wasn't deserving? What if they noticed my issue? What if this ended my journey? That's the challenge with mental health—even when you feel healed, negative thoughts can still sneak in and make you doubt yourself. My fox is dark too, and I secretly worried about that when I saw the pure white of the other animals. But I pushed those thoughts deep down. Even after Baren declared me a member of the Agni clan, I still fretted. Even when I understood that my clan symbolized fire, and fire produces smoke, and that smoke matched the dark bands, I still worried. It wasn't until I saw Riya's magic resembling mine that I felt at ease. I wanted so desperately to belong here. I adore everything about this journey, and that's not typical for me. Some mental health conditions have ups and downs, but mine are usually just downs. So this isn't a high—it's a true appreciation for life at the moment. I'm even beginning to love myself, to love the person I see in the mirror, something I can't recall feeling before.

Playing in the swimming hole with Archer was the first time I had "played" since childhood. I had completely forgotten what that felt like, but there I was, splashing around like a kid. I need this to work; it's the only thing that has worked for me. I can't return to where I was before. The few hours of downtime we had were fantastic. We all gathered as a group, sharing parts of ourselves, laughing, sharing our excitement, and bonding. Lunch was just as delicious as every other meal we've had here. We ate until we were stuffed. It's incredible how much energy magic drains from us. We eat, we burn, and then we eat again. Baren says this will subside as we practice more. I hope so—I can only fit so much food in my body!

That afternoon we reconvened on the wide patio. Baren walked us through the risks of training—and eventually fighting—with our magic. We could burn out, strain ourselves, or worse; the list was long. He ran us through safety protocols and made us repeat them back—knowing we were still drunk on the thrill of our newfound powers, which is exactly when accidents happen. We promised to push ourselves, but only at a controlled pace. He reminded us that our bonded spirits already had much to teach, so we'd begin by learning the basics of our connected magic. Then he dismissed us to our clans. Riya and I were assigned to the desert region—apparently they didn't want our fire magic getting out of hand. The Jala clan would head to the lake, Aria and the Vayu clan to the mountains, and the Prithvi clan into the forest.

Nyterian, Riya, Zuri, and I set off toward the desert. From the cottage rooftop it looked close, but once we plunged into the woods, I realized it might take until nightfall to reach the dunes. We'd just disappeared from sight when Zuri and Nyterian halted us for our first lesson. "Speed and long-distance travel are essential in battle," Zuri began. "Riya, I can carry you—so you must learn to ride at my pace. Kat, you can ride me— however, neither of us is small enough. Instead, you'll draw speed from Nyterian's magic. She moves faster than any of us, especially without someone on her back, so you must learn to stay within her reach. If you stray too far, your channel will falter until your own power strengthens over time. We'll start slowly and build up until we can travel flawlessly." Nyterian's voice was soothing as she added, "Flawless synchronization keeps you safe. If we scatter in battle and one of you falls behind, the Siphon will single you out. If Riya tumbles from Zuri, he'll target her. He's crafty—he seeks out any weakness. That's why our training will include spotting and shoring up those weak points. We're not picking you apart; we're learning to protect each other. None of us is at full strength without you two."

Riya climbed onto Zuri's back, easing into the rhythm of her stride, while I closed my eyes and reached for Nyterian's energy. Almost at once we felt the bond—enough to nudge up our pace. It wasn't perfect, but it was a start. Zuri shifts into second gear, and I match her pace with Nyterian's speed to keep us together. For me, it's just like running normally; only — I have to stay focused on our bond with Nyterian. Riya, meanwhile, must learn to grip Zuri's fur and brace with her legs, so we hold this speed until she feels secure. Before we push any faster, our instructors add obstacles: Riya has to anticipate Zuri's moves and steady herself, while I practice maintaining the bond as I leap over or duck beneath barriers. We each stumble a few times—just enough to lose a split second, but not enough to slow us down.

As we accelerate, the falls grow rarer—until we suddenly hit a new level of speed. I steal a glance at Riya and realize we're moving so fast we cast trailing shadow like bands — like you would see on TV. The trees and ground blur around us, making me a bit dizzy, yet my feet find the earth without missing a beat. Through Nyterian's bond, I sense each obstacle the moment it appears and react almost instinctively.

"Wait!" Nyterian cries. "Riya fell off!"

I look back and see Riya lying beside a log. She's breathing, which is a relief, but there's blood at her hairline. I dash over and inspect the cut. "She slipped on that log and smacked her head," Zuri says. "In battle, this is when we're most at risk—the siphon can sense our distress and will come for us. You need to push aside your panic and stay calm while you handle this. Katerina, you can fix her—use your magic." I understand, but I'm uneasy. My healing magic isn't fully under control—what if I turn Riya into a frog? Zuri senses my doubt and soothes me. "Trust your intuition, focus on the intent to heal, and the magic will flow."

I hover my hand over the cut and draw power inward. I envision Riya whole again, without a mark. My fingers tingle as a soft blue glow seeps from my palm, spreading over the wound. Warmth pulses through me as the gash closes, tendrils of her skin weaving its way back together, leaving only traces of dried blood in her hair. A wave of exhaustion rolls in—but just as quickly, it fades. Riya sits up with a confused look on her face. "What happened" she asks while looking at each of us waiting for an answer "I just healed you! With magic!!" I say excitedly.

"You all possess the power to heal, and although we demonstrated it today as a lesson, you must reserve it for true emergencies. Minor wounds are simple; major injuries demand far more from you. Also you must know...If the person is dead, the magic will not work, and will cost you your life as well. So never attempt it on a corpse," Nyterian warns. We stand and brush ourselves off, ready to move on. Riya gives me a grateful look, then grins, "Full speed now."

Her fall must have helped both of us. We surge forward at top speed, the wind pressing into our bones. A shimmering cloak of magic wraps around us, holding back the force that tries to hold us back. It is as we are trying to push through the sound barrier, and it pushes back against us, but the magic opens a door. In an instant, we burst from the dark forest into the open desert, the sun slashing across our faces so fiercely it stings our eyes. I have no idea how far we've traveled in those seconds, but charging through felt like tearing through a dense jungle. Glancing back, the trees already vanish behind us. It's pure exhilaration—who needs horses or cars when we outrun them all? Riya and I exchange a look, then erupt in laughter. Nothing's funny, yet everything is. We collapse onto the warm, yielding sand, surrendering to the desert's symphony. Each breath draws in the heat of sun-baked stones and the resinous perfume of hardy shrubs. Sunlight—liquid gold—dances across our skin, reminding us of our bond to this timeless land.

Around us, tall yellow-and-green grasses sway in the breeze, weaving a living tapestry. Their hushed rustle becomes a lullaby for our restless souls. In this moment, time seems to pause, and the urge to escape life's fleeting pleasures drifts away. Here, amid the ebb and flow of desert life, we find solace in the earth's embrace, woven into its fabric like threads in a grand tapestry. The swaying grasses remind us how transient we are— mere spectators in nature's theater. Nyterian and Zuri interrupt our reverie, urging us back into the training we came to master. I'd expected our fire magic to be as tame as lighting campfires. I was wrong. For hours, we fling fiery tendrils through the air, coil them around dead branches, then snap them in two. At one point, I stumbled and caught myself with my hand on the ground. A burst of energy flares from me, turning the grasses to ash. It's terrifying at first, but Zuri reminds me that sometimes you must burn the old to make way for new life.

As the sun dips below the horizon, Riya mounts Zuri, and I crouch for the run home. With the speed we discovered on the way out, we'll outrun the coming darkness. I give Riya a sly wink—no falls today! I settle into a runner's stance while Riya leans forward on Zuri's neck, her fists buried in her midnight mane. "Let's go!"

Before we know it, we're back at the cottage, spirits high. We make our way out to the back patio to join the others for dinner.

Archer and his team are already gathered; we're still waiting on Jaliah's and Arias's groups. We swap tales of today's power drills with Archer's crew, everyone practically buzzing with excitement. A few minutes later, Jaliah and Callan arrive, equally triumphant. As dusk deepens into night, we linger, expecting the rest to show up. Soon, Baren appears and asks how our training went. We answer in turns, each story hinting at our personal victories and setbacks on this journey. But even as we talk, a nagging unease prickles at me. I watch Baren's eyes drift toward the distant mountain peaks. His look isn't casual—there's something unspoken behind it. Is he merely taking in the view, or does he have a hidden motive? Doubt creeps in, fraying the trust we've built.

Then an eagle's piercing cry shatters the desert's quiet, and we snap alert. Heartbeats racing, we scan the moonlit horizon until three dark shapes materialize against the sky: Ophelian, Atticus, and Isador, gliding swiftly toward us. Aria and Greyson sit astride their feathered mounts, silhouettes bathed in silver moonlight, one on each side of Atticus. As their forms draw near, a grim sight emerges: Vega, limp and lifeless, dangling from Atticus's talons. My breath catches, disbelief and sorrow crashing in on me. I look to the others, shock plastered all over their faces. I feel a hand slide into mine, I can tell it's Archer's; there is no need to look. I can name the feeling that comes over me, it's not lust … it's — safety. Under that desolate desert sky, broken only by the wind's whisper and the eagle's lament, we stand together, united in grief by this cruel turn of fate.

Thirty-Seven

Aria

This morning marked our first lessons in mounting our connected creatures. Under the guidance of Atticus, Ophelian, and Isador, we absorbed the essentials: the art of grasping firmly, maintaining balance mid-flight, and discerning the feathers that could bear our weight. As we practiced in a field nestled beneath towering mountains, caution tethered us close to the ground, primed for any mishap. Once we mastered the fundamentals, our aspirations soared higher. Positioned on top of Ophelian, I nestled my fingers into her plumage for stability, clutching with my legs tucked beneath her wings. Alongside Atticus, Vega, Greyson, and Isador, we formed a row, poised for takeoff. Ophelian, her gaze piercing in its owl-like intensity, scrutinized my readiness with a turn of her head. "I'm good, promise," I say with a gentle nod to her.

With a powerful takeoff, we soared straight into the sky, quickly embraced by clouds that were thick and invigorating as they filled my lungs. Breaking through the misty barrier, our creatures leveled into a smooth, horizontal flight, cutting through the air with effortless grace. Ophelian instructed me on how to keep my hold steady as we practiced turning maneuvers. As she banked left, I leaned slightly to the right to maintain balance among her feathers, with the others trailing us a short distance behind. We refined our skills with various directional changes and even rehearsed some combat tactics before settling atop snow-covered trees at the mountain's summit. There, we paused to absorb the breathtaking view while Ophelian educated us about the different terrains surrounding us. Our next lesson took me by surprise. Our avian companions taught us how to merge our magic, drawing strength from them to enhance our vision.

While I knew birds of prey had exceptional eyesight, experiencing it firsthand was eye-opening. With this newfound clarity, I could make out every detail of the landscapes around us, as if viewing them through a powerful telescope.

They challenged us to identify animals on the distant plains below and deduce their actions. I was amazed when I spotted a chipmunk scurrying across a log miles away. As we took flight again, our mentors encouraged us to strengthen our connection to this magic, allowing us to foresee what lay ahead long before we reached it. Given our creatures' ability to cover vast distances quickly, developing the skill to anticipate upcoming challenges became essential. This heightened perception would be invaluable in battles, improving our reaction times and enhancing our strategic edge. Next, we delved into formations tailored to suit our needs on the battlefield. Positioned at the center, I led the formation, with Vega flanking the left and Greyson on the right.

Utilizing their enhanced sight in both directions, they scanned the surroundings while I focused on the front line. Every half-minute, Ophelian prompted me to rotate slightly, ensuring I could maintain vigilance over our rear.

We soared over jungle canopy, glittering lakes, and parched deserts before looping back to the mountains. This time, instead of perching in trees, we landed on a sheer cliff face, our bird's talons biting into stone. Now that we could both fly and see clearly, it was time to learn to wield magic. We traced looping patterns at different elevations to avoid collisions, our task simple: knock loose the boulders clinging to the ledges. Each pass sharpened our timing and accuracy, laying the foundation for this vital skill. Under Ophelian's guidance, I tried to draw my intent inward and project it outward with precision. My first effort sputtered into a weak puff of air—my focus tangled by doubt and old habits. "Again—focus your intent and wield. Don't simply imagine the rock moving.

Launch your magic like a projectile from your palm," Ophelian called.

I cleared my mind and dug deep, picturing currents of energy streaming from my hands as my gaze locked on a single boulder. Brilliant, ice-like shards spiraled outward. It fell just shy of the mark, but nearly there. Summoning every ounce of resolve, I willed it again—this time hitting dead center and sending the rock plummeting down the slope. Our cheers died the instant a piercing scream broke through the air to my left. I whirled and saw Atticus plummeting toward Vega. "Ophelian!" I cried. In a blur, we dove toward them. My vision honed in—Isador banked from below, twisting to cradle Vega in his talons while Greyson hovered overhead. They saved him, but he lay limp in Isador's grasp.

We dropped to the valley floor, skidding to a gentle stop. I sprinted from Ophelian's back without a second thought. Vega's lips—once the rich pink of dawn-bright berries—were now a deathly blue. I pressed my fingers to his neck, but there was no pulse. "CPR, now! Don't let him die!" I urged. "What happened up there? Someone tell me!" My voice cracked with fear. Atticus's urgent cry cut through the panic: "Mount—now!" He scooped Vega's inert form into his claws and launched skyward. I froze. Ophelian glided beside me, tilting so I could jump on. When I still hesitated, she barked, "Climb up!" My hands shook as I clutched her feathers. We shot upward into the widening sky. Even if only seconds passed, each pulse throbbed like an eternity as we rose, dread weighing on every wingbeat.

The sun slipped quickly behind us, turning the once-luminous sky into a suffocating darkness. Silence enveloped us as we made our way to the cottage, and my eyes stayed locked on Vega, his form growing more ghostly against the fading light. Only when we neared the door did I realize—I can see perfectly in the dark. Baren must have spotted us; he'd cleared a spot near the swimming hole for our landing. Atticus set Vega gently on the patio, and Baren rushed over, sensing the crisis at once. We all stood frozen, tears turning to ice on our cheeks as the cold wind cut through the night. Baren raised his hands over the swimming hole and unleashed a swirl of white magic that cloaked the water. Gradually it churned into a vortex, silver fish dancing in its center. Steam curled skyward, weaving a spellbinding scene in the frigid air.

Shifting his power, Baren lifted Vega as if he weighed nothing and carried him to the water's edge. He placed Vega on the surface, where he floated, cradled by unseen hands beneath the waves. Baren held him there with unwavering concentration, then spoke to us in a steady voice. "He'll be all right. We got him here in time. Magic can overwhelm you if you're unprepared. We anticipated this and know how to fix the damage." He went on, "Vega's magic froze inside him, trapping him in a sort of cryogenic sleep. If it went unchecked, it would kill him." His words offered a flicker of hope.

"Why couldn't they heal him like we did Riya?" Kat asked, surprising me with her question. Did we really wield such power? Baren answered evenly. "Their abilities aren't that strong yet. Riya's injury was limited, so healing her was possible—Zuri and Nyterian guided you because of that. Trying to mend Vega fully would have shattered their strength and caused permanent harm."

He added, "We do possess healing magic, but not on every scale. We can't restore an entire body alone. That's why we use conduits—like this swimming hole—to aid the process." As Baren keeps Vega submerged until color returns to his flesh, he informs us that Vega may not awaken until morning. Using his magic, he lifts him from the water and transports him to his room. Despite the thoughts of others, my determination is steadfast—I am going with them. Quietly trailing behind Baren, we ascend the stairs to Vega's room.

Upon entering, I find myself surprised by the decor. Unlike my own vibrant and cozy space, Vega's room exudes a contemporary aura, reflecting what I imagine his style would have been in the real world. Baren's words catch me off guard as he addresses me. "I had a feeling you would come, and I also have a feeling that you won't leave his side," Baren remarks perceptively. "I sensed the connection between you before you ever made it here. Would you like me to have your dinner sent up?" His offer is met with a silent nod, gratitude swelling within me for his understanding and support during this trying time. As I settle into the room, my thoughts remain with Vega, hoping for his swift recovery and silently vowing to stand by his side until morning light breaks through the darkness.

With gratitude, I thank Baren and accept his offer. Shortly afterward, two of the woman with long hair—whose name I plan to learn—enters the room. They gather dry bedclothes from the closet and gently change Vega out of his wet clothes, using their magic to settle him into bed. As Baren and the women leave, a feeling of solitude envelops the room. I quickly retreat to my room, changing into comfortable sleepwear with urgency, fearing I might miss Vega waking up. Returning to his room, I find him still deeply asleep. Without delay, I pull back the covers and slip into bed beside him, pressing close, offering comfort and reassurance in the darkness. Despite the long night, I stay by his side, silently willing him to sense my warmth even in his dreams.

As exhaustion overtakes me, I fall into a deep sleep, so profound I don't even hear when they bring my dinner. Throughout the night, I remain beside Vega, my body protectively curled around him as if shielding him from the darkness's looming shadows. In the night's stillness, I pray for Vega's quick recovery, yearning for the moment he awakens and the world feels right again. With every breath, I cling to hope, trusting dawn will bring the promise of a new beginning, where light will cut through the shadows and guide us back to the sun's warm embrace.

***

The morning light slips through the full-length curtains of the cottage as dawn arrives. I blink awake and lie still for a moment, letting my eyes adjust. Last night I bedded down in Vega's room; he's still fast asleep, unmoving from the position I laid him in. He looks calm—hardly what you'd expect from someone who nearly died only hours ago. I resist the urge to stir him, instead watching: my nursing instincts flicker to life as I check his skin tone, count his breaths, and feel for his pulse. Everything falls within normal limits. As I keep vigil, I finally notice the intricate tattoo winding up his arm. Like me, he belongs to the Vayu clan, his design unfolds from his wrist upward with delicate mountain peaks that climb toward his shoulder. There, a blazing sunset arcs across his skin in glowing yellows, fiery oranges, soft purples, and deep blues, woven through with threads of shimmering gold. A great falcon's wing rises from the panorama, its feathers sweeping seamlessly into the sunset behind it.

My own Vayu tattoo mirrors the vast heavens. From my wrist a band of tall grass stretches upward, parting to reveal a radiant sunrise at its heart. The reds and oranges of dawn bleed into indigo and midnight blue as the scene reaches my upper arm, where tiny silver stars glint against the darkness. Rays of golden light stream skyward, tracing a path toward a grand white-and-gold owl's wing that arches over my shoulder and brushes my clavicle. I can't help marveling that no earthly artist could capture such beauty—yet here we are, our clan's magic made manifest in living art. A sharp knock at the door pulls me from my thoughts. A woman with long hair enters, carrying a tray of breakfast. She smiles. "Baren asked me to bring this up," she says, setting the tray on the stand and removing the untouched dinner plate.

"Is it normal for him to still be asleep?" I ask.

She shrugs, voice calm and steady. "Miss Aria, I really don't know. Baren would be the one to ask. But if he weren't okay, he'd be more worried. Recovery takes time." With that she steps back into the hallway.

"And here I thought you were worried about me, Miss Aria," Vega murmurs, his tone soft and sarcastic.

"You're awake!" I fake a scowl. "I'd hit you for joking, but since you nearly died, I'll let it slide. How do you feel?"

"Tired. Happy. Sore."

"You've been out for hours—probably the longest you've slept since the trip began. Sore makes sense, and I'd be happy too if I'd almost died but didn't."

He chuckles. "No, dummy. I'm happy because we didn't miss a sunrise together."

I glance out the window. "We kind of did—the sun's fully up now."

"True," he admits, voice soft. "But we were together when it rose. Thanks for staying by me. If I didn't know better, I'd think you might like me a little."

"Sarcasm won't get you far, sir! I was worried!"

He grins. "I'll take 'worried' as code for 'like.'"

I reach for the breakfast tray—he snatches my hand and pulls me back onto the bed. "Hey! I was going for the food!"

"Food can wait," he whispers, wrapping me in his arms. "I haven't kissed you in hours, and I fear I might die if I don't right now." Then he kisses me.

I try to stay tough, but relief floods me. He's alive. The thought of losing him would have broken me. I won't say so, but I'll drop the act long enough to savor this perfect kiss.

With each heartbeat of the kiss, he seemed to come alive more fully. His fingers wove through my hair, tangling in the soft strands. I surrendered entirely, pouring all my emotions into that kiss, sharing my secret heart with him. My hands found his jaw without thought, holding him as if to freeze time itself. He circled me with his left arm, drawing me close—so tight I feared he might crush me, yet grateful for his grip. I molded myself against him, craving nothing but this closeness. He eased his hold just enough to slip his hand to my knee and slide beneath it, guiding me astride him. Under the thin fabric of my gown, his palm crept up my thigh to grip my hip as his kisses deepened. Every ounce of me longed to cast aside every concern and remain suspended in that suspended moment.

Breaking our kiss, he trailed his lips along my jaw and down the side of my neck. I sighed softly as he planted gentle kisses on my collarbone. Driven by a shared urgency, my hips began to roll against his, matching the swell of his desire. With nimble fingers, he undid the tiny clasps at my neckline, exposing my breasts to his hungry gaze. When his lips brushed against my nipple, a fierce ache bloomed inside me. I tangled my fingers in his hair, ensuring he stayed lost in this moment with me. His hand tightened on my hip, pulling me closer with every rhythm of his kiss. His low growl shook through me as he wrapped both arms around my waist and lifted me clear of his lap, laying me gently on the bed. Hovering above me, our eyes locked before he claimed my mouth again. One hand slipped beneath my gown to hook my underwear and slowly peel them away, interrupting the kiss only when essential.

He kissed a path down my chest and across my stomach, pausing to tease my belly button before venturing lower. His other hand climbed my inner thigh until it reached its destination. Pleasure coursed through me, arching my back in anticipation. He paused at the bare edge, then, with a breath, his tongue brushed the most sensitive spot. Every nerve ignited; I gripped the sheets with one hand, the other tangled in his hair to hold him close. I blinked against the soft glow of gold in my tattoo as it pulsed in time with my racing heart, mirroring my pleasure. He explored deeper with practiced precision, and waves of bliss washed over me. In that haze, I saw birds rising from grass, colors of dawn swirling around us. Warmth unfurled between my thighs, my stomach fluttered— and then I could no longer hold back. An orgasm crashed through me, primal sounds escaping my lips. He felt my shift and moved to meet me, capturing my mouth in a heated kiss.

His hips found their rhythm, each thrust sparking another tremor of release. Moments later, it surged through me again, from toe to crown, a small cry woven into our kiss. We unraveled together, his kisses soft now, gentle caresses where urgency had once driven us. He eased off, and we lay entwined in the tangled sheets, his fingers drifting through my hair, his lips pressing tender kisses to mine. We lingered in our quiet aftermath—but the world beyond our bed called, and with a shared look, we knew we'd have to answer.

Thirty-Eight

Archer

Yesterday was a day filled with new insights, and if that was just the beginning, I can barely imagine what lies ahead. Unlike the usual first-day orientation of a "class," our experience was anything but typical. Together with Talon and Annalise, I embarked on an adventure through the jungle landscape where our learning journey commenced. From the outset, our lessons were practical. We learned to ride our animals skillfully without falling—a challenge that many of our peers struggled with. Within the thick foliage, we mastered the art of utilizing the forest's shadows, allowing us to move almost invisibly. While Talon and Silas elegantly navigated the canopy, Annalise and I stayed nearer to the ground, climbing into the trees only when the branches could sustain our animals' weight. Each moment in this intricate environment revealed new layers of skill and comprehension. We progressed to learning how to nurture the earth beneath us. Much of this involved using growth as a tool in battle, but we also learned the importance of respecting the land. We moved beyond just nurturing a small plant in a pot, and can now cultivate entire trees, even forests. Additionally, we learned to wield this power while riding. If Annalise and I are moving from branch to branch, we can create new, sturdy branches ahead of us. Talon developed the ability to grow thick, rope-like vines for Silas to swing across, moving from tree to tree above us.

We learned how to restore damaged land by extracting pollution directly from the ground, a skill that will be invaluable when we return to Earth. My personal mission, once the chaos subsides, is to travel from place to place, repairing the harm we've caused to our planet. It might take a lifetime, but it must be done. Today, we gather on the patio again, waiting for our assignments from Baren. We're starting a bit later than yesterday because Vega was injured. Initially, I didn't care much for him, but I don't want anyone hurt, and he's starting to grow on me. My first impression might have been off, and for Aria's sake, I hope he's a decent person. Soon enough, Aria and Vega rush out of the cottage as if they're late, seemingly unaware that the morning was delayed to allow Vega to recover. The group collectively breathes a sigh of relief when Vega assures us he's fine.

"Everyone, please take a seat," Baren interrupts our celebration, guiding us into the semicircle. "I understand magic is still new to you, and when something's fresh, you're eager to experiment. We're not here to stifle that curiosity—but we must also dedicate time to learning how to wield this gift responsibly." Positioning himself at the gap in our formation, he continues, "With that in mind, let's begin today's lesson."

"Remember: everything in life is connected. So we'll start at the source—your own bodies. To harness magic at full strength, you must maintain both physical health and mental clarity. These aspects feed into each other—your fitness affects your state of mind, and vice versa." He lifts a hand to capture our focus. "Let me give you an example. Suppose I hand each of you two identical pots and two identical seeds. We'll pretend the soil in each pot is exactly the same at planting. Now, every day you water the left pot with pure water and the right pot with the full range of substances humans typically ingest—coffee, alcohol, processed food residues, and so on. What do you predict will happen?"

He pauses, letting the question settle. "Assuming both seeds sprout, which plant will blossom more vibrantly?" Heads nod in agreement: the one nurtured with clean water. Baren smiles. "Exactly. In this metaphor, the soil represents your inner environment, and the flower is your outward form. If you supply your 'soil'—your body and mind—with wholesome nutrients, your exterior will flourish accordingly." He gestures at the surrounding landscape. "This principle applies to our world as well. Imagine what this realm could look like if we cared for it as attentively as that left-hand plant. Instead, pollution and toxins choke the land. While pockets of beauty endure, they can't match the untouched splendor these places once possessed—before humans arrived with their ambition to build and dominate." His voice grows firm. "Everything is intertwined. When you commit to nourishing yourselves, that intention radiates outward, shaping the world around you. Your example sparks a ripple effect, inspiring others to follow the same path."

"Now, let's turn our attention to your mental well-being," Baren says, his tone steady. "Just as everything in this world is connected, so is your mind. If you feed it uplifting truths and positive insights, it will flourish. But if you swallow lies and chase greed, your inner world will suffer. Look at that flower on the right—it's choked by pollution, poisoned by falsehoods, and is slowly dying." He lets that sink in before going on. "It's up to you to change this course. You must nurture a mental space rooted in authenticity and growth, not one clouded by deception and decay."

"Remember," he adds, "perception becomes reality. For so long humanity has been blinded by a warped view of the world, and that has shaped Earth's fate. The Siphon never sought to destroy the planet outright; it feeds on the chaos we've created—the very chaos it once ignited. Left unchecked, this turmoil will be our undoing, whether through war, climate collapse, or species extinction. The end result is always the same: ruin." A heavy silence follows. We realize our mission isn't only to confront the Siphon, but to heal the Earth itself. Baren shifts gears. "That concludes your personal lesson. Now for your joint lesson." He smiles slightly. "You must keep honing your individual abilities—

but also learn to combine them as a team. No one clan's gift is greater than another's. Each of you is essential. Let me give you some examples."

He turns to Talon. "You can extract pollution from the land—what do you do with it afterward?" Talon shrugs. "We practiced extraction yesterday, but I never thought beyond that." "With good reason," Baren replies. "Pollutants don't vanish on their own. You could have Katerina or Riya burn the toxins, but then you'd wind up with polluted air. Luckily, Aria, Grayson, and Vega can cleanse the atmosphere afterward." He continues, "There's no step-by-step guide—only an understanding of how each power works. In battle, for instance, Agni might shape fire into a blade, Vayu could boost its force, then Jala could douse the flames, and Prithvi could heal scorched earth." He grins. "It's like a puzzle with infinite solutions."

"Here's another scenario: a coastal town faces a hurricane. The Jala Clan could raise a seawall by manipulating waves, cutting storm surge. Meanwhile, the fire wielders might generate small heat bursts to thin the storm clouds, lessening wind and rain as the hurricane rolls in."

"The Vayu could join forces with the fire group, bending the wind to carve out calm pockets amid the storm. Those sheltered breezes would give townsfolk a brief haven and let rescue teams escort the vulnerable to safety. At the same time, the Prithvi could shore up the town's defenses—fortifying walls, stabilizing the earth beneath, and preventing landslides or structural collapse from relentless rains and fierce gales. Your powers won't always be needed for battle," Baren reminds us, revealing how we might serve as heroes in any crisis.

"The Siphon wields immense power—otherwise he couldn't have bent humanity to his will. He latched onto our world when we'd never learned debate, when defense wasn't even a concept. That was our weakness.

When you return to Earth, he'll sense you instantly. As you strive to restore balance, he'll strike at you and at humankind. He thrives on chaos, and to stop its spread, he'll unleash more. We've gathered every scrap of intelligence, but facing him in combat is uncharted territory. We must prepare for anything."

Baren's gaze sweeps the hall. "Soak up everything you've heard today. Let it guide your training. We'll devise scenarios, but you must sharpen your own minds—no exercise can cover every threat. And remember, here you're shielded from the Siphon's reach, but not from all dangers." With that, he rises, motioning for us to stand. As we do, the Tribunal ascends the platform, signaling the start of practice. Each of us moves to our element stations, preparing for instruction. Argus and Ethos join us to announce today's exercise: we'll assemble as a full team in the valley by the water within the hour. They order us to don battle attire and fetch packs from the kitchen—supplies for an overnight stay. We break to our rooms to get ready.

Heading for the stairs, Kat falls in beside me. "So… have I done something wrong?" she asks. "Not that I know of. Why?" I reply.

"You've barely spoken to me since the swimming hole. I thought you were angry, so I kept my distance."

"Absolutely not," I assure her. "It's just been a lot to process, and I didn't mean to shut you out. I actually want to hear everything you learned yesterday."

She exhales with relief. "Okay, I was worried. I can change fast—want to head down together? Maybe we'll snag thirty seconds to catch up."

"Perfect. Meet me here in five?" I suggest, and she calls back yes before sprinting off. I pause, guilt prickling at me. Ignoring her wasn't intentional—it's just been overwhelming. I still don't know how she truly sees us, nor how I want her to. Part of me still feels attracted to her; another part treats her like a little sister. For now, I guess a friendship will have to do—and we'll see where it leads.

Thirty-Nine

Jaliah

I ought to feel guilty—Vega nearly died yesterday—but all I can remember is how incredible the rest of the day was. I don't know why it never occurred to me that Kobin was a real polar bear; perhaps the sheer magic and beauty of it all kept me from thinking straight. The moment we dove into the water, everything shifted. I could sense my body adapting the instant we submerged. It was as if my skin had changed—like those movie scenes where a mermaid's tail appears at the touch of water. I didn't sprout fins or scales, but my skin felt different. The cold didn't bother me; I adjusted instantly. I could see as clearly underwater as I could in the air, and the water no longer stung my eyes. Fish flocked around us without a hint of fear, and the sea grasses and rocks glowed with vibrant colors. Most astonishing of all, I discovered I didn't need to breathe. It wasn't that I was inhaling; I simply had no need for air.

I marveled at being able to stay submerged for over thirty minutes. When I finally did need oxygen, the aquatic life would form a precious air pocket for me, or Kobin would surge to the surface so I could refill my lungs. Water has always been my passion. Mom used to say I was like a fish when I was little, and this freedom to explore its depths felt like the greatest gift imaginable. Kobin and I moved as one, our strokes fluid and graceful, gliding with effortless ease. Callen and his python, Kyson, wove through our path in perfect sync. Beneath the waves, the realm looked unlike anything I'd ever seen. Kobin told me it wasn't just this place's natural feature but a magical endowment— the power to perceive true reality. He reminded me that Earth would be equally breathtaking if humanity hadn't scarred it.

Learning to command water proved intricate. Slicing streams through the air like a sword felt intuitive, but parting currents or shaping air pockets demanded painstaking control and finesse. Yet with each exercise, we realized that water manipulation lay at the heart of every battle tactic. It offered formidable offense and impenetrable defense, granting fluid movement and adaptability that could turn the tide of any fight. By mastering this power, we unlocked an arsenal that would shape every confrontation to come.

Im not trying to be an asshole —Vegas' accident was tragic, but he pulled through— and now that we're all safe, I'm itching to get back out there. I was the first one changed and back downstairs, Callan right behind me, I want to say its a shared excitement for practice, but also I sort of think he is checking out my ass. We swung up onto Kobin and Kyson and headed straight for the lake, hoping to squeeze in some extra practice before anyone else arrived. We tore through the woods, our pace smoother than running but not quite as fluid as water. A rustling behind drew my attention—Talon and Silas were swinging from branch to branch, limb to limb, effortlessly keeping pace. We all wore the same eager expression: ready to master whatever came next. When the forest opened into a meadow, Silas dove toward the ground, the impact sending a low rumble through the grasses. I braced for them to slow as we neared the shore—they didn't.

My heartbeat quickened as the bank rushed toward us. I thrust my hands forward, channeling magic through my veins. A ribbon of water rose from the lake and arched toward me; with a flick of will, it froze into a solid bridge. Silas and Talon stepped onto it without hesitation, striding confidently across the ice, while Kobin and I slipped beneath the surface, cutting through the water in perfect sync. Above us, the bridge hovered, a translucent guide tracing our every move. Without warning, Callan and

Kyson burst from the depths, vaulting over the bridge in graceful arcs. Their trajectories intertwined with ours, drawing us into a protective ring. We circled back toward shore, anticipation building for the rest of the team. Just as we broke the waterline, Kat and Riya lobbed waves of heat at the ice beneath Silas and Talon. The bridge cracked; they tumbled into the lake with startled yelps. Laughter exploded as the girls collapsed in giggles and Silas surfaced, drenched but grinning.

"All right, all right, I see how it is," Talon teased, wiping water from his eyes as he joined Silas on shore. "Just remember—payback's a bitch." His wink promised future mischief. We all knew the lessons here were intense, but a little fun kept us from burning out. The rest of the group gathered at the water's edge, laughter and banter knitting us closer. Then Ethos and Argus appeared, and the easy mood snapped into tense silence. They watched us with inscrutable eyes, as though we were players in some grand performance. The air grew heavy with expectation.

"If you've vented your energy, let the games begin," Argus said, his voice surprisingly warm, stripped of its usual ancient echo. "You'll be tested on your ability to work together. This isn't a competition against one another—you'll be evaluated on reaction speed, creativity, and how you use your skills. Though our lessons carry real weight, we want you to enjoy yourselves." His words settled over us, blending responsibility with promise. Then he added, "We'll play something like what you call capture the flag —only there's a twist." Ethos stepped forward. "There are multiple flags, and you're all one team. We've hidden them throughout the valley, both above the surface and below these waters."

"These flags won't stay put," Argus asserts with authority. "The Aviaphids, creatures of both land and water that we have crafted, will be their protectors. Do not fear; they are magical constructs and can be defeated. Their sole mission is to guard the flags and prevent you from claiming them. They will engage in battle and can cause you harm, yet they remain dedicated to their task." He pauses to let this information settle, then adds, "Once you capture a flag, bring it back here to the shore and secure it on a spear in the sand to demonstrate your victory and skill in this challenge."

"Although there is no fixed time limit, remember that the longer you take, the more the Aviaphids will adapt to your strategies," Ethos warns solemnly. "They learn from every encounter, making each capture progressively more challenging, just like the Siphon will do. Note that there is a limit they cannot cross." He gestures broadly to outline the playing field, which spans the entire valley, stretching into the jungle on the right and partway up the mountains on the left. "For those skilled in water," Ethos continues, "the lake may be familiar, but you must learn to assist your air-breathing teammates. The same applies to those navigating the jungle and climbing the mountains. Teamwork is pointless if you can't adapt and cooperate across different elements."

"If the challenge lasts into the night, as we assume it will, your packs contain supplies to sustain you for days," Argus assures with a calm, steady voice. "You might grow tired and need rest—don't push past your limits, as tomorrow brings new chances. Each clan has four flags, totaling sixteen: Agni's are red, Jala's are blue, Prithvi's are green, and Vayu's are grey." He pauses before concluding, "We wish you success in this venture, and hope you find growth and friendship in this exercise. Though we are unseen, know that we are observing your every action." With these final words, the challenge commences, setting the stage for a test of skill, teamwork, and resilience that will shape our journey ahead.

"So… I guess we will be staying the night out here… in the woods. Dont worry, I will make sure nothing scary gets you" Callen says nudging me in the side with his elbow. "You fucking wish, Im sure it will look more like *me protecting you* the moment things go bump in the night and you scream like a little bitch" I shoot back at him.

Forty

Vega

Ethos and Argus leave us at the shoreline, their final instruction being that we'll start when the horns sound, and then they vanish into the forest. We gather calmly to devise our battle strategy. It seems the team took some pity on me, as they unanimously chose me as the team leader. We realize discussing strategy is futile without knowing what lies ahead, but we do decide to split into two groups, with me leading one and Greyson leading the other. Initially, I considered appointing Archer but concluded Greyson was the wiser choice. With his ability to scout from above and his background in the U.S. Navy, he brings valuable battle experience. We organize into our groups so everyone can recognize their teammates. The primary rule is to keep communication open within our squads. Our plan is to focus on capturing one flag at a time to conserve energy. My team will go for the first flag, while Greyson's team sets up camp in case we remain here. The day is moving quickly, so if we take more than a couple of hours for the first flag, the other team will prepare dinner. Magic use tends to drain us, so meals will be crucial, and thankfully, our packs are stocked to sustain us.

Atop Atticus I surveyed the sprawling terrain below. Aria hovered at my side with her owl, her quiet confidence a steadying force amid our uncertainty. Riya's fiery wolf paced restlessly, eager for action, while Callan's python coiled next to him, its unblinking gaze ready to strike. Beside me, Talon and his great ape companion emanated power and resolve.. Together, we formed a formidable team, each member contributing unique strengths. As we weighed our next move, anticipation thrummed through our ranks. The Aviaphid—our dark-winged adversary that we havent seen yet—stood guard somewhere over the clan banners we sought. Success would demand precision and coordination. Exchanging silent nods, we fixed our eyes on the valley below, its wide basin awaiting the first strokes of our victory. Our journey had begun, and as leader, I was determined to guide us through every challenge.

Aria and I ascended into the sky to scan the jagged peaks, while Riya and Talon plunged into the rugged ravines beneath. Callan and Kyson slipped through narrow fissures between our paths, their senses alert to every hidden crevice. From my vantage, Aria's sharp eyes spotted the first flag—a solemn gray of the Vayu clan—tucked deep in a shallow cave near a snowy summit. At its entrance, Aviaphids blended into the shadows, almost invisible. I raised my hand, and we moved in unison. I scaled the cliff face with Talon clinging to my back as Zuri carried Riya, leaping from boulder to boulder. Callan and Kyson threaded through cracks, securing flanks and tightening the noose. Once we'd taken our positions, Riya summoned a blazing orb that filled the cave with light, banishing the shadows and revealing four Aviaphids lurking within. With a swift arc of her hand, she carved a blade of flame across the mountaintop, melting the snowpack into a torrent of rushing water. Callan shaped that runoff into a spiraling funnel, cutting off the Aviaphids' line of sight, while Talon and I hurled jagged boulders to drive them into the open. As the clash began, Riya and Zuri slipped forward under the protective canopy of clouds Aria had woven, inching closer to the cave's deepest chamber.

Talon and I unleashed a relentless duet of earth and wind magic, keeping the Aviaphids off balance with swirling dust and cracking stone. Callan angled the watery vortex toward their ranks, its powerful pull tugging at the creatures' feet. Just as Riya gripped the flag and began her descent, a lone Aviaphid dove from above, talons outstretched and fury in its eyes. Our hands were full, and neither Callan nor I could react in time. In that split second, Silas sprang into action, slamming into Talon with all his strength. Propelled forward, Talon called up a surge of emerald magic: thick vines erupted from the earth to form a living barrier mere moments before impact. The Aviaphid struck the verdant wall and reeled, stunned, as Talon wove the vines tighter to cage it. With swift precision, Callan and I drove the remaining Aviaphids into the earth-forged prison.

Exhausted but exultant, we made our way back to the shore, Riya holding the flag aloft. The moment its tip pierced the sand, a golden light shot into the sky—a radiant signal of our triumph and a surge of pride pulsed through us all. Despite every danger, our unity and resolve had carried us to the first victory in this war game. We returned to our beachside camp to debrief. Our aggressive advance left no time to study the other team's magic, so we warned the second squad to vary their approach. We knew our own powers would sharpen with practice, but also that rest was crucial—none of us could afford another spell-misfire like yesterday's. As the sun dipped behind the mountain ridge, the lengthening shadows threatened to tip the balance. Thankfully, each team boasted a fire wielder who could hold the darkness at bay. Though fatigue tugged at us all, we tweaked the plan: before the second team launched their assault, we would send out recon parties.

The Prithvi clan slipped into the forest depths, moving like living shadows through undergrowth and hollow trunks, seeking hidden flags in every nook. The Jala group submerged beneath the waves, gliding through the currents with silent grace, eyes trained on the murky depths for any telltale glimmer. Above them, the three of us from the Vayu clan took to the air, our silhouettes traced against the twilight sky as we scanned the land below with unwavering focus. And under the cloak of dusk, Kat and Riya prowled the fortress corridors, their forms melting into the half-light as they hunted for secret passages and concealed alcoves, determination lighting their path. With a collective understanding, we set a time limit of one hour, knowing that what remained undiscovered would remain shrouded in secrecy for the time being. As we dispersed into the night, our resolve remained unshaken, for we knew that with every passing moment, we gained knowledge that would only help us complete this challenge.

It's freezing up here in the clouds. I expected it to be cold, but the night air has a sharper bite. "Are you warm?" I ask Aria as she tucks her hands into Ophelian's feathers. "Of course not, but if it were comfortable, it wouldn't be a challenge, right?" she replies with a smile. For a moment, I can't take my eyes off her; she's truly beautiful. A sudden rise into the sky pulls my attention away. I know I need to concentrate, but a larger part of my mind eagerly anticipates crawling into the tent later to sleep beside the most amazing woman in the world. What the fuck has happened to me?

Forty-One

Jaliah

As night descended and we captured the first flag, our attention turned to the challenging task before us. With shadows stretching and time slipping away, we divided into smaller teams for a quick reconnaissance mission, each group aiming to locate at least one target before complete darkness set in. Callen and I were given the crucial job of exploring the lake and its enigmatic depths. Knowing the Aviaphids were drawn to both air and water, we understood the importance of our mission. Driven by determination and urgency, we ventured into the night, our senses sharpened and our resolve firm. As we navigated the calm waters, our eyes swept the surface, searching for hidden flags or potential threats beneath. The lake, cloaked in darkness, held untold secrets, its depths concealing mysteries waiting to be uncovered. Each moment added pressure to our mission. With fifteen flags still out of reach, time was critical. We knew success required swift and decisive action, as the challenges ahead demanded our full dedication and perseverance.

This lake is no ordinary stretch of water; it embodies every conceivable aquatic realm— truly awe-inspiring. Its expanse reflects the oceans' diversity, from intricate coral reefs teeming with vibrant life to secluded coves reminiscent of hidden natural springs. Dark, murky swamps, with dense foliage, have twisted roots that delve deep into the earth, resembling gnarled fingers reaching for secrets buried below. As we navigated its depths, we discovered a maze of hidden alcoves and shadowy recesses, each one a potential hiding spot. The water swirled around us, and in the darkness below, we noticed rocky formations etched with markings that looked like ancient runes.

Within these runes, we spotted the distinct blue glow of a flag. Carefully noting its location and the solitary Aviaphid standing guard, I mentally recorded every detail, knowing that each observation could be vital to our strategy. Honestly, I wanted to swoop in and grab it—I was sure I could do it, but if something went wrong, I didn't want to be the one to piss off the group.

Callen and I moved towards the swamp area, our senses alert to the hidden dangers lurking in its murky depths. Despite our thorough search, the second flag eluded us, prompting us to head towards the spring-filled lagoons that beckoned with their serene beauty. The first lagoon greeted us with its turquoise waters and sandy bottoms, where small bubbling springs added a whimsical touch to the scenery. Even though the vibrant plant life hinted at hidden treasures, our efforts were fruitless, as we couldn't find a flag. Unfazed, we continued our methodical search, dividing the lake into sections to explore every inch of its vast area. As we approached the eastern coral reefs, we were captivated by a stunning display of glowing blue fish, their graceful movements highlighting the lake's enchanting beauty. Amid the swirling currents, we spotted the second flag, nestled among the towering coral structures rising from the depths. Sea fans in shades of purple and dark red offered scant cover, barely hiding the flag from view. Two Aviaphids stood vigil atop the coral towers, their keen eyes scanning the depths below. Taking note of every detail, we quietly moved toward the beach.

Armed with the information we had gathered, we returned to camp, ready to regroup and strategize for the upcoming challenges. Katerina and Riya were busy with camp preparations, carefully laying out a large blank canvas on the table and marking the camp boundaries and the landmarks they had explored. They had circled an area with a flag at the base of the mountains, where the range emerges from the forest. Callen and I returned, eager to add our discoveries to the map. With quick strokes, we marked the locations we had searched and the two flags we had found. We'd just completed charting our own finds when Vega, Aria, and Greyson arrived, faces set with resolve and edged by weariness from their reconnaissance. Without delay, they began adding mountain and aerial markers to the map—each one a flag they'd uncovered. The first sat precariously atop the furthest peak's summit. The second hid in a high-altitude pool nestled between twin mountains, its overflow tumbling down into a gentle creek. Their third mark pinpointed a flag floating in midair, tethered to a small island drifting among the clouds. The last rested on the map's western edge, tucked within the canopy of a colossal redwood, its ancient boughs offering perfect concealment. As each symbol went down, our shared purpose tightened around us; with this section of the map complete, our next moves were already taking shape.

Shortly after, Archer's team strode back into camp, determination still bright in their eyes despite their fatigue. They wasted no time filling in the forest's terrain, each icon revealing another hidden flag—six in all. One lay in a secluded meadow, cradled by thick foliage. Another stood at the heart of a natural tree "village," where intertwined branches formed a secret enclave. The third awaited us in the depths of a vine-draped canyon, concealed beneath layers of climbing greenery. A perfect circle of boulders sheltered the fourth, its flag planted square in the center. The fifth wound around the soaring aerial roots of a banyan tree. But it was the sixth that tested us most—hidden in a haunting grove where twisted trunks reached like gnarled fingers and veins of lava glowed across the forest floor, all under the watchful gaze of prowling Aviaphids. With every new mark, excitement mingled with a flicker of unease, but our unity and determination only grew. With a complete map, we quickly devised a strategy. Since the forest contained multiple targets and we had two Prithvi specialists on hand, we'd secure the woodland flags first—both to capitalize on our earth magic and to conserve my water powers for the flags hidden beneath the lake's surface. Not everyone could dive without oxygen gear, so it made sense for me to focus on the aquatic objectives once we regrouped. United by our plan, we stood ready to face whatever trials lay ahead.

By doubling our efforts on the water flags, we'd smooth out our coordination and lean on everyone's unique strengths. Our first target sits in the meadow. After Archer and Greyson forge their airborne magic link, Greyson lifts into the sky, out of sight but ready to dive into the meadow on command. The rest of us slip through the forest under Kat's dark haze—her magic muffles our noise and cloaks our presence, giving us the element of surprise over any aviaphids lurking nearby. Near the meadow's edge, we huddle in Kat's shadow to hear Archer's update: Greyson is circling above and has eyes on the flag. A couple of aviaphids drift in the vicinity, but none stand guard. Archer outlines the plan: those of us on the ground will form a magical barrier so Greyson can swoop in, grab the flag, and head straight back to the beach. One by one—Archer, Annalise, Kat, and I—we fan out around the perimeter of the clearing, pausing just inside the tree line. Then, we extend our arms, channeling protective magic outward. Our individual bands weave together into a glowing ring encircling the meadow. Confident in its strength, we push our combined magic upward until it arches toward the sky, forming a luminous tunnel.

At Archer's signal, Greyson plunges down through our tunnel. Behind him the aviaphids pour in, but Archer directs Greyson to keep going. Just as Greyson snatches the flag and brakes inches above the grass, Archer ruptures the tunnel wall on one side, giving Greyson an exit. The moment Greyson is clear, Archer seals the breach. Now trapped inside the tunnel, the aviaphids swarm upward against our barrier. Shifting our intent from protection to containment, we cinch the tunnel shut at the top, imprisoning them. With Greyson safely airborne, Kat shouts that she has an idea. She steadies the barrier with one hand, freeing the other to summon fire magic. In a brilliant flash, she fills the tunnel with flames. The aviaphids collapse to the meadow floor, incinerated.

We release the barrier, panting as our magic drains away. For a heartbeat, we stand in stunned silence—then realization dawns. We did it. Moments later, Greyson returns, exhilarated and already thinking ahead to the next flag. He tosses each of us a small packet of viscous goo. "Tear it open and drink it down," he urges. "The texture's weird, but it's packed with glucose and a bit of protein—my go-to on long runs."

We tear open the pouches of goo and gulp them down—mine's chocolate-flavored, just like icing. We'd already decided our next target was the Banyan tree on the far side of the forest; recon showed only a light aviaphid patrol there. We mount up and slip into the shadows toward our goal, though by now the aviaphids have probably caught wind of us. Ethos and Agnus warned they learn from every engagement, so our old tactics won't work twice. Suddenly Greyson's voice rings in our minds—he's extended his communication spell to the whole squad, something he couldn't manage before the last battle. "Any ideas beyond our usual tactics?" he asks as we hurry on.

"I do, actually," Annalise replies.

When we're just out of sight of the Banyan's flag, we pause to run through her plan: a classic distraction. Kat, Archer, Annalise, and I cluster beside a young sapling. Annalise and Archer channel Prithvi magic, coaxing it into a massive Banyan tree whose tangle of branches hides us completely. Greyson lifts off, spiraling overhead at high speed, whipping up a fierce windstorm. As soon as the aviaphids swarm toward the vortex, we spring into action. The hidden Banyan shudders, its roots writhing free from the earth like great tentacles. It strides across the ground in a smooth, swaying motion, carrying us straight up to the flag. When our tree's limbs entwine with the Banyan's, Nyterian—small and nimble—scurries along the downward-reaching boughs, plucks the banner, and slips back into the leafy cocoon. With the flag secured, our animated tree glides us out of the aviaphid zone. We signal Greyson; he breaks his circle, rocket-lifts into the sky, and draws the creatures off in the wrong direction. Meanwhile Annalise leaps onto Cassius, grasping the flag, and rockets toward the beach at an impossible speed.

We head back toward the beach as Greyson speeds off, drawing the creatures away. When our boots hit the sand, I'm flooded with relief at the sight of three flags planted in the dirt just where the water meets land. We've still got a long way to go, but it's progress. I shouldn't need long to rest before diving with Callan to retrieve the submerged flags. Meanwhile, Greyson tells Aria and Vega he's got enough stamina—thanks to his military years—to help them fetch the mountaintop banner while I recover. I grab a quick meal and sit with Callan at the table, studying the map. We brainstorm strategies and decide which magic users will be best for each scenario.

"I hope those things stay gone long enough for you to bounce back," Callan says with a smirk. "I don't want to have to drag you through the water when you burn out."

"Don't flatter yourself," I shoot back. "Even on my worst day, I'll still kick your ass."

"Oh, such a tough girl, aren't we?" he teases.

"You want to test that in my tent? I could use a little post-battle release," I challenge.

"So you admit you need me," he replies, raising an eyebrow.

"Don't let it go to your head, big guy. There aren't exactly bodies lining up here—you'll do in a pinch," I counter.

He leans back, grinning. "I'm not above letting you use me, but fair warning: once you've sampled my unique skills, nothing else will do."

I say nothing—victory is mine before we even begin. I push away from the table, dab my mouth with a rag, and toss it onto my empty plate, meeting his eyes as I stand. Then I turn and head to my tent. Out of sight of the others, I shrug off my shirt and let it drop at the entrance. Inside, I make it my mission to show him exactly how thoroughly I can win.

As Callen steps into the tent, his breath catches at the sight of me, fully bare and sprawled across the bed, legs splayed wide in invitation. His eyes trace the curves of my body, pausing at the apex of my thighs where I am already glistening with anticipation. I can see the hunger in his gaze, the primal need that matches my own. He drops to his knees at the edge of the bed, his hands gripping my ankles as he drags me closer to him. His touch is firm, possessive, and it sends a thrill through me. I prop myself up on my elbows, looking down at him with a smirk. "This is how you should always be," I tell him, my voice laced with command. "On your knees, worshipping me."

Callen grins, his eyes never leaving mine as he leans in, his breath dancing across my skin. His hands slide up my calves, his fingers tracing a path of fire along my skin. He pauses at my knees, pushing them further apart, opening me to his gaze. I can see the hunger in his eyes, the sheer desire that makes him want to devour me whole. He leans in, his breath hot against my inner thigh, and I can feel the slight graze of his teeth before he bites down, a sharp, exhilarating pain that makes me gasp. His hands move higher, gripping my thighs with a bruising force that makes me feel owned, possessed. I love the roughness of his touch, the primal need that drives him to claim me so fiercely. He licks the spot he just bit, soothing the sting with his tongue before moving higher, his breath cool against the wet trail he leaves behind.

I tangle my fingers in his hair, gripping tightly I force his mouth to my clit, he doesnt fight back, he devours me. His hands slide under my ass, putting me in the perfect position for him to carry out this mission. His tongue dances over me, exploring every fold and crevice with a hunger that leaves me breathless. I can feel the pressure building, the tightening in my core that begs for release. He sucks my clit into his mouth, his tongue flicking against it with relentless precision. My hips buck against his face, grinding out an orgasm that crashes through me like a tidal wave. Callen's grip on my thighs tightens as he drinks in every last shudder, his eyes locked onto mine, reveling in the pleasure he's drawn from me. I pant heavily, my body still quivering with aftershocks as he slowly pulls away, a satisfied smirk playing on his lips.

"That was just the warm-up," he growls, rising to his feet. His hands move to his belt, deftly unbuckling it before pushing down his pants. He springs free, hard and ready, and I can't help but lick my lips. Callen sees my reaction and his smirk deepens, knowing the effect he has on me. He leans down, his body covering mine as he captures my mouth in a fierce kiss. I can taste myself on his lips, a mixture of us that is intoxicating. His hands roam over my body, touching every curve and dip, claiming every inch of me. I wrap my legs around his waist, pulling him closer, feeling his hardness press against my entrance. He teases me, rubbing against me without entering, building the anticipation until I'm practically begging. "Please," I gasp against his mouth, my nails digging into his back. He chuckles, a low rumble in his chest, and finally gives me what I want. He pushes into me slowly, inch by inch filling me completely. I arch my back, pressing my breasts against his chest, desperate for more contact, more friction, more of him. He obliges, his hips beginning to move in a steady rhythm, each thrust driving me higher, pushing me closer to the edge.

His mouth trails hot kisses down my neck, pausing at the sensitive spot where it meets my shoulder. He bites down, a raw marking that sends a jolt of pleasure-pain straight to my core. I cry out, my nails raking down his back, urging him on. His pace quickens, his thrusts becoming harder, deeper, as if he can't get enough of me. I meet him thrust for thrust, our bodies slick with sweat, our breaths mingling in ragged gasps. The tent fills with the sounds of our passion, the sound of flesh on flesh, the whispered pleas and growled commands. The intensity of our connection is overwhelming, pushing us both closer to the brink.

Callen's hand finds its way between us, his thumb pressing against my clit, circling with the same rhythm as his thrusts. The added stimulation sends shockwaves through my body, my moans growing louder, more desperate. I can feel the tightening in my core, the building pressure that threatens to consume me. "Come for me, Jal," Callen growls into my ear, his voice rough and commanding. "Let me feel you come undone around me." His words are my undoing. With a final, deep thrust, I shatter, my orgasm ripping through me with an intensity that leaves me breathless. My body convulses around him, my inner muscles clenching and releasing in waves of pure bliss. He pulls out of me instantly, letting his own orgasm splash onto my stomach in puddles. "Fuck, I feel a thousand times better about this whole magical war game already" he says as he drops his sweat covered body onto the bed next to mine. He slides his arm under my neck, placing my head in the crook of his arm and chest. For a moment, I lay there, absorbing the sensations that just coursed through me. When I realize that we are crossing the lines from sex to cuddles, I push up off the bed, grabbing a tshirt and wiping the evidence off me before tossing it to him. "Clean yourself up, we have shit to do." I say to him nonchalantly. "Okayyy, we just pretending that wasn't phenomenal or something?" he asks as if I just deflated his ego. "Dude, it was sex, it was needed, and its done." I say smiling at him as I pull my shirt back over my head. Sex is good, its necessary, but the strings that tend to follow it are outside of my comfort zone.

Forty-Two

Aria

" Alright, here's the situation. We've already found three flags, which is fantastic, but we still have more ground to cover. The next flag is up on the mountain, and it's quite a hike. So, Riya will ride with Greyson. Her fire skills could be useful up there, and the high altitude makes it easier for her to ride instead of taking Zuri," I explain to the group. Greyson, Riya, Vega, and I will handle this flag while the others rest and plan our next move. Jaliah mumbled something under her breath and shot me a look like she was offended she wasn't on this mission, but they have been on all of them so far, and we have to make sure everyone gets rest so they don't burn out. Greyson positioned Riya at the front on Isador's back, making sure she had a secure grip for the journey. Meanwhile, Vega and I mounted Ophelian and Atticus, ready to set off from the shoreline. Without a solid plan yet, our first goal was to reach the peak nearest to where the flag was located. From there, we could survey the area and devise our strategy.

Before departing, we made sure Riya was comfortable and ready. With a determined nod, we signaled it was time to start our climb. As we climbed higher, the cold intensified, especially with the sun now set. The wind howled fiercely, making my eyes water and the tears freeze on my face. Despite the freezing conditions, we continued, resolved to reach our goal. With the rendezvous peak just five minutes away, the biting cold threatened to penetrate my core. I tapped into the magic linked with Ophelian, allowing me to scout our landing spot from above. The area was covered in untouched snow, with no sign of the feared Aviaphids nearby.

I signal to the team that our landing zone is secure, prompting us to initiate our maneuver and bank left, circling slightly around our designated area. We navigate carefully through the shadows of the night, making sure to stay out of the moonlight that could reveal our location. The wind stirs up swirls of snow as we approach the peak for landing, heightening our awareness of the imminent risk. Upon landing, we move cautiously, aware of the Aviaphids nearby. Greyson, Vega, and I use our wind magic to create a quiet bubble around us, allowing us to communicate without attracting attention. "I see two creatures on the peak and one flying above," I inform the group.

Greyson proposes a plan: we approach the Aviaphids in a V formation, each taking a strategic position. As we advance, we manipulate the atmosphere to drop the temperature to subzero levels, while Riya counteracts the cold with her warming powers to protect us. It's not foolproof, but it's a solid plan given the uncertainties we face. Vega establishes a line of communication between us, ensuring we stay connected throughout the mission. After a final check, we mount our companions and take to the skies, ready to face whatever challenges await.As we approach the peak in Greyson's formation, the Aviaphids react quickly, converging and launching silver magic bands toward us. Instinctively, I raise my hands to create an invisible shield between us and the attack. Through our linked magic, I signal the others to drop the temperature. Together, we channel our powers, causing the air to buzz with magic as the temperature plunges.

Riya's magic grabs ahold of us in a gentle warmth, shielding us from the biting cold. The Aviaphids, slowed by the sudden temperature drop, struggle to maintain their magical grip, their bands weakening under our combined assault. Seizing the momentary distraction, I urge Ophelian to guide us forward, skillfully weaving under the formation of creatures ahead. With a swift move, Ophelian veers sharply to the right, bringing us close to the flag. I reach out and grab hold of it, marking the completion of the first phase of our mission. Now, our main focus is to make a quick and safe escape from this dangerous scenario.

As they employ their magic to immobilize the creatures, I quickly assess how much distance we've gained. Suddenly, I sense a threat from above. Before I can respond, a solitary Aviaphid emerges from the shadows and crashes into me, knocking me off Ophelian's back. Clinging tightly to the flag, I plummet through the air as Ophelian lets out a chilling screech. Looking back, I see the Aviaphid sinking its claws into Ophelian's wing, trying to bring her down too. With little time left, I attempt to use my magic to slow my descent, but before I can act, I hit something solid. The impact is jarring, and everything goes dark as my senses fade.

***

When consciousness returns, I find myself on Atticus, held securely by Vega as we speed through the air. My head is pounding, and I notice blood on Vega's shirt, uncertain if it's his or mine. The wind's roar drowns out any attempts to speak, and my whole body aches. Before I can fully comprehend the situation, darkness overtakes me again. I wake up in a tent, Vega's body shielding mine protectively. The pain has lessened, the headache now a faint whisper, yet still persistent. As I regain my senses, memories of recent events rush back, and a wave of dread hits me. Ophelian —the last I saw her, she was fiercely battling the Aviaphids, her screams piercing the night. I reach up to touch Vega's face, silently thanking him and seeking reassurance. When he opens his eyes and sees I'm awake, he lets out a relieved sigh.

"Ophelian?" I ask softly.

"She's fine," he assures me. "Isador helped her, and she's resting outside." He kisses my forehead. "We got the flag back, Riya and Kat healed you, Ophelian is safe, everything is alright." I kiss him, overwhelmed by his care and gratitude. Though I'm not a damsel in distress, if I need saving, I'm grateful he is there. Still, I can't express my feelings to him as he did to me. I need more time to be sure of who he truly is now, not who he was before. I pull him close, wrapping my arms around him tightly. He hugs me back, planting soft kisses on my neck and whispering gratitude to God for my safety.

"Although staying here in this tent just like this is tempting, we should really join the others and assess our situation. If this were an actual battle, every second would be crucial, and as pleasant as this is, we need to concentrate," I softly tell him. He nods in agreement, helping me to my feet. As we leave the tent, Kat quickly grips me in a hug.

"Oh thank God, I was so worried. I'm not exactly experienced in healing, so I was just improvising, but you're okay, everyone's okay," Kat babbles rapidly.

Archer approaches, holding my shoulders and gazing into my eyes to ensure I'm truly fine before giving me a tight hug. "You gave us all quite a scare back there," he remarks.

We gather around the table, examining the makeshift map and counting the flags we still need to collect. While I was unconscious, Callen and Jaliah managed to capture two flags from underwater and also snagged a bonus flag from an aviaphid that tried to attack Callen. This puts us at seven flags collected, with eight more to go.

I mentally list the flags we still need:

- Top of the waterfall

- Floating island

- Top of forest trees

- Boulder circle

- Haunted forest

- Forest canyon

- Tree village

- Base of the mountain

That leaves two unmarked flags yet to be found, hopefully, simple bonus ones. We anticipated the lack of daylight would hinder us, but so far, it's been advantageous. With about four hours of night left, we need to press on. I suggest we head to the top of the waterfall, but Vega disagrees, saying I need more rest, and that we could use water magic, plus Callen and Jaliah just returned and need rest too. The group decides to aim for the flag at the mountain's base and we'll reassess after that. Archer, Kat, Annalise, and Greyson prepare to leave, and Riya joins their team to give Jaliah a break. They quickly mount up and head out after deciding where to go.

Since I'm on rest duty, I think I should check on Ophelian, feeling a bit guilty for not doing it sooner. She's resting peacefully just outside the camp, so I grab a bowl of food and go to her. I choose not to wake her, sitting beside her and leaning back against her wing while eating. Atticus comes over to check on Ophelian too. I thank him for helping rescue me, not wanting to imagine what could have happened without him and Vega.

"It was my honor and duty, Miss Aria," he replies wisely.

Ophelian wakes up upon hearing us talk, saying she feels fine and that the damage from the aviaphids is mostly healed. She also assures me she's ready to fly. I tell her that Vega put me on bed rest for the time being, so she has some time to continue to rest, but that I would stay right here with her. She curls around me, making the perfect recliner of warmth and softness — and before I know it I am fast asleep.

A voice thunders through the air, ripping through every sense I possess. "This version of your world is a mere illusion. Perfection has never existed. You have been fed an endless stream of deceit, but I am here to reveal the truth. Join me, and I will unlock powers within you that defy imagination. I can transform you into something beyond your wildest dreams." The voice declares with an overwhelming intensity. I am uncertain, but I suspect it is the Siphon himself infiltrating my dream. How did he find me here? How is he reaching me? I desperately need to wake up, yet I am trapped in this shadowy realm.

"It would be wise to keep our conversations to yourself," the voice warns, laced with a seething anger. "You may feel one way now, but I assure you, you will return to me with questions. You will crave to join me. The more you reveal to others, the more difficult it will become for you. But make no mistake, you will join me, eventually." With his final words, the oppressive darkness retreats from my mind, and I jolt awake, gasping for breath.

Forty-Three

Archer

❝ We're going in for this one swiftly," I say, my words nearly lost in the biting mountain wind as our small band advances toward the flag nestled in the rocky foothills. Moonlight glints off the jagged peaks above us, and each step crunches over frost-hardened stones. I can still feel the tremor in my chest from last night—the image of Aria's limp form, her once-bright eyes closed forever until we brought her back from the brink. Without magic healing her, I dare not imagine how close we came to failure. We fall into formation as if rehearsed a thousand times. Annalise and I hug the circling tree-licked slopes, our hands crackling with restrained magic. We are the shield, the warning bells at the edge of the circle. Ahead, Riya's hair flickers crimson in the glow of her gathering flames. Kat, cool and focused, feels like a torch held steady against the dark; her every breath seems to stoke the blaze dancing on her knuckles.

Above us, Greyson hovers against a starless sky, perched on currents of air. His sharp eyes sweep the shadows for movement, for any sign that we've been spotted. Down here, the stillness coils tightly around us—anticipation, fear, resolve. Suddenly Riya exhales a burst of fire that snakes along the ground, and Kat follows, her own flames bursting like twin suns. We barely have a moment to exult in the heat before the Aviaphid—a hulking creature with insectile carapace and malevolent yellow eyes—erupts from the boulders and throws up a shifting, opalescent shield. Our fire licks at it, then recoils, leaving the night unmarked. Kat melts into motion. She darts forward in a fluid arc, weaving beneath Riya's flare. Sparks rain off the Aviaphid's barrier as she slips under, her blade springing from a hidden sheath at her thigh. The edge is alive with magic, humming like a living thing. With a single, precise stroke she severs the creature's jointed legs. Its screech is a ragged crack in the night. It stumbles, collapsing onto its forelimbs.

Time slows as Kat plunges the blade upward. Viscous, inky blood bursts from the wound, splattering dark ribbons across the stones. The metallic tang of it fills my nostrils. Under the torrent of gore, the Aviaphid's defiant flickers fade into a final, gurgling rasp. We stand frozen in shock. Kat wipes her blade on the hem of her pants, slides it back into its sheath, and steps over the twitching remains. I realize I no longer see her as the little sister I need to protect. She is steel forged in fire—unyielding, fearless. She strides to the flagpole, her hair aglow in the dying embers of her magic, and plucks the banner from its stake with one hand. With a swift motion, she hurls it skyward and Greyson snatches it in midair, Isador's wings beating fierce currents that carry him toward the distant shoreline.

A rumble tears through the sky. We look up to see hundreds of Aviaphids cresting the mountaintop, their bodies black silhouettes against the moon. Greyson veers first, streaking toward the beach. Riya yells instructions through the connection of magic; Kat vanishes in a flare of orange light, teleporting toward the opposite ridge to seal the flank. Annalise and I twist orbs of shimmering energy over our palms and launch them into the night, luring the first wave of creatures toward us. Moments later, having confirmed Greyson's safe descent in the distance, we pivot uphill and converge on Riya and Kat. Our spells link into braided strands of power that snake through the air, ensnaring the horde in glowing cords. The creatures shriek as the bands tighten, pinning them like twisted metal. "More!" Kat cries, her voice a sharpened blade. We pour every ounce of magic into the weave. The bands flare gold, then burn fierce orange as they constrict. One by one the Aviaphids sag, their limbs going limp though life remains within. Kat steps back, sparks crackling off her fingertips as she ignites the perimeter ring of the energy field. Flames erupt, consuming the fallen beasts in a roaring inferno. Smoke coils into the sky, and in the sudden lull, all we can hear is our ragged breathing. We take that precious respite and make for the beach, hearts still hammering, flag in hand, knowing that—together—we turned back the night's darkness once more.

We move so quickly that the rest of the landscape turns into a blur around us. As we make our way back to the beach, my thoughts are consumed by Kat's remarkable display of skill and bravery. Her swift and decisive actions were instrumental in securing our victory over the Aviaphid. I can't help but feel a sense of admiration and gratitude for her leadership in the heat of battle. As the shoreline comes into view, a wave of relief washes over me. The sight of the eighth flag standing proudly on the beach fills me with a profound sense of accomplishment. Despite the challenges we faced, we emerged victorious, one step closer to completing our mission and securing the flags for our team. I slide off Lexora the second we stop at the camp, running over to grab Kat and lifting her into the air.

"Where on earth did all of that come from" I say to her with excitement

She smiles and gives a soft shrug "I didn't want anyone to get hurt again, so I did what I had to"

"Well, it was amazing, you were amazing!" I say to her while setting her feet back on the ground and hugging her. She squeezes me in the embrace before letting me go to high-five Riya as she approaches. Everyone is so pumped that they decide to run off of pure adrenaline and go again. Kat's bravery not only helped us defeat that part of the challenge, but it fueled everyone to press forward as well.

Aria and Ophelian come back into the camp, looking rested and well. They both agree that it's time to put a dent in the flag collection, but something doesn't look normal about Aria. She looks concerned or scared even. As everyone is busy getting things together for the next run, I pull her to the side, asking her if she is ok.

"I am fine, I wouldn't have said I was ready if I weren't" she bites at me

"I did not mean it like that, I just meant that you look concerned," I say gently

"I'm not, I just had a bad dream is all," She says a little nicer this time.

"Ok, well if you need to talk, you know I'm always available," I tell her

She doesn't reply, she just moves along with getting ready for the next mission and keeping to herself. I try not to worry as I get my own stuff ready, but I will keep an eye on her.

The flyers set off ahead of us to see what it would take to get the flag from the tree top while the rest of us moved in the shadows of the forest towards the circle of boulders that held another flag. Hopefully, we are able to get these quickly, the sun is starting to come up and we really do not want to spend all day out here. As we approach the boulders, we find it completely abandoned. It could be possible that the creatures are distracted by the flyer's flag retrieval, but unlikely. Annalise whispers for us to stay back as she slides off of Cassius and calls forth her magic. Suddenly, we cannot see her at all. She has used her magic to completely camouflage herself into her surroundings. The only thing that gives her away is the slight indentions of the leaf-covered ground as she stalks toward the flag. I call forth my own powers, attempting to do the same. It is hard at first, but with focus I achieve it. Talon watches me, knowing it has to be part of our earth magic, he too tries and succeeds. Both of us in unison step carefully towards the location that Annalise is in. At least if she gets noticed she won't be alone.

I use the magic connection to tell Annalise not to move the flag but to try and extend her magic into it like Kat had done with the blade, camouflaging it as well. Moments later, there is no flag to be seen, as it is safely hiding within Annalise's magic. When we exit the circle, a loud noise rings out without ceasing, stabbing our minds and causing us to fall to our knees. With the sound staying constant, it takes us a moment to get ourselves together. Annalise keeps moving slowly toward the rest of the group, keeping the flag camouflaged with her magic, while Callen uses his power to place a sound shield around us. The sound can still be heard, but it's dampened by the shield, just enough for us to use our own magic to reinforce it. We group together and continue moving through the woods away from the boulders as much as we can. We cross back into the forest and out of sight of the boulders — the sound stops. Annalise and Talon take off towards the beach letting us know they will get the flag back. They disappear as their magic camouflages them again. A bright beam can be seen through the treetops, letting us know that the fliers have retrieved the tree-top flag and made it to the beach. They should be headed towards us at any moment to regroup. As we race through the forest, the trees seem to quake with anger, dropping branches and leaves in our path. It's as if the forest itself is resisting our advance, but we can't afford to wait. Delaying our mission would only give the Aviaphids an advantage.

When we reach the outskirts of the woodland village formed by the trees, we spot six Aviaphids standing guard. Fortunately, one of them is holding an extra flag, turning our mission into a two-in-one opportunity. As we wait for Annalise and Talon to return, we discuss our plan of attack. Those of us with Prithvi magic can use vines to restrain some of the Aviaphids, while the others can target specific ones to trap, allowing us to grab both flags simultaneously. Each of us contributes ideas through our magical connection, preparing ourselves mentally for the impending confrontation.

Suddenly, we hear rustling behind us, and relief washes over me as Annalise and Talon return. But my relief turns to terror as I see them wrapped tightly in vines, barely able to breathe, controlled by an Aviaphid using the forest itself as its weapon. Before we can react, Kat and Riya leap forward, hurling flames at the creature, only to have the vines tighten around their throats. In desperation, I use my magic to camouflage myself while Aria, Vega, and Greyson take to the sky. Jaliah summons bands of water, freezing them into shards to attack the creature, but it proves futile. Callen manages to sneak behind the creature with Kyson, using his python's strength to constrict the Aviaphid and disrupt its control over the vines. However, our momentary victory is short-lived as three other Aviaphid guards join the fray, picking up where the first one left off. In that moment, despair sets in, and I fear that we may be facing our doom.

Right when I think everything is over, I feel a wave of magic come over my skin, coating my entire body, rain falls from the sky, but it isn't regular rain. As it lands on the skin of the creatures, it simmers and begins to melt into their flesh. The Vayu powers are being used to influence the atmosphere creating rain… of acid? The film covering my body is the same as the others have, preventing the flesh-melting rain from harming us. As the creatures retreat in pain, the remaining vines fall to the ground, and we can regroup. Greyson swoops down on Isador claiming the flag from the now writhing in pain aviaphid while Vega grabs the flag from the village-like group of trees. We do not wait around to see the outcome of the creatures, instead, we make a straight beeline in the opposite direction, regrouping when we are far enough away. We agree that no one needs to return the two new flags alone, So Vega and Greyson agree to make the run while the rest of us wait and rest a moment. When they return we will head to the haunted-looking section of the forest and work as an entire group to retrieve that flag.

Twelve flags have been found, and only four remain. No one has been fatally injured yet, but we have come very close. Tension grows in my bones as I realize that the danger has increased with each flag we have found. We need to go back and rest after this flag, though the rest of the group is ready to be finished. I worry because Aria does not seem herself, and when it is time to retrieve the floating island flag, it will be limited to the fliers, leaving them without the rest of the group's full support. It is not long before we're all gathered back together, and we are making our way quietly to the darkest part of the forest. Let's just hope that this one looks worse than it really is. The world around us turns from a magical woodland feel to a knotted, dead, soul-sucking atmosphere. The forest exudes an eerie aura, its bark cloaked in a hue as dark as the night itself, while its branches contort and twist like the gnarled fingers of some ancient creature. The air is tainted with the acrid scent of sulfur, mingling with wisps of burning lava that snake along the ground like tiny veins of fire. Thick and oppressive, the atmosphere weighs heavily upon us, devoid of the usual woodland chatter, leaving only the mournful howl of the wind in its wake.

Amidst the desolation, the flag stands defiantly at the heart of this decaying forest, encircled by the bubbling source of molten lava seeping from beneath the surface. Though no creatures guard the flag, we understand all too well that danger lurks in every shadow. Heat radiates from the scorched earth, yet our breath crystallizes in the frigid air, sending shivers down our spines. An unsettling feeling grips me as I stand alongside my comrades, our footsteps measured and cautious as we traverse the treacherous terrain, mindful to avoid the boiling depths below. Unbeknownst to us, a low growl rumbles beneath our feet, growing louder with each step toward the flag. In an instant, the earth beneath us convulses, erupting violently as if possessed by some unseen force. A great rift tears open between us and our goal, its jagged edges consumed by molten fury.

This is the moment my deepest fears violently erupt into reality. A blood-curdling scream from my right tears through my soul like a jagged knife. Time warps and distorts, each agonizing second dragging out as I watch in sheer horror, utterly paralyzed and helpless, while Kat hurtles over the precipice. The ground, once solid and unwavering, has transformed into a monstrous cliff, its jagged edges menacingly jutting into the sky. Below, a river of molten lava seethes and roils, its fiery surface casting a malevolent, hellish glow. Desperation floods through me like a tidal wave, and I stretch my arm frantically, my fingers clawing desperately to capture her hand. But my efforts are futile, and she slips from my grasp, vanishing into the gaping maw of the abyss, consumed by the violent, churning inferno below.

Forty-Four

Aria

We had a feeling that the haunted-looking forest would present us with problems. What we did not anticipate was that it would swallow one of us whole before we could even begin. None of us can breathe as we watch Kat slip from the edge being consumed by the boiling lava below. I see now, how much Archer cares for her. He cannot move, he cannot breathe, and he is on his knees at the edge of the cliff, frozen in panic.

"Vega - grab him before he falls too" I shout out. The last thing we need is to lose him as well. "I know how you all feel right now, but we all have to save it for later so that more losses do not happen" I demand to the others. On the other side of the split earth stands a group of aviaphids, and while we knew they were dangerous, this whole time we have been viewing this as a game, and those creatures as just made-up opponents. That all changes as we stand there watching the group merge into one, creating a massive beast capable of squashing us, and to add to it, it breathes a vicious fire.

Ophelian, Atticus, and Isador force us to mount, flying high above the creature, so that we have a better placement for attack. I attempt to manipulate the atmosphere and flood the ground with snow, but it doesn't work. The heat from the creature and the lava turn the snow to steam before it can even get near the ground. The three of us try again, combining all of our magic into one so that maybe it is strong enough to work. The heat still melts the snow, but ice-cold water makes it to the ground, putting out some of the small veins of lava, but dissipating when it reaches the larger pools. Riya steps forward from the line, sending bands of fire towards the large creature pushing it back slightly for a moment. Archer, Talon, and Annalise use their Prithvi magic to form weapons from the trees, launching blades and arrows toward the creature to keep it at bay.

Callen and Jaliah are manipulating the snow-turned water, forcing it to stay moving and cold in an attempt to cool the lava. The creature raised its giant head back, inhaling all the air from around them, and spitting it back in an electrifying ball of flame, striking Jaliah and Callen moments after they threw up their protective boundaries. The fire does not harm them, but it takes a toll on their protection boundary, throwing them back about 100 feet. With every step the creature takes, the ground rumbles with the sound of thunder.

I use the magic to communicate with the others, maybe instead of pushing it back, we should be trying to draw it forwards so that it will fall from the cliff into the lava. Annalise is the first to make a move, circling around to the creature's side, throwing forth a bridge of earth from her side to the monster's side. Moving fast, she crosses the bridge before it turns to ash, sliding under the creature and slicing into its flesh to anger it. She doesn't wait to see its reaction, instead, she throws another bridge and crosses back toward the rest of the team. The monster takes a step toward the ledge but stops when the bridge falls into the lava. She tried to trick it, and it almost worked, but the aviaphid caught on. While it stood on the edge, Archer and Talon threw vines from the trees behind them, thrusting them across the river of lava and wrapping them around the creature. Even though their magic is not strong enough to pull the creature, it does manage to keep him at the edge. Annalise follows suit, casting more vines to reinforce. Jaliah and Callen split sides, throwing a barrier of protection in front of the others right before the monster throws another ball of flame.

"We have to push it while they pull" I shout to Greyson and Vega.

We hurl ourselves with unyielding force towards the creature's back. Our birds thrust their talons with ferocious intensity, making contact with the beast's spine. As it lurches forward, the others yank viciously on the vines, pulling with every ounce of their strength. The creature teeters dangerously on the precipice of the molten river below, the earth itself trembling with rage. In a cataclysmic eruption, liquid fire explodes from the depths, engulfing the creature in a relentless inferno. From the core of this fiery chaos emerges a figure, cloaked in flames yet pulsating with life, driven by an unstoppable purpose. With a blazing sword gripped tightly, the fiery apparition surges forward towards the creature's menacing face. With unwavering determination, the flame-enshrouded figure drives the scorching blade deep into the creature's skull—a final, fatal blow that seals its doom. With a thunderous crash, the beast succumbs to the blaze, its colossal form plunging into the roiling river of lava below, devoured by the seething flames.

As the aviaphid meets its demise, the earth seems to sigh in relief, closing in over its fallen form once more as if to erase its presence from existence. The once vibrant veins of lava, now bereft of their fiery glow, transform into a slick, obsidian black. Lying amidst the aftermath of the battle, Kat's prone form rests where the creature once stood, her body no longer engulfed in flames. With her blade still clutched tightly in hand, she lies motionless, a silent figure amid the chaos. Rushing to her side, the rest of us form a protective circle, anxiously scanning for any sign of life. In a voice strained and faint, Kat breaks the tense silence with unexpected humor, her words tinged with exhaustion. "Is someone going to at least grab that flag I almost died for?" she quips, eliciting a wave of relieved laughter from our weary group. With Kat's survival assured, the defeat of the creature, and the capture of the flag, victory becomes palpable.

Without hesitation, Greyson retrieves the coveted flag while Vega gently lifts Kat into his arms carrying her towards Lexora. Swiftly, Archer mounts Lexora, prepared to whisk Kat to safety. With Greyson soaring above as a watchful guardian, and Nyterian leading the way, they embark on the journey back to camp, their spirits buoyed by the triumph over adversity. The rest of us re-group. We are all tired, but the sun has made its way high into the sky, and if we do not press forward, we will be out here for another night. We agree to at least scope out the canyon flag while we are in the forest. Maybe it will be possible for us to capture it with what is left of the group. We still have members from each clan, so we at least stand a chance. We take a moment to suck down a couple of packs of Greysons running goo he left us before heading out.

As we journey into the depths of the forest where the canyon lies, a profound transformation greets our senses. While the forest still stands tall around us, its demeanor has shifted from one of desolation to an enchanting wonderland. No longer do we encounter the skeletal remains of trees; instead, the landscape exudes a whimsical allure. Trees adorned with vibrant leaves cast a kaleidoscope of colors overhead, while mushrooms with luminescent undersides spiral upward like staircases crafted for mythical beings. Golden embers dance and twirl on the gentle breeze, infusing the air with a sense of magic. Vines, adorned with clusters of purple blossoms, cascade from the treetops, weaving a tapestry of ethereal beauty.

Guided by smooth stepping stones, we tread along a pathway that winds toward the canyon's entrance. Here, we are greeted by arches draped in jasmine, their fragrant blooms beckoning us forward. Descending into the canyon, a breathtaking scene unfolds before us. At the base, a pool of water shimmers with an emerald glow, casting an enchanting light upon the surroundings. Lush vegetation sprouts from the rocky walls, transforming the canyon into a hidden sanctuary, where nature's splendor flourishes in every corner. This mystical realm, adorned with its own brand of magic, invites us to explore its secrets and bask in its otherworldly charm.

As our eyes fixate on the flag nestled amidst the rocky formation at the heart of the shimmering pool, a sense of caution tempers our awe. Despite the serene beauty surrounding us, we remain mindful of the lurking perils that may lie beneath the surface. Halting our advance, we take a moment to scan our surroundings, vigilant for any hidden threats that may emerge. Suddenly, the tranquil waters stir, and from their depths emerges a figure of unparalleled grace and beauty—a woman whose ethereal presence commands our undivided attention. As she addresses us, her words resonate with a mesmerizing authority, drawing us closer with each syllable.

"I have been expecting you," she declares, her voice carrying an otherworldly allure. "I have safeguarded this flag on your behalf, fending off the creatures that sought to claim it. It now belongs to you. Take it and continue your quest."

As Talon steps forward, his senses are ensnared by the mesmerizing beauty and captivating words of the woman before him, and a sense of enchantment flows in the air. Entranced by her allure, he finds himself drawn closer, his gaze fixed upon her radiant form. With a voice laced with admiration, she addresses Talon, her words echoing with genuine admiration. "You, sir, are a vision of exquisite beauty. I would gladly offer you sanctuary here, as a token of gratitude for safeguarding your flag."

As the woman inches closer, her attire glistening with the remnants of the tranquil waters, Talon's attention is captivated by every subtle detail. Her garments, fashioned from sheer cream silk, cling to her form in delicate cascades, revealing glimpses of her supple curves beneath. His gaze descends, ensnared by the allure of her figure, the fabric molding to her contours with a tantalizing transparency. Her lustrous hair, cascading in wet tendrils around her, frames her features with other worldy grace, accentuating her bare skin. Talon's vision is obviously captivated by the fact you can see her nipples perfectly through her clothing. A sheer skirt adorns her hips, while a chain of dangling medallions adorns her waist, adding a touch of mystique to her captivating presence.

Adrenaline hammers in my veins as Annalise glides past the oblivious enchantress, her form wreathed in an invisible shroud of magic. Every heartbeat drums out a warning: one misstep, one ripple in the water, and she'll be exposed. I force myself forward, matching her pace, feigning rapture at the sorceress's side. My toe breaks the pond's glassy surface just as Annalise's does. The woman's head whips around, her eyes glinting at my feigned wonder. "If he will not stay, you will do just fine," she purrs, her voice velvet laced with danger. Her fingertips trail a frosty path along my arm, sending ice through my bones. Each syllable she breathes coils tighter around me, her stare burrowing into my spine. She leans in, and I can taste the cold breath ghosting across my throat. Panic sparks in my mind, and I pour it through our magical bond: Move now—before she claws any deeper. "Make it quick before this creature advances further," I whisper into the silent current that links me to Annalise. The enchantress's other hand curves beneath my jaw, tilting my face to hers. Her tongue, slow and deliberate, slides up the side of my throat, igniting a furious heat that battles the chill of her skin. My pulse drums loud between us, but I don't resist—my body is her bait. All that matters is Annalise and the flag tucked beneath her robes.

Suddenly a howl rends the air. Annalise's fingers snap shut around the flag's pole. The sorceress's lovely mask fractures, her mouth unhinging into a jagged scream. Bones crack beneath flesh as she erupts into her true horror: a rotting aviaphid, every feathered wing a blade of nightmare. Talon's enchantment shatters like fragile glass. Callen and Jaliah surge forward in perfect unison, summoning a coiling wall of water that slams around the beast before its talons can slash free. Enraged, it batters itself against the watery prison, its form warping into something even more hideous—an elemental terror born to guard this flag. I stand rooted, my mind reeling at the transformation. Annalise tucks the stolen banner under her arm and dashes toward the canyon's mouth. I break free of my stupor and rush after her, only to feel strong hands clamp around my waist. My heart leaps—has the monster caught me? But it's Vega, his grip firm and reassuring. With one motion he swings me onto Atticus's back; moments later his wings unfurl in a thunderous roar.

We ascend, every mighty beat lifting us farther from the cacophony below. The wind tears at my hair and flushes my cheeks with triumph and relief. Far beneath, the dark forest shrinks into a tangled blur of panic and shattered magic. Here, high in the open sky, danger falls away. Only freedom remains.

As the tumult of the recent events begins to settle, clarity dawns upon me, and I piece together the sequence of events that led to our escape. The realization strikes me that the creature had ensnared my thoughts, holding me in its grasp even as we fled the canyon. Glancing around, I notice that our trajectory isn't directly towards the beach, and a sense of understanding washes over me. It's as if Vega, with his intuitive understanding, recognized my need for a moment of respite amidst the chaos. His arms encircle me, providing a sense of security and grounding as we soar through the sky atop Atticus.

Gently, I shift my position, turning to face him, intertwining my legs with his to anchor myself firmly. Nestling against him, I find solace in the warmth of his embrace, my head resting against his chest as his steady heartbeat soothes my frayed nerves. In the quiet expanse of the sky, Vega breaks the silence, his words a testament to his unwavering concern and care. "I know you're more than capable, but when that creature targeted you, I couldn't just stand by," he confides, his voice soft with sincerity as he presses a tender kiss to my hair

"I'm not upset, I was simply going to say thank you. Also, it only targetted me because I let it. I has some kind of feeling it was all a trap, that it was an adaptation the Aviaphids were using. I was pretty sure that Talon was actually enchanted, so I was faking it to draw the attention away. It still messed with my head in some ways, but I was still mostly in control. But I do thank you, for pulling me out and all, and for always watching out." I reply.

Forty-Five

Katerina

We make it back to the camp, where Archer carried me into the tent to rest. I told him I could walk, but he insisted on helping me. He sets me down, letting me stand, before gathering fresh clothes for me to change into. As the adrenaline of the harrowing ordeal begins to ebb away, I become aware of the state of my attire, or rather, what remains of it. The fabric is riddled with holes, proof that the whole fiery trial wasn't a dream. While I may be physically unharmed, my clothes bear the scars of the inferno's wrath, their once sturdy fabric now worn and tattered. The realization settles in that while I may be fireproof or something like that — my clothing is apparently not. With a sense of humility, I acknowledge that despite my resilience, the image of my apparent demise in the depths of the lava pit has left a lasting impression on my companions. At this moment, I recognize the importance of allowing Archer to offer his support and assistance. With a nod of acceptance, I turn to Archer, silently conveying my gratitude for his steadfast presence. As Archer kneels before me, his hands gently removing the remnants of my melted shoes and tattered socks, I am struck by the depth of his vulnerability.

"I couldn't move, I reached for you and couldn't catch you, so I stayed there, frozen in fear and pain" he admits to me as he rises.

His confession lays bare the turmoil that gripped him in the throes of our shared ordeal. In his eyes, I see a reflection of my own disbelief, a shared acknowledgment of the gravity of the situation. His words resonate with a raw honesty that pierces through the veil of our shared silence, revealing the depth of his care and concern for my well-being. It's a feeling I'm not accustomed to, the sensation of someone truly caring for me, and it stirs a tumult of emotions within me. As he rises to meet my gaze, I sense the weight of his unspoken words hanging in the air, the unspoken question of what might have been had our fates taken a different turn. The thought gnaws at the pit of my stomach, a haunting reminder of the fragility of life and the bonds that tether us to one another. Gently, I reach out, my hand cradling his chin as he meets my gaze. "Thank you," I whisper, my voice barely above a hush, gratitude, and warmth infusing my words. "Thank you for caring, for reaching out, even when the fear threatened to consume us both."

In the charged hush of our stolen moment, our gazes lock like magnets drawn to the same fierce core of need. Archer's breath hitches, and he inclines toward me, his fingers tangling in my hair as he claims my mouth with a kiss long denied, gentle at first but swelling into an urgent, searing hunger.

My pulse hammers in my ears as I press closer, fingertips clawing at the hem of his shirt, desperate to feel every ridge and plane of him beneath my touch. His own hands rip at the frayed edges of my blouse, peeling it away so eagerly it feels as if flame follows his fingertips. Heat crackles between us; every grazing brush of skin sends shivers that roar into wild desire.

We stagger back toward the floor pallet—our tiny haven amid chaos—until we collapse in a tangle of limbs and breathless want. Archer's lips abandon mine only to trail scorching trails of kisses along my collarbone, down the hollow of my throat, unleashing sparks that ignite in my veins. He undresses me with reverent ferocity, each torn scrap of fabric falling away like the last barriers to our mutual unraveling. Then, in a moment of tender gravity, he cradles my feet, his thumbs pressing into the arches with deliberate, exquisite care.

"I know emotions are heightened right now," he murmurs, his voice a soothing balm against the backdrop of our passion. "I don't want you to think I am taking advantage of you in a desperate moment." His words resonate with a depth of sincerity that touches my soul, a reassurance that transcends the physical realm. With each tender stroke of his hands, he unravels the knots of tension that linger within me, moving from my feet to my calves, to my thighs, then my hips. He turns me over, running his hands up my back, working out the knots that formed in my muscles along the way. With my head turned to the side I reply "I do not think you are taking advantage of me, and I truly know that if I wanted to stop at any moment, you would." I take a deep breath in "But I do not want you to" I turn to him, the need of desire burning bright in my eyes. "I'm telling you not to stop," I whisper, my voice a soft plea laden with longing and yearning.

My words fan the blaze in his eyes. He hovers, lips brushing my earlobe as he whispers my name like a prayer, and then he's on me again—his mouth trailing fire across my jawline, down the slope of my neck, setting my skin ablaze. His hands slide up my thigh, warm and commanding, and I arch into him, the world narrowing to the slick press of his body against mine. With a swift, powerful motion he wraps my leg around his waist and lifts me onto him, our chests flush, our groans colliding in the stifling air. I grind down onto him, every heartbeat pounding with the delicious ache of fulfillment, lost entirely in the white-hot intensity of our union.

His lips consume mine with an insatiable, ravenous hunger, a ferocious declaration of our shared yearning. His hand grips possessively the curve of my lower back, pulling me closer, our bodies merging into an inseparable tapestry. In the throes of ecstasy, I surrender completely to the intoxicating rhythm of our union, my body moving with his in a frenzied dance of shared delight. Every breath, every movement, propels us deeper into the primal embrace of unrestrained desire. I ride him with relentless intensity, my nails clawing into the taut skin of his back, driven by the mounting crescendo of pleasure surging within me.

As the intensity of our passion reaches its zenith, I hover on the brink, the tantalizing promise of release just out of reach. With every heartbeat, waves of ecstasy swell within me, threatening to crash over the shores of my consciousness. In a final, desperate kiss, he ignites an inferno of sensation that consumes me entirely, his lips seizing mine with an urgency that mirrors the tempest raging within. A fierce nip of his teeth against my bottom lip unleashes a torrent of ecstasy, an earth-shattering wave that engulfs us both in its tumultuous embrace. In the aftermath of our shared climax, we collapse onto the pallet, our bodies entangled in a chaotic embrace of limbs and insatiable desire. Completely spent. Completely satisfied. Completely breathless.

Forty-Six

Jaliah

The team decided to attempt the flag on the floating island next, which left me sitting down below on watch. There isn't much I can do from here, but if there are attacks on their way down, I can do my best. As I sit here skipping rocks across the perfectly still lake, my mind races with so many questions. I know I come off as though I don't really care about much, and it looks as if I just go with the flow, but deep down I do care.

Life was always tough for me, I didn't have any silver spoons or platters in life like most people I know. I had to work for everything I got. It made me hard, it made me learn to just live and not ask much. "So.... the world has been a mess for a long time, what made you guys choose now to intervene?" I inquire, my curiosity piqued as I turn to Kobin."It is not that we chose this moment; we have tried in the past, but the time was not right," Kobin responds, his gaze sharp, scanning for any signs of movement from above.

"What do you mean you guys have tried?" I press further, intrigued by the notion of previous attempts.

"At one point we tried to integrate Earth. We chose different tribes and cultures to blend in with, but with all of those societies, one of two things happened: either they became basically extinct, or - worse. War struck their lands, and they wanted to use us as a power to feed their greed. So we left," he explains, his voice tinged with a sense of regret. "So, ya'll just gave up on Earth for a while?" I probe, though I immediately recognize that my question might come off as more blunt than intended.

"No - we tried again. We attempted during the medieval era - obviously, it did not work. People who were gifted the powers loved being seen as wizards more than they wanted to fix anything. We tried again in the late 1600s - it worked for a while, and change started happening. However, those who did not want to believe it, due to their own power struggles or religious persecutions, viewed the magic as blasphemy and put them on trial, burning most of them on pillars tied to posts," he recounts, his voice carrying the weight of history. "Don't get me wrong, I am not putting human religion down by any means. You are all created by a higher power, the same one who created us. It is not God's wish for evil to exist the way it does, but it is the evil that corrupts man into believing that anything outside of their beliefs is, in fact, evil," Kobin states with conviction.

"Are you referring to the Salem witch trials?" I ask, completely consumed by this eye-opener. "They were part of it, the part that history chooses to teach at least," he says. "We tried many more times though they are not all noticeable. The 1960s and 70s were noticeable. We tried helping, you know, during the hippie era, but the use of drugs ran high at that time as well, which made the boundaries of magic and usage blur, so the label became derogatory," he explains, his tone tinged with a hint of lamentation for missed opportunities.

Just as our conversation hits a fever pitch, a savage gale rips down from the floating island, yanking me off my feet and slamming me into the jagged earth. When I glare skyward, a monstrous tornado plummets from the clouds, its black vortex looming like a death sentence. I vault onto Kobin's back, scanning the storm's roiling eye. There— Greyson, Aria, Vega—hovering effortlessly in the cyclone's heart. The aviaphids pummel the swirling barrier, helpless. Behind Aria's shoulder I glimpse the gray banner, whipping triumphantly in the wind. One more flag down.

With a victorious smirk, Aria drives the staff into the sand at the water's edge. Vega reines us in, eyes blazing. He rattles off strategies with razor-sharp focus. "Plans change on arrival," he growls, "but every angle counts when we hit that summit." We spit out ideas —ambush points, diversion tactics, fall-back routes—each suggestion layering our battle plan with lethal possibilities. Our voices fuse into a single, determined roar. Then we launch ourselves toward the mountain. The world blurs—rocks, wind, shouting friends—a symphony of adrenaline and purpose.

At the base, Callen and I slam our hands into the river's surge, twisting water into solid, earthen steps. Beside us, Aria and Greyson exhale crystalline blasts, freezing each step rock-hard. United by elemental power, we carve a stairway up the living cliff. We surge upward, hearts hammering. At the summit's edge—a churning pool encircling the final banner—time shatters. Leaves hang suspended. Muscles lock mid-leap. The air crackles with tiny bolts of electric magic, summoned by unseen guardians. In that suspended heartbeat, Riya steadies herself. Flame flares in her palms—slender, determined. She threads a ribbon of fire through frozen droplets, striking the electric arcs like a lightning rod. The barrier shatters.

Suddenly, movement floods back. We drop to the ground, wind roaring in our ears, bodies battered but spirits ignited. Stunned for a heartbeat—then ready to seize the last flag at any cost. At this critical moment, a single creature stands before us, its presence radiating an overwhelming aura of power that demands our collective confrontation. Kat charges forward with fierce determination, unleashing rapid torrents of flames at the beast. Riya shadows her, their fires merging into a blazing inferno. Aria joins the fray, her magic conjuring a violent cyclone that propels the flames around the creature, amplifying their destructive force.Recognizing that ordinary water attacks are futile against a creature capable of thriving underwater, we concoct a daring strategy to freeze it solid. Aria, Vega, and Greyson pool their powers, ice spreading like a merciless tide to encapsulate the creature. Meanwhile, the Prithvi group channels the earth's might, crafting an unyielding cage from the soil itself. I urgently communicate our plan through magic, exchanging a decisive nod with Callen as we command the waters to form a bubble, entrapping the aviaphid.

Simultaneously, Talon summons robust vines from the mountain's depths, while the others weave hardwood through the gaps, sealing the creature within an impromptu wooden frozen prison. With swift precision, Riya seizes the moment, snatching the flag as the icy grip weakens, leaving the aviaphid ensnared. Greyson, with deft agility, transports the cage back, as Riya and Kat channel every ounce of their fiery magic into the structure, igniting it in a brilliant, all-consuming blue blaze. With the threat of further dangers hanging heavy in the air, Aria unveils a powerful new trick. Her hands stretch forward, summoning a small circle that rapidly expands into a swirling portal. Beyond it lies the sanctuary of the beach where Greyson awaits, his landing confident and assured. "Damn okay then Aria, show out a little" I say to her with a wink. Without hesitation, we leap into the portal, the promise of safety pulling us through. As we emerge onto the familiar sands, triumph floods our senses. The final flag is driven into the ground, its light piercing the sky in a radiant beam, a signal to Ethos and Argus that our mission has reached its victorious conclusion.

United on the shore, we stand as one, forged by adversity and bonded by victory. With the final flag secured, we can finally let out a breath of relief, our spirits emboldened by the trials overcome and the glory achieved. "You know what this calls for" Callen says through our magic to where only I can hear him. "I can only imagine what is about to come out of your perverted ass mouth" I send back to him. "I think that we both worked so hard out there, and it would only be proper to have some type of relaxation as a reward, maybe in the form of — you know… release" he send back. "You are a fucking moron. And as far as releases go, that was a one time thing" I reply. "One time my ass. There is no way you don't come back for more at some point. You can pretend all you want, but I know you enjoyed it. Lets just say… your enjoyment was all over myface… and other places" he replies. "Awe, you think you are actually amazing don't you? I hate to break it to you, I can do that for myself just as well whenever I want." I say to him. "Want to put money on it? I bet you a thousand dollars that at some point you come back for more" he says with a laugh vibrating through the connection. "Don't count on it lover boy, you served your purpose, I will give you that, but I am not so desperate, you are not the only option around here you know" I say, this time sending a little frost through the connection. "So a challenge it is then… I had a feeling you were one who enjoyed games. I accept your challenge. You will beg me — again, at some point" he says sending waves of pleasure through the connection that take aim right for my center. Our banter is quickly cut short when Baren and Ethos arrive on the beach. "Game on" is all I reply back before standing up to hear what comes next.

Forty-Seven

Aria

The moment the last banner fell into our hands, a wild cheer rose from our weary lungs—and almost before the echoes died, Ethos and Argus were on us. Ethos's eyes glowed with approval as he ticked off each power he'd witnessed—our crackling wards, our synchronized strikes, and the fleeting spark of aether we'd barely harnessed. They urged us to break camp and hurry back to the cottage for supper. By the time we stumbled through the low door of the cottage, our clothes reeked of smoke and sweat. Inside, long wooden tables sagged under platters of roast fowl, steaming loaves of crusty bread, bowls of roasted root vegetables, and pitchers of ruby wine. The golden candlelight danced along the ceiling beams, casting our hungry shadows onto the rough-hewn walls. We collapsed into chairs and nearly lunged into the feast before Baren glided in, the room hushed at his approach.

He lifted a slender goblet, his voice calm but heavy with purpose. "Well done." Every syllable carried weight—ours was a victory, yes, but a small one against the tide of the Siphon's influence. He spoke of the games we'd just completed: exercises meant to temper our teamwork and awaken our latent gifts. Yet, he warned, the Siphon's corruption was a deeper sickness—one that would not be cleansed in a single battle, or even by these ten alone. Somber faces surrounded him as he spoke of time slipping through our fingers, of generations needed to heal the wounds sown long ago. With that, he rose and traced a pattern in the air. A rift shimmered open beside him, revealing a grand mansion perched at the edge of a mist-veiled cliff. Its circular walls of pale stone curved around a central courtyard, where vines crept along marble columns. On one side, a dense forest marched down to the lawn; on the other, the land dropped away to pounding surf. The structure seemed alive, breathing in the salty breeze and exhaling wisps of magic that made my heart stutter.

"That will be your haven between missions," Baren continued, voice softening. "Room for you ten—and more." Each of us would choose an apprentice, someone who could one day shoulder this burden. They won't arrive with their own bonded spirit at first; that gift will awaken only as the world's balance shifts and new bondable creatures are born. Until then, you'll teach them all you know—your basic arts and whatever clan techniques you've claimed—so they can stand beside you when the time comes. I cleared my throat. "But how will we know where to find them, or whom to choose?" Baren offered a gentle smile. "It will come, as all things do. Trust your connected—that inner bond guides you more surely than any map. Wait until they prove themselves before bringing them to the sanctuary. More guidance will follow as you need it. For now—dine well, rest deeply, and steel yourselves for tomorrow." He raised his glass in a final, resonant toast. The clink echoed through the hall as we lifted ours in turn, hearts pounding with anticipation of the trials to come.

Initially, everyone eagerly delved into the feast spread across the table, with conversation kept to a minimum as we absorbed everything Baren had just divulged. The notion of taking on apprentices evoked both relief and apprehension within me. Given my nature, I knew I would become protective of them, and the prospect of sending them into battle filled me with anxiety. Yet, it was also a relief; the past few days spent engaged in battle simulations had left me drained, and I could only anticipate how exhausted we would be when faced with the real thing. Moreover, none of us possessed any real insight into what the impending battle would entail. The specter of the siphon haunted my dreams, or so I believed, but I hadn't even had the chance to fully comprehend it. And right now, I had no desire to dwell on it. Tonight was for enjoyment. Gradually, the chatter around the table picked up, mostly light and inconsequential. The wine certainly aided in loosening tongues. I had already made up my mind that once I finished eating, I would retire to my room; the oversized bathtub beckoned to me. My entire body felt as though it had endured a thrashing, and a soothing soak with Epsom salts seemed like the perfect remedy.

In the midst of the room's lively chatter, my attention is drawn to Vega, who isn't engaging in conversation but rather studying me with a curious gaze, as if nothing else in the world matters except for us. It's dawning on me that I need to confront what exactly is happening between us; he's bared his soul to me, yet I've offered him nothing in return. What if his continued interest in me hinges on my lack of reciprocation? What if I confess my feelings, and he loses interest once the chase is over? I don't know how that would affect me, but I know it would cut deeply. Undeniably, I care for him deeply; beyond his undeniable physical appeal, there's so much more to him that captivates me. Jaliah and Callen discreetly slip away from the table after finishing their meal, though their intentions aren't lost on the rest of us. There's an unmistakable air between Archer and Kat as well; the way they exchange glances across the table mirrors Vega's gaze directed at me. It's heartening to witness their budding connection. As for any other potential "love connections" within the group, I attempt to gauge everyone's interactions, but if there are any, they remain elusive.

As I finish my meal, I bid everyone a good night and gently push back from the table. Vega's unwavering gaze follows me as I make my way towards the stairs leading to my room. The thought of departing from this place saddens me; the room holds a certain perfection that I'll miss. Perhaps when we transition to the mansion back in the earthly realm, I'll be fortunate enough to find a room sort of like this one. Even if I don't, I can't complain—it's an entire mansion, after all. Leaving here hasn't been something I've given much thought to. I left behind an entire life when I arrived here, and the idea of returning to it now seems unfathomable. Knowing what I do now, returning to a normal existence would be impossible. Moreover, restraining my abilities in conventional nursing practices would prove challenging; the temptation to utilize my powers for healing would be constant. Then I would become a science experiment. When the time comes, I'll likely have to fabricate a family emergency as an excuse for not returning to work. But how will we sustain ourselves financially? I suppose those concerns will present themselves in due time. God, I am literally just now realizing that it is impossible for life to ever go back to what it was. We have crossed a threshold, a point of no return. As I think about life before... half the things we worry about in life seem so stupid now. It actually gives me anxiety to even picture being normal again. I have discovered something mind blowing, normal is never an option again. I am giving myself over fully to this new life, there is no going back for me.

I turn the faucet and watch the water churn into frothy warmth, steam curling around me like a seductive promise. I peel off my clothes, the fabric whispering against my skin, ready to sink into the tub's soothing cradle—when a sudden rap at the door shatters the hush. My heart lurches. Of course it's Vega; I should have left the door unlocked. I snatch a robe from the closet, its softness a poor shield against the sudden chill that slithers down my spine. Something isn't right, theres something….. wrong. Each step toward the door feels impossible, the floorboards groaning underfoot. A rancid cold presses against my throat, and the lights flicker as if protesting. My breath hitches; the air tastes metallic. Something is very wrong. Desperation claws at me—run, hide—yet my feet won't obey. I slide to my knees before the door, voice tangled in my chest, unable to call out Vega's name. I reach inward for our shared magic, but the well within me has run dry. My pulse thunders in my ears. Fear constricts me like iron bands. Then comes the tug—a vertigo so profound I feel myself plunging even as my knees remain planted. The room tilts, walls bending and bleeding into darkness, as though I'm being dragged headlong into an infinite pit. The world dissolves into a formless void, and an icy wind howls through me. Im spinning through oblivion and nothing I try is stopping me. I reach again deep within me to grasp my magic, there is nothing there. What if this is me losing magic, right when I decide to completely embrace it. It feels as if there is a massive hole inside of me where it used to reside.

Abruptly, the plunge halts. I open my eyes to find myself on cold stone, the air dank with rot and damp. A single, sickly glow slithers from a far corner, revealing dripping walls and rusty shackles. This is no longer my sanctuary but a subterranean cell. My tongue feels swollen; attempts to speak die in my throat. I lift trembling hands, willing a mote of light to spark, but the darkness swallows even my intent. A weight settles across my shoulders, tethering me to the spot. A voice slithers through the gloom: "You don't realize it yet, but I do. You will stand by my side." The words echo, each syllable dripping with authority and menace. "I have seen the future. Everything you believe true is nothing but a lie." I flinch, every hair on my body snapping upright. The voice continues, soothing yet cold: "Forgive me for sealing your lips, but I could not risk you rallying your pathetic allies." A faint radiance creeps nearer, carving his silhouette from the shadows. Tall, impossibly elegant, he exudes power. Despite the obscured features, I sense a predator's grace.

He intones, "Loqui." Miraculously, I understand: speak. My voice works again.

"Why me?" My voice trembles into the gloom.

"You are the balance to my chaos," he says, stepping into the weak light. Bright blue eyes burn with intent. His platinum white hair cascades like a ghostly waterfall, framing a face that seems untouched by time, a chilling paradox of ageless beauty. His skin, though sun-kissed, holds an eerie perfection, as if sculpted by a hidden hand that defies nature. There's an unsettling intensity in his features, an otherworldly allure that whispers of secrets best left buried, casting shadows that dance in the dim light. "With you at my side, we will cradle Earth in equilibrium. Without you, chaos would devour everything." He reaches out, fingers cold as stone yet bringing fire to my skin, trailing across my cheek. "Chaos is the marrow of this world. The only way to rid the chaos is for humanity to die. Resist me, and you doom all you love. Embrace me, and you preserve us both." His touch is a vice—terrifying in its intimacy.

"You feed on chaos. Why would I join you?" I whisper, though each word feels like a betrayal.

"Because you belong to me." His breath puffs warm against my ear, a whisper of brimstone. "It is writ in fate. That worthless creature you call your lover must be torn away. I do not tolerate rivals. You are more than you know, and your earthly life is a waste." My heart hammers. His hand slips behind my ear, tucking my hair with predatory gentleness. My body quakes, torn between revulsion and an inexplicable longing.

"Are you forcing me, or compelling me, controlling me?" I choke out.

"No," he murmurs, stepping closer, eyes ablaze. "In time, you will choose me. The power buried inside of you matches me, it is drawn to me."

My limbs freeze in a chilling rigidity as he leans in to kiss me. A surge of desperation propels my palms against his chest, seeking liberation, yet an electric current races beneath my skin, ensnaring me in a web of forbidden allure. My eyelids flutter shut, seduced by the dark promise of his touch. I command myself to resist, to banish this spell, but panic rips my eyes open again, thrusting me back onto my bedroom floor. The door shudders with another ominous knock. My breath is a chaotic symphony, jagged and broken, punctuating the oppressive silence of the house—broken only by the relentless drum of my racing heartbeat, echoing like a sinister premonition. I try to call out, but my voice is choked, and before I can pull myself to the door — darkness swallows me whole.

Forty-Eight

Vega

"I don't know what is wrong, she has not spoken a word since I found her like this," I tell Baren.

"Go through the whole thing, what exactly happened?" Baren asks

"She left the dinner table and headed up here. Shortly after I knocked on the door to tell her goodnight, I could hear the water running, but she did not answer. At first, I figured she was in the shower and couldn't hear me, but before I walked away, I heard a sound that resembled someone falling. I pressed my ear to the door, and it sounded like she was choking. I tried to use my magic to open the door, but it wouldn't budge, so I kept pounding on it. A few moments later, I heard her whimper like she was being hurt, so I used my magic and broke the door knob. When I came in she was lying there, she responded with her eyes but nothing else. Then —, I ran to get you." I explain.

Baren gently places his hands on Aria's temples, his lips moving in a silent incantation, eyes shut tight with the weight of concentration. After a tense moment, he swiftly withdraws his hands, shifting his intense gaze toward me. "Close the door," he commands with an urgency that brooks no delay. With a fluid motion, he harnesses his magic, lifting Aria's limp form from the floor and gently cradling her onto the bed as if she were made of glass. Baren prowls around the room, his eyes scanning the walls with an intensity that suggests he sees beyond the visible realm. Positioning himself at the room's center, he begins to chant, his voice a low, resonant hum, while his hands extend outward, pressing against unseen forces. A soft blue luminescence unfurls from his fingertips, enveloping the room in a protective embrace, the light cascading down the walls and rippling across the floor and ceiling before fading into the ether.

"This room is shielded. Nothing spoken here will escape its confines," Baren declares, his voice a mix of triumph and caution. "Her memories are partially obscured from me—a dark barrier blocks my way. The Siphon has breached our defenses to reach her. This revelation implies two critical possibilities," he explains, his words tumbling out in a fervent stream of consciousness. "First, he fears the success of your group, as we predicted. What we failed to foresee is the existence of a bond he has somehow forged with her. The Tribunal meticulously examined each of your mind spaces prior to linking you, yet he slipped into her consciousness unnoticed, between the bonding and your arrival," he concludes, his expression shadowed with foreboding.

"So what does that mean?" I ask, my voice barely above a whisper, laden with the gravity of the situation.

"I am not yet certain," he admits, a rare glimpse of uncertainty in his eyes. "We must rally the others to sever this mind bond, or at least fortify it with protections. Without intervention, the Siphon will know every secret, every plan you devise while here. Go now, gather the group. Locate one of the house ladies, instruct them to prepare the nightshade brew to soothe her," he directs, his voice a blend of urgency and resolve.

I burst from the room, breathless and adrenaline-fueled, relaying Baren's urgent request to the women with their cascading hair. My heart hammers relentlessly, like a war drum echoing in my chest, as I dash off to gather the others. Most have already sought refuge in their quarters, but as I near Riya's room, I notice the door hanging slightly ajar. A soft rap nudges it open further, and I'm greeted by a startling sight— Talon is there with her. Stunned, I swiftly retreat, pulling the door shut as my mind spins from the unexpected intrusion. In that fleeting moment, I've gleaned a secret about Riya's tattoo—it sprawls beyond her arm, resembling claw marks from her leopard, stretching from her shoulder down to her breast, flames licking at the edges. I can only hope she didn't catch my lingering gaze.

"Ummmm, guys, sorry to interrupt - but Baren urgently needs us in Aria's room," I announce, my voice tinged with embarrassment as I pivot back towards Aria. She remains mute, her gaze locked on some distant, unreachable horizon, as though ensnared within the confines of her own mind. Baren directs me to sit at the head of her bed, cradling her head in my lap. As I gently lift her head and slide in, an overwhelming urge to kiss her consumes me. It's astonishing how profoundly this woman has altered me, without a hint of effort. I'd forsake all the magic we've uncovered just to share a life with her, to forge a future together. A chill of fear grips me as I ponder the devastation the Siphon might have wrought; if he can reshape the world into its current chaos, imagine the havoc he could wreak on a single soul. We must stop this before it's too late.

Riya and Talon slip in last, their eyes offering silent apologies as they enter. Baren swiftly updates them on the situation and instructs us to form a protective circle around Aria. We don't wield magic as we would in combat but instead channel it, feeding it to Baren, who murmurs an incantation over her. As I watch, a solitary tear escapes Aria's eye, tracing a glistening path down her cheek.

As Baren's whispers continue to weave through the air, a gradual flush of color returns to her once pallid cheeks. The room begins to tremble subtly, an ominous sign that something within her is mounting a fierce resistance against our efforts. It feels as though an unseen force is repelling the very magic we are desperately infusing into her. Baren is aware of this, yet he remains relentless, his determination unwavering.

Moments later, Ophelian strides into the room, pressing firmly against Baren's back, channeling her own potent magic into the fray. Whatever malevolent entity resides within her is retaliating with vigor, and a cold dread seeps into my bones at the thought that this struggle might originate from her own spirit. With a final, resonant word, Baren halts his incantations and commands the others to leave, sparing only me from his directive. His instructions are clear: speak nothing of this beyond these walls. The rest depart, their bewilderment palpable, leaving a heavy silence in their wake. He offers me no insight into his thoughts or the sensations that have gripped him, only instructing me to remain by her side, for when she awakens, she may seek answers.

I gently pull the covers over her and extinguish the lights, the darkness a shroud of solace. Sliding in beside her, I draw her frail form into my embrace, my arms encircling her in a protective cocoon, as if my presence alone could ward off the shadows that linger. I battle against the turbulent storm of negative thoughts swirling within my mind, commanding them to silence as I summon the elusive balm of sleep to descend upon me.

***

I was lost in the velvet haze of sleep when I first felt her stir—a hesitant curl of fingers around my arm that soon tightened with urgent need. Half-awake, I sensed her press against me, the weight of her body shifting until she'd flipped me onto my back and settled astride my hips. Her touch, once feather-light, sharpened into something hungry and insistent, as if she'd starved a lifetime for this moment. The world narrowed to the heat of her lips crashing against mine, her teeth grazing my lower lip with a delicious bite before she tore away any barrier between us. She trailed fervent kisses along my jaw, each press of her mouth a promise of darker delights. At my throat she lingered, breath warm and urgent, then dipped lower to my chest. Her teeth sank into my nipple, a sting that bloomed into exquisite fire. She paused to look up at me, eyes smoldering, then let her tongue slip down my stomach, planting teasing kisses at the rim of my pants. I'd never known this side of her—so bold, so ravenous—and even as my pulse thundered with desire, a flicker of dread stirred inside me.

Any thought of caution evaporated the moment she engulfed me, her mouth a wet, disciplined vortex of pleasure. Her tongue swirled around me like a serpent, sucking with practiced expertise that sent my head rolling back. My fingers tangled in her hair, holding her close as waves of ecstasy coursed through me. Her nails scored slow, deliberate trails down my abdomen, each scratch a delicious mix of pain and need. Then she rose, shifting her weight with feline grace, guiding me into her with a rhythmic roll of hips that felt both possessive and liberating. Every thrust drove me closer to the brink, her hands pressing over my heart, sending sparks of something electric rippling through my veins.

And then the shadows began to seep—dark tendrils oozing from her skin, curling through the candlelit air, filling the room with an oppressive hush. Yet she moved on, fierce and unblinking, as if empowered by the very darkness she exuded. When our eyes locked, hers were empty pits, the fierce light I knew extinguished, replaced by that uncanny void. Her body swayed against mine with a raw intensity, her breath mingling with mine in the heated air. Her hands, like whispers of silk, traced a path from my chest, up her body to grip her own breasts, her fingers kneading the supple flesh as if drawing strength from within. Her head fell back, exposing the graceful curve of her throat, while delicious moans tumbled from her perfect mouth, each note a symphony of desire. The dark bands of shadow danced around us, a wild and untamed force that mirrored our own fervor.

My fingers dug into her hips, pulling her down on me with a hunger that matched the rhythm of our shared heartbeat. She moved a hand to her mouth, her gaze never leaving mine, as she slid her fingers in, the gesture both bold and intimate. Her eyes were a challenge, daring me to look away as her fingers trailed down her body to her clit, swirling in measured, tantalizing circles that stole the breath from her lips and sent shivers through my spine.

Her climax hit like a tremor, an earthquake of ecstasy that shook her to her core. Her body quivered against mine, a shudder of release that left the air crackling with electricity. As if she sensed my own release coming, she slid herself off me, staring into my soul as she glides her body down mine and takes me in her mouth. She slides a hand down to her center, keeping her own orgasm burning while she claims my own into her throat. Moments later, she collapsed on my chest, her form a darkling embrace that gripped me completely. I lay still beneath her, my mind racing with the knowledge that something primal—and possibly perilous—had been awakened within us both. The shadows lingered, proof of the night's passion and the depths of desire we had dared to explore together.

I hover at the edge of the bed, my heart still racing from the sight of her collapsed on the floor earlier in the night. "I was worried earlier," I say softly, leaning forward so she can see the concern in my eyes while I gently stroke her hair. "Do you want to talk about what happened?" She remains silent, her gaze fixed on some distant point in the shadows. I brush a strand of hair behind her ear, my fingers lingering against her scalp as if willing comfort into her. "Baren mentioned the Siphon affecting you. I want you to know I'm here if you need to talk."

At last she lifts her head, frustration flaring in her eyes. "How did he know that?"

"He could see it in your mind," I admit, willing honesty over half-truths.

Her lips curl in a bitter twist. "Does everyone feel entitled, like it is just okay to access my mind whenever they please?"

I wince. "Aria," I murmur, cheeks warming with guilt. I hadn't stopped to consider how violated she might feel. "I found you on the floor—unable to speak or move. I thought you were choking. I didn't know what was happening, so I went to get Baren." I pause, gathering courage to explain. "He didn't know exactly what happened either, but he sensed a Siphon block in your mind."

Her shoulders slump, the fight draining from her posture. "It's not like I asked for the Siphon to target me."

"I promise, none of us even considered that," I say quickly. "We were just worried about you. Baren secured your room, then protected your mind so no one else could intrude while we're here."

She presses her palms to her temples, breathing shallowly. "It was terrifying. I heard you knock—then the room went dark, and I was falling. When I came to, I couldn't speak." She blinks, searching her memory. "I don't remember much, except feeling the Siphon there... wherever that was." A lump rises in my throat. I shift closer on the mattress, pulling the covers around us. "Well, don't take this as a complaint," I begin, nerves tightening. "But waking up to... sex isn't exactly a hardship. Still—before you finished, I saw dark shadows seeping from your pores."

Her body twitches. She whips her head toward me, eyes wide with fear. "What does that even mean?"

"I don't know," I confess, my voice gentle. "Baren's the expert. Maybe you should ask him. All I know is, you weren't entirely yourself. Not that it wasn't incredible, because it was…" I trail off, reaching for the right words. "You seemed angry—like you needed to release something. Maybe those shadows were part of that."

She closes her eyes and exhales a shaky breath. "Maybe. I felt furious when I woke, but also… I needed you more than anything." She turns to the window, moonlight painting her profile in silver. "I felt like you were the only person who could help me cast out that anger."

"Hey," I say, sitting up against the headboard. I sweep her into my arms, her head resting against my chest. I press a soft kiss to her hair. "I'm always right here for you." Her tears soak into my shirt, warm and salty, and I hold her tighter. A small, wry smile tugs at my lips. "You've got me, Aria. And if hot sex is what it takes to sweat out dark shadows, well —I'm fully on board."

She lifts her head, her eyes searching mine with a fierce intensity. "Vega, I—I think I'm in love with you. Or at least falling in love. And I feel like this Siphon is trying to come between us. I need you to know—that's not what I want. I want to save Earth. I want you. I want all of this."

My pulse hammers in my chest. "You have me," I tell her, my voice steady despite the storm of feelings inside. "I think I've been in love with you for a long time." She leans in and kisses me—soft at first, then with growing urgency. This time there's no anger driving her, only the pure, aching need of two hearts finally finding each other. And as our lips meet under the gentle glow of the moon, I know there's no force in the universe that could come between us now.

Forty-Nine

Aria

I confessed to him that my memory was a blank slate when the Siphon appeared, but deep down, I was concealing the truth I wasn't yet prepared to face. The creator of chaos himself exuded a captivating allure—an allure that blinds at first glance, much like the initial impression people have of chaos. Think about it—humans have entire festivals dedicated to chaos, which they fondly call music festivals. In a whirl of lights and sounds, we surrender ourselves to the tumult, some even resorting to substances to amplify the disorder. We find beauty in the pandemonium, yet we cannot deny its inherent chaos. We willingly endure the madness of serpentine lines just to sip the first brew from a newly opened coffee shop. We tarnish the purity of oceans, gathering on sandbars to revel in the chaotic euphoria of summer. In truth, humans have an unspoken reverence for chaos. It is only when we pause to survey the wreckage left in its wake that we recognize its hideous reality. Still, a part of me was drawn to it, and I despise that part of myself. When I laid eyes on him, an unsettling emotion churned within me. A concealed corner of my being yearned for his kiss, and I detest that yearning as well.

I can't bring myself to tell Vega; it feels like an unforgivable betrayal. My own body has turned traitor, and the mere thought of him perceiving me as such makes me nauseous. When I awoke to find him in my bed, his arms wrapped around me with a tenderness that I felt I no longer deserved, all I could think about was my desperate need to make amends. I longed for him to desire me so intensely that everything else faded into insignificance. I was trying to use the intimacy between us as an unspoken apology, though he remained oblivious to the reason behind it. I can't quite grasp what possessed me when I climbed on top of him. Every fiber of my being ached to make him want me, to bring him pleasure, yet amidst that fervor, something darker emerged. It was as if a foreign force within me seethed with anger, perhaps even jealousy. My blood simmered, transformed into molten fire coursing through my veins, unleashing a rage I didn't know I harbored. Vega had explained that Baren safeguarded the sanctity of my thoughts and the space around us, yet I couldn't shake the feeling that the Siphon was insidiously working its influence through me.

I truly yearn to leave all this turmoil behind. I confessed my feelings to him, a revelation I hadn't intended to share, but it seemed the opportune moment, as if destiny had nudged me forward. Today, I resolve to concentrate solely on the positive, to erect mental barriers against the encroaching shadows of negativity. Gently, I slip out of bed, taking care not to disturb Vega's peaceful slumber. He looks achingly perfect nestled beside me, his serene expression untouched by the chaos that plagues my mind. I turn on the shower, holding my hand under the cascading water until it's just the right temperature. As the steam swallows the room like a comforting cocoon, I step in, allowing the scalding water to wash over me, painting my skin a vibrant, reassuring red.

I was so captivated by the sensation of water cascading over my skin that I almost failed to notice his silent entrance behind me. His hands, warm and reassuring, encircle my body as he leans close, his lips grazing my neck with tender kisses while whispering a soft "good morning." The familiar scent of him mingles with the steam, wrapping us in a fog of intimacy. He reaches for the soap, letting the water wash over it until a rich lather forms, then begins a meticulous ritual of cleansing, his touch gentle yet deliberate. Starting at my neck, his fingers glide with practiced ease over my arms, back, chest, stomach, thighs, and legs, each movement infused with care and devotion. Once I am thoroughly washed, he turns his attention to himself, continuing the ritual. He pours a generous amount of shampoo into his palm, working it into my hair with a gentle, rhythmic massage that starts at the roots and moves with precision to the very ends. The water streams down, carrying away the suds, and he tips my head back with tenderness to ensure every trace is rinsed clean. With equal care, he repeats the process using conditioner, his fingertips weaving through my hair as if composing a melody. After rinsing my hair again, he turns me to face him, gently adjusting our positions so that he stands beneath the warm cascade. He swiftly tends to his own hair, mindful of keeping me enveloped in warmth.

Our previous shared shower was unforgettable, yet this moment surpasses it in its quiet, profound intimacy. There is something deeply comforting about these interludes of normalcy amidst the chaos of battles and turmoil. I find myself gazing at him, utterly entranced—his presence a perfect amalgamation of strength and grace. His physique, honed by relentless training, is more defined than ever, his skin kissed by the sun to a deeper shade of bronze. His tattoo, a masterpiece, adds to the allure. "Can we skip today and just stay here under the water? I'm pretty sure we could use magic to keep it warm forever," I suggest with a wistful smile.

"I'm all for that idea," he replies, laughter in his voice, "but Baren would probably counter any spell, and we'd still end up down there for practice."

We share a laugh, a harmonious blend of amusement and resignation — a nice long bout of laughter mixed with splashing water and throwing of bubbles, before finally surrendering to the inevitable. We turn off the water, wrapping ourselves in plush towels, preparing to face the day. As I open the shower door to grab some clothes, a chuckle escapes me. Everything here seems meticulously planned, no doubt with a touch of magic. I would assume it was Baren or the house ladies forsight, has placed clothes for Vega right next to mine in the closet. With a playful grin, I toss them to him, relishing the small joys that punctuate our extraordinary lives.

Once we are dressed we head down to the join the rest of the group for breakfast. There is a different feel this morning as if last night's happenings have Baren on edge. We aren't being rushed to eat, but the sense of urgency lingers in the air. Everyone can feel it, so there is not much conversation going on around the table, just the sounds of everyone filling their bellies in preparation for the day. When we are done, Baren asks us to gather on the back patio. When we head to our normal sitting area for practice, we notice a new person joining us. It is a woman, she is tall with long dark hair, she is wearing battle clothing but it is white instead of black like ours. She introduces herself to us right away.

"Good morning, my name is Seraphina, Though I am here with you, I am not as you are. I am in a way, like Baren, a conduit that was made in the case that one day my services would be needed. In my time, I was also with magic, but I also was a muse as well. There were those of us in the past that were both blessed with magic and also other worldly gifts that were passed down as our birthright." She calmly explains. "At one time, we assumed that those gifts died off over the centuries, with the absence of magic, the elders thought that the gifts would be severely limited and unrecognizable. Over time, we identified some who we believed had gifts, but with no way to interact with the person, it was hard to tell. We have identified one of you that possesses a gift. With some study of lineage, we believe that the gift is like mine, a muse. That is why I am here, to help guide the gift." She pauses, placing her hands together to collect herself before her next statement.

"Aria, we believe that you possess capabilities like mine, which is why the Siphon could get to you," She says directing her attention to me. I feel like it was yesterday when I learned that magic existed, now I am being told I have other powers on top of it. It is a lot to take in.

"What does being a muse even mean?" I ask her.

"Well, it means a lot of things. It is likely that the Siphon knows that you did not know about your gift. We believe that is why he targeted you, to control you before your gift was discovered so that he could use it for his own agenda. A muse possesses a great deal of power once practiced. We will be working on that today" she says before Baren walks up.

"Now that you have met Seraphina, we can move on to today's practices. While most of you will be working on an array of tasks, Seraphina and Aria will work alongside you.

We will reconvene in the meadow in twenty minutes sharp. Gather your lunches that have been prepared for you and head out." Baren instructs us as he motions to the sacks arranged on trays that the ladies with the long hair are holding.

We all grab our lunches and head down the stairs to meet up with our animals to make our way to the meadow. No one talks, mostly because there is nothing to say - yet. Maybe I am blessed with an extra gift, but it also means that I am targeted. Part of me feels a ping of anger, but also sadness. The Siphon only came for me due to a gift, nothing else. The moment the thought enters my head, more anger fills me, this time towards myself. What is wrong with me that creates these feelings? The Siphon is evil! I don't want him to want me, or come for me, but something inside of me does.

It only takes us all moments to make it to the meadow. We all left together, but when I got there, Vega was nowhere to be seen. Kat is standing with Archer, Callen with Jaliah, Talon with Riya, and Analise with Greyson.

"Where is Vega?" I ask Greyson

"He was right behind me, maybe he had to go back for something?" He replies

Maybe so. But something about it doesn't feel like it. At least we are in this realm, so he is safe wherever he is. Moments later Baren and Seraphina emerge from the shadows of the woods with Ethos. Seraphina is holding a golden staff with a deep red crystal on top of it. It is wrapped in a black filigree that matches the style that our animals wear. She taps the staff against the ground and instantly the landscape around us changes. There are still signs that we are in the meadow, but a large factory of some sort, with two huge silos, connected by metal walkways that have rusted out. Everything is in desecration as if the world ended and the factory has rotted. Pavement covers the ground where grass once was, but it is cracked and broken apart as if something crashed down into it. The air is different, thick and heavy, smelling of chemicals and rot.

"This is what happens in your world when man tears the land to build, and then eventually moves on. While the earth will try to reclaim the land, it will never be the same again. In this practice, you will all be tasked with restoring the meadow back to its original form. This may seem like a meaningless task, but every bit of earth that is reclaimed is like a wound healing. I will not instruct you how to do it, that is up to you, the only instruction I have is that Aria works with Seraphina to do so" Baren instructs.

"Sir, Vega is still not here. Should we wait for him?" I ask

"He is here, he has alternate instruction. He is the catch, the longer it takes the team to complete the mission, the longer he is in danger. You will find him within the challenge. As gruesome as it may seem, we needed to raise the stakes so that real implications are felt." My heart pounds at the sound of Baren's words. Vega is in danger, and while I am sure they won't let him accrue any serious harm, I am still worried, since I am stuck with Seraphina, there is nothing I can do to help. I mean, I think that they won't allow any real life threatening harm, but then I also think of when his power consumed him, when Kat fell into the lava, when I fell from Ophelian... all of these could have been serious without intervention. I have to be the intervention. The team disperses, heading straight to work on the meadow. They work together to help re-grow and nurture the parts of the meadow that lack concrete, Riya and Kat use their fire to burn off what part of the factory that they can while Greyson works alone to funnel out the smoke and pollution.

"You must be frustrated that you cannot join them," Seraphina says to me

"Yeah, I feel worthless not joining in" I reply

"Aria, you do not yet know it, but you will become the most valuable part of your team. I have set this scene you see before you not with my magic, but with the muse capability. What you see though, is more than just a scene, I have changed the reality of this meadow, and I can change it again at any time I please," she says to me.

"So basically everything they are doing is pointless because you can just snap your fingers and change it completely? I ask

"No. It is not without a point. While I can change the reality, I cannot hold it forever. When I leave, it returns to the reality that it truly is. When they leave, their work stays." she says

"So then this means when in battle I can change the reality to better suit the team?" It makes sense how this gift can help us.

"Yes. But you can also use it to guide others, maybe to show them what is to come, or what something could be. There are endless ways your gift will help you. But I must tell you, your powers are not just this. As a muse, you can use your gift to influence the thoughts of others. Sometimes that will be on purpose, and sometimes it will be accidental." She pauses to let it sink in, watching me closely as I process what she is saying

"Let me give you an example. Let's say you are in a battle and your team is on edge, your power would allow you to change their feelings. Baren chose Vega to be the one in danger on purpose. If you are scared for him, you can imbue those feelings into the team, so that your importance becomes theirs. Once you learn how to do it, we will practice controlling it. I am sure he is important to the others, but I have a feeling that importance is heightened for you," she says, making it clear as to why they planned this the way they did.

"Ok, well aside from sharing my feelings, what can I do to help them," I ask in haste.

"There are words from a forgotten language that can help direct your gift. For this exercise, use the word "Transema" which is Lumoren for Transfer. Think and feel what you want them to feel, and then silently whisper, where only you can hear, the word transema. This will guide those feelings and thoughts to them."

I turn away from her, facing the meadow and my team. It is not hard to conjure up the thoughts of saving Vega. Even if the harm isn't permanent, the thought of him suffering at all pulls on my soul. The dire need to find him consumes me.

"Transema" I whisper silently.

Everyone on my team hesitates for the briefest heartbeat—then unleashes everything they have. Riya and Kat thrust their arms skyward, violet runes spiraling around their wrists as they wrench slabs of cracked concrete upward. Blue-white fire ignites the rubble, turning jagged chunks into ash that Greyson's hands—glowing with smoky black energy—draw in, funneling it into a void between worlds. Above us, thunder rolls and sheets of rain pummel the ground as Callen and Jaliah race over torn earth, their hands glowing emerald as they force the rain down into the soil. Archer's sinewy arms rip the factory walls apart plank by plank, while Talon—defying every rule we knew—flickers small, his silhouette shrinking until steel beams fold in on themselves like blown-out candles. It's astonishing, really, what flickers of love can do when someone dear is trapped beneath a tomb of concrete. As the last great slab hinges outward, Silas pounds his massive, ape-like fist into the floor. A radial fissure tears through the foundation, rattling the world beneath our feet. Riya and Kat lift the final pieces of debris—then I see him. Vega, half-buried, his breath ragged. If we'd hesitated much longer, the weight above him would have been his death knell.

Riya's violet flames vanish in an instant as she lunges forward, her fingers trembling as she scoops the dirt from his chest. She brushes grit from his jaw, checks his pulse, her brow wet with rain and relief. Vega wheezes up words of thanks, but before he can finish, Riya's arms coil around him. Her lips settle soft and urgent against his—fierce gratitude and concern mingling in a single, burning kiss.

Rage condenses in me like an ice spike at my heart. What the actual fuck? My knuckles tighten so hard my nails dig into my palms. But before I can roar, everything near us freezes—rain suspended in midair, the wind stilled. Seraphina stands to my side, her silver eyes calm, a thin line of power around her fingertips. "Stop," she says softly, and the single word echoes in my chest. "You're seconds from unleashing that fury on everyone here—and that would hurt more than this moment ever could."

I taste iron on my tongue. My ears ring with the threat of my own power. "But he didn't—he didn't stop her," I choke out, tears cutting cold tracks down my cheeks. Seraphina lays a hand on my shoulder. Her voice is patient. "When you transfer emotion through our gift, you often send more than you intend. Right now you've transferred anger, jealousy, confusion—and they're all as raw as your fear. If you'd been the one who found him, wouldn't you have thrown yourself into his arms just the same?" I swallow, voice small. "Yes. Of course I would."

"So you must learn to sift what you send. Share only what you choose: relief, hope, calm. If you wish to end the transfer altogether, you need but whisper 'Finitora.' It means 'finish.'" Her eyes hold mine until my pulse steadies. She releases her hold on time, and the world blurs back into motion. I turn to face Riya and Vega, still caught in each other's arms, and in one breath murmur, "Finitora."

Riya jolts apart, her hands flying to her lips as realization flashes across her features. Vega blinks, confusion and something like panic surfacing as he scans the circle of our team. His eyes meet mine—unsettled, uncertain. I inhale the cold, electric air and speak aloud, voice measured. "I need to master this gift before it hurts anyone else—especially those I care about. I can't risk unknowingly swaying hearts. I must learn to guide it, to separate true emotion from illusion...and to harness it on the siphon."

Seraphina inclines her head, a sliver of pride in her expression. "Agreed. Come on." She extends her hand, and together we move away from the ruined factory, the storm rolling on behind us.

Fifty

Aria

After what felt like endless days holed up with Seraphina, I finally wrestled my muse side into submission. We ran through a dozen mock scenarios—moonlit gardens, cavernous libraries, storm-lashed cliffs—to test every edge case, and still made it back in time for dinner. Now that I know I can flip the switch at will, I feel a surge of confidence. I'm no longer at the mercy of that wild power; I can cloak myself in it or turn it off completely. If I'm ever dragged into the Siphon's realm, I'll reshape the landscape — softening its jagged edges or painting it in pastel hues, to suit my own strength. I've even learned to weave my magic through it, bleeding my muse energy into every spell I cast, or intention I conjure, amplifying each incantation. Best of all, I discovered the off button. No more runaway transformations. I hold the reins.

Seraphina insists this gift was mine from birth, lying dormant until now. She says others like me wander the world, oblivious to their potential—people who, under a different sky thick with magic, might have mastered powers of their own. Without arcane currents pulsing through the earth, our gifts are whispers in the dark, easily mistaken for madness. Without a teacher, without guidance, most never realize what they're capable of. A single doubt claws at me: Did my gift draw Vega to me in the first place? Had I unknowingly coaxed his heart with a flicker of muse magic the moment I saw him? I replay our first meeting over and over, terrified I manufactured his feelings. The only solace is that he spoke his truth before I could even acknowledge mine—he said "I love you" when I was still fumbling for the words.

This gift can be a blessing or a curse. What if every flutter of attraction I've felt sparked some enchanted feedback loop, pulling him closer because I willed him there? At least I can silence the gift—I only wish I could do the same to my racing thoughts, switch off this relentless self-doubt. Baren has instructed us to dress formally for tonight's dinner—a rare decree, last heard on our arrival. I step into the bathroom and let a steamy cascade wash away my worries. I wrap myself in a towel, tucking the tail between my collarbone and chest, and study the reflection. The face staring back feels both familiar and entirely new. Muscles I never knew I had ripple beneath my skin. My shoulders square, my posture radiates power. This Aria is stronger, more beautiful, more herself than ever before.

I let my hair fall in soft waves around my shoulders, pinning back a strand at my temple. From my closet I draw a gown of translucent, shimmering fabric, threaded through with delicate gold filigree that curves around every contour. I slide into it—and, as if by magic, it molds perfectly to my frame. The metal-like vines skirt all the places that should stay modest, leaving just enough to make me feel irresistible. I slip into matching metallic heels and clasp slender golden cuffs around my wrists. In another life I would have trembled at the thought of wearing anything so bold. Tonight, I stand tall. A dusting of rose-blush warms my cheeks, a swipe of mascara curls my lashes, and a feather-light gloss polishes my lips. Satisfied, I open the door—and there he stands, Vega. My pulse spikes; I steady myself, tamping down any stray muse energy.

He takes me in from head to toe, and his dark eyes soften. "Aria," he breathes. "You look… like a goddess. If you didn't already have my heart, you'd steal it now." My chest swells. I step forward, take his hands, and brush a kiss against his cheek. "Care to escort me to dinner?" He grins, warm and easy. "Hell yeah I do."

We enter the dining room together, and every inch of it has been turned into an ode to refinement—silk-draped tables, crystal chandeliers, gleaming silver. The others sit waiting, each one a vision in formal attire. Baren stands at the head of the table, resplendent in white with a gold tie, and welcomes us with a graceful nod. Vega pulls out my chair, slips a single crimson rose into my palm, and settles me in. As I sink into the cushion, I realize: I may have questioned everything tonight, but one truth remains unshakable. I am here. I am powerful. And I finally believe in myself.

"You're probably wondering why tonight's gathering is so formal," Baren's voice rings out over the flicker of candlelight as he holds his goblet aloft for the attendant to fill. Around the long oak table, raised brows and hesitant nods ripple through the group—an unspoken chorus of unease. "Unfortunately," Baren continues, his gaze sweeping each of us, "this shall be our final meal together. Tomorrow, you return to your realm."

Silence settles like a weighty fog. No one dares speak; even the crackle in the hearth seems to pause. My heart hammers against my ribs—have we truly become the warriors we set out to be?

"You're asking two questions," Baren says quietly after a long pause: "Why now, and whether you're ready. The answer to the latter is both no and yes. Of course we wish you more training, but the reason—why you must go—is what truly matters." He steeples his fingers. "When you arrived, chaos stood at level one—ish. In the weeks you've spent here, it's surged to level seven—cataclysmic. The Siphon senses this growth. He feels the approaching storm and redoubles his efforts. Tomorrow, your world will not resemble the one you left. We'll brief you fully before dawn. For now—eat, drink, laugh if you can. This may be the last time you hear that invitation for a good while."

I want to ask more questions. What does he mean the world isn't the same? I start to ask questions, but Baren catches my eye, giving me a nod that says the time is not now. I decide to just let it be what it is, there is nothing I can do at the moment anyways. The wine attendant drifts down the table. One by one, we lift our glasses. As the ruby liquid warms our chests, the dread loosens its grip. Murmurs bloom, laughter peals, and for a moment the looming mission dissolves into shared jokes and memories. When the final plate is swept away, a soft melody drifts across the threshold. Baren motions us to the patio, and we follow him past stone archways dripping with ivy. Outside, strings of iridescent lights hover overhead, each bulb a mote of captive magic. The music hums through the air, directionless yet enveloping.

Vega offers his hand. His fingers are warm against mine as he draws me into a sway beneath the lantern glow. His confidence steadies me; together we trace gentle arcs on the cobblestones. "Look who has hidden talents," I tease, letting myself be led. He grins, tight and proud. "Fancy upbringing means I attended my fair share of balls."

The words tumble from my lips before I can stop them. "I love you." It feels as natural as breathing. Vega pauses, his gaze anchoring me. Then he cups my face and presses his lips to mine in a kiss that hums with promise. "I love you, Aria," he whispers against my mouth.

A soft voice glides between us. "Mind if I borrow her a moment?" It's Seraphina. "Go ahead," Vega says, flashing me a playful wink. "But we resume this dance." I smile at him, then drift after Seraphina to the garden's edge. She holds out a small, ornate box of burnished gold. "I made you something," she says, voice laced with bittersweet regret. "I wish I could journey with you, but I exist here only as a conduit, possibly one day we will figure out how to cross into your realm, but for now, it is on you and your team." Inside, nestling in crimson satin, is a pendant: a blood-red crystal cradled by filigreed gold. Serenity settles in my chest as I lift it out.

"It's a conduit for your muse powers," Seraphina explains. "When the crystal glows, your gifts awaken. Whisper 'Arthelys' while holding it, and your magic answers. Whisper again, and it rests." I turn it over in my palm, astonished. "What if I drop it… or can't reach it in time?" She smiles, gentle as starlight. "Then speak the name twice, and the crystal obeys you regardless. If it slips free? You'll rely on your abilities as you do now—no more, no less."

I fasten it around my neck, testing the clasp and the chain's unyielding strength. Seraphina's laughter lilts through the night air. "Arcannian gold," she murmurs. "Unbreakable." Heart thrumming, I slip back into the circle of lights. Fingertips grazing the pendant, I whisper "Arthelys." A soft glow pulses from the crystal, and the music shifts —beats grow deeper, lights pulse in time, and soon the patio transforms into a neon-hued sanctuary.

If this is truly our last night of freedom, then we will seize every shimmer of it with a fervor that defies the impending dawn. We will dance as if the world is ending, our feet pounding out a rhythm of defiance against the ticking clock. We will laugh with abandon, the sound echoing like a symphony of rebellion. We will indulge in unabashed fun, for if the fate of the world rests heavily upon our shoulders, we deserve at least a fleeting moment of pure, innocent joy.

As the bass beats pulse through the air, vibrating in harmony with our beating hearts, the others drift in, carrying with them the elixir of the night—small shot glasses brimming with amber liquid. Tequila? I raise an eyebrow at Callen as he hands me another shot. "How did you manage to find tequila in an entirely different realm?" I inquire, curiosity piqued. "Girl, who are you kidding? Did you forget we have magic?" he responds with a mischievous grin. Jaliah chimes in, a playful smirk on her lips, "He thinks he's a fucking genius, but really—it was my idea." We take turns showcasing our dance moves in the center of our intimate circle. Laughter bubbles up, mingling with the sweat that glistens on our skin, as we exhaust every ounce of lingering energy. This is how I want to always remember us—our faces adorned with wide, genuine smiles. We might not spend hours braiding each other's hair or delving into the depths of our souls, but this is what true friendship feels like. It feels like home and Christmas, all wrapped into one joyous bundle.

As the night wears on, and our dance moves become more awkward, our words slurring into a delightful mess, we recognize the need to seek rest before the world shifts beneath our feet come morning. I extend my hand to Vega, inviting him to join me, a silent plea shared between friends. He meets my gaze with a gentle smile but bypasses my hand, opting instead to sweep me up into his arms.

He carries me tenderly to the room, laying me on the bed with a look that speaks volumes beyond my comprehension.

"You tucking me in or what?" I tease through the haze of tequila. "Darlin', don't you remember? This is far from casual, and there's no way I'm casually leaving you in this bed alone. If this is our last night of freedom, then we're going to do it right," he says, his smile warm and genuine. With a gentle touch, he slides my heels from my feet, tossing them aside, and in that moment, I know that whatever tomorrow brings, tonight is a memory carved into the tapestry of my heart.

Fifty-One

Vega

The sun's gentle rays seep through the curtains, casting a warm glow on my skin, coaxing me from my slumber. Aria's body is entwined with mine, her presence a comforting anchor. We had danced until near dawn, losing ourselves in the music and the moment. This is the life I yearn for—one filled with joy and togetherness, a respite from our relentless mission. Last night was a celebration, a final hurrah, and I am quite certain none of us slept alone.

"Are you awake?" she murmurs, her voice a soft caress.

"Yes, but I'd rather not be," I reply, my eyes still heavy with sleep. "After a night like that, we deserve a day of rest."

Her voice, though gentle, carries an urgency as she says, "You might want to wake up."

A smile plays on my lips as a mischievous thought flits through my mind. I roll towards her, cracking open my eyes just enough to catch her gaze. But her expression is not what I expected. We aren't in her room, nor mine.

"How wild did we get last night?" I muse, bewildered. "I could have sworn we spent a wonderful night in your bed."

"I have no idea," she replies, slipping out of bed and heading for the closet. The room resembles hers in layout, yet the decor is an uncanny blend of both our tastes. "Our clothes are mixed together in the closet," she notes.

Curiosity piqued, I rise from the bed, wrapping the blanket around my waist, and approach the door. I intend to peer into the hallway to discern where we are. But when I open it, the sight before me is startlingly unfamiliar. It is not our hallway. We are in an entirely different house, one shrouded in mystery and leaving a lingering question hanging in the air: How did we end up here?

Peering out the hallway window, I noticed the outside world was unrecognizable, a jarring reflection of my own internal chaos. That's when the thunder started to rumble in my chest, an unsettling crescendo of fear and doubt. What if this is all a deceitful ploy orchestrated by the Siphon? What if we've been abducted, pawns in a sinister game? As these thoughts spiraled wildly through my mind, Riya's presence broke through the haze. "Get dressed. We all need to talk," she commanded, her tone leaving no room for hesitation.

It was clear something significant had transpired during the night. Hastily, we donned our clothes and ventured out of the unfamiliar room, navigating the labyrinthine halls in search of the others. Around the corner, a modest sitting area came into view, where Riya and Talon awaited us.

"Where is everyone else?" I inquired, a hint of apprehension in my voice.

"Getting dressed, hopefully," she replied, her words tinged with an urgency that mirrored my own unease.

Gradually, the rest of our group gathered, each face etched with anticipation and concern. Once assembled, Riya rose from her seat with a deliberate grace, a piece of paper clutched in her hand. "I found this outside my door when I woke up," she announced, her voice steady yet weighted with the gravity of the moment. "I suppose they knew I'd be the first to rise, so I'll read it to you all."

With a pause that seemed to stretch into eternity, she began.

"After careful consideration, we extend our sincere apologies through this letter. We believe this transition is for the best. Welcome to your new home, where you may dwell together for as long as you desire, perhaps even indefinitely. Every necessity for living is provided, along with dedicated staff. While the rooms you woke in are temporary, feel free to choose any room you want; our staff will ensure your belongings are arranged to your liking. The world has evolved, and as I mentioned last night, it is time for your return. Not every day will be a struggle, so focus on nurturing the Earth and seeking apprentices amidst occasional battles. Not all confrontations will involve the Siphon, and not all of humanity will readily embrace your gifts. On the lower level, you'll find a briefing room equipped with a portal screen for ongoing communication and guidance, if you feel you need it. The fate of Earth now rests in your hands, and I trust you will steward it well. Sincerely, Baren"

As her voice trailed off, Riya looked up, her eyes scanning the room, eagerly awaiting the group's reaction. The air was thick with the weight of the unknown, each of us grappling with the enormity of our new reality.

"Okay, so they've decided to jump-start the grand reunion of exiles by dumping us all back here," Callen mutters, his voice laced with equal parts sarcasm and something like relief. He stands just inside the threshold of the main doors, hands shoved into the pockets of his worn leather jacket, scanning the vast foyer as if measuring it against the one they'd left behind.

Jaliah rolls her eyes but can't suppress a wry grin. "Before we all have time to truly appreciate how fucked the world is outside these walls, why don't we take a moment to explore our new crib?" Her tone is light, but there's a flicker of genuine excitement in her gaze as she gestures down the long corridor. Around her, the rest of the group—half-reluctant, half-curious—exchange nods of agreement. The house itself is breathtaking. Impossibly vast, its wings form a perfect circle around a central courtyard. Seven sectors fanning outward, each with its own purpose: a cavernous dining hall where long wooden tables could seat hundreds, a sparring arena with reinforced walls and gleaming weapon racks, and a briefing room whose doors stand heavy and expectant. Above these three, a mezzanine level unites into a single, soaring commons—a space for laughter, music, and the kind of camaraderie they've been starved for.

Four remaining sectors branch off like silent sentinels, each a labyrinth of stairwells and corridors leading to private quarters. The architectural styles vary wildly—one sector is all marble and wrought iron balconies, another is panelled in warm cedar with stained-glass windows casting kaleidoscopic patterns on the floors, a third resembles a forest glade with living vines winding up stone columns, and the last feels almost monastic, with simple stone walls and narrow

arrow-slit windows. Aparently when they designed this place, they used our elements as the theme for each house.

"We'll meet in the courtyard," I announce, falling into step with everyone else. Through an arched gateway we step into a lush, sun-dappled oasis. Flowers in every color imaginable carpet the ground, and slender, ornamental trees sway lazily in a breeze scented faintly of jasmine. In the very center glints a koi pond, its glassy surface broken by the gentle ripple of orange and white fish. It feels almost too peaceful—an artificial Eden in the heart of this fortress. As we all take in the massive place we get to call home, we decide we should pick rooms. The plan is simple: the original seven of us will claim the larger bottom-level rooms, one per sector, so that when we recruit new apprentices we're already dispersed. And if any fool tries to sneak in trouble, at least we're on the front lines.

Just as Baren promised in his letter, the house staff materialize at that moment: a line of women with hair cascading like molten silver down their backs. They glide forward, faces serene and unblemished, halting just shy of the garden's stone benches. Aria clears her throat, stepping forward with her trademark confidence. "Ok, so if you're the staff—or…" She glances around, smirking, "…the Ladies of the Manor, do you even have names? Or do we stick with 'you there' and 'silver-hair'?"

The woman in the center inclines her head, voice soft but resonant. "No names have been given. You may address us as you wish. We are constructs of the manor's magic, bound to its needs and commands." Jaliah offers a shrug that somehow seems both amused and resigned. "Staff, then. Or Ladies of the Manor—your choice." The lead attendant's eyes flick to us, immaculate and unblinking. "Have you selected your rooms?"

"Sort of," I say, glancing back at my friends. "So like, since we are now at a version of Hogwarts, and the reliquary was our sorting hat - and the mansion is literally themed with our elements, dividing shouldnt be hard. We should all take space in the lower levels. One apt per sector or element — whatever— the lower levels have the bigger rooms anyways... kitchen, two bedrooms. Who wants which?"

We divvy up the apartments quickly: me and Aria claim the one nearest the briefing room —strategic, and also because we'll be sharing. She bumps my shoulder playfully. "Guess we're roommates now. Gosh... thats a big step in the real world" she says with a laugh. "Just promise you won't snore me awake," I tease, and she laughs more, a bright sound in the hush of the courtyard.

Moments later, we're settled around the massive table in the briefing room—its surface polished to a reflective sheen. The lights dim, and with a low hum, a giant screen flickers to life at the front. The single display fractures into fifty windows, each looping a different news channel: burning cities, panicked anchors, scrolling emergency alerts. We sit in stunned silence, our reflections mingling with the tapestry of global panic. None of us speaks. The portal awaits, but for now, we're prisoners to the jarring reminder of how desperately the world beyond these walls needs us—and how much we have to lose.

I feel stupid slightly, we have been enjoying ourselves since last night, and have been blessed with this massive house, while the world around us is in shambles.

Countries are launching nuclear missiles at one another, like a chain reaction.

Major cities are burning, what is left after bombs is ravished from riots.

Law enforcement in most of the U.S. does not exist anymore, shit the military barely stands.

Rebellions have launched globally, all fighting for a different goal.

Oil stations have been bombed, massively dumping pollution into the oceans.

Most forms of digital communication have been cut off in many areas.

Commercial ships have run aground on all major beaches, pouring out waste and debris surrounding them.

Food and supplies are being rationed around the world - causing more riots.

The list goes on. They said the Siphon turned the heat up, but at this pace, there won't be an earth from which he can feed on much longer. Baren had mentioned that there was a protective barrier surrounding the manor, I guess that is why we don't see it here. I would assume that if the earth is destroyed, so is the barrier.

We brace ourselves before turning the orb in the center of the table, opening a holographic-type portal for Baren to speak to us.

"I trust that you found your new living quarters suitable, and by the look of your faces, you now know the reason we sent you back so soon. You have a lot of work to do, and it will not be easy. I would advise that you stay together as a group as much as possible, remember you are not in this realm anymore, and when alone outside of the barrier, you will be a target for the Siphon. There is a doorway at the other end of this room, it is a portal within your realm. To use it, you hold the orb next to it and tell it where you need to go, then the door will open - allowing you to pass through to your destination. Be careful with this though, it is very easy to get lost in its own power, or even lost at your destination if you lose the orb." Baren says before being joined by Argus.

"We acknowledge the profound responsibility that now rests upon your shoulders. Your bonded companions stand ready by your side; a simple call will summon their support. You are all now esteemed members of the Tribunal, We can call you the Second Tribunal, integral to our collective mission. You will all be the leaders of anything that comes. There are others out there, cherish that, nurture them. I offer my genuine well wishes as you embark on this journey. The moment for action has arrived," Argus says before signing off.

The entire room sits in silence. Some with tears, other with blank stares. We knew we were preparing for something, the reality just had not slapped us so hard in the face like it has today. Panic taps at the back of my consciousness, what about my family, what about thier families. Selfishly I want to find a way to check on my own, but I know this is far bigger than just my family, just their families. This is the entire world.

"Dude. I think I am just now realizing that Earth is fucked. Completely and utterly Fucked. Are we really ready for this? Anyone else secretly having a complete meltdown internally that this is on us? No? Just me?" Jaliah says as she blankely stares at nothing.

"No. Not just you. How does this all happen in just a few weeks. How is humanity supposed to be so smart but we also let shit like this happen. Like did no one sit at any roundtable meeting and say "hey this won't work out like we think it will"... did they think bombing each other was truly the answer?" Riya says with tears slipping down her face.

More silence fills the rooms, the only noise is the chattering of news casters playing on the TV's. Even as we are watching, the newscast for Seattle turns to static. Another one lost. We know we are somewhere near the coast in South Carolina, but as the news screens show, there isn't much left around us. Atlanta isn't far, but as older broadcast come across, Atlanta is barely even there now. I feel like this is some kind of fucked up dream and at any moment I will wake up. The world was a mess before. We had our work cut out for us even then, now… its far more than "just a little mission" for us to tackle. The noise from the screens become all I can hear, like it is drowning out even my own thoughts, taking over my entire concioussness. Aparently it is doing the same to the others because Callen stands up and hits the power button shutting them all down before moving to look out the giant window on the other side of the room. Now the silence swallows us whole.

"OK then. I guess let's suit up and go save the damn earth or something" Talon says as slaps his hands down onto his thighs… pulling us out of our trance.

To be continued…………..

Epilogue

Dear Diary,

I haven't heard from my sister in a week. She always texts me to check in. Mom says she went on some retreat, but this is the worst time for her to disappear. The news keeps talking about war and other scary stuff. I'm not great at politics—I didn't even like the subject in school. Mom and Dad are worried, I can tell. I get the same speech every time I leave: "Drive straight there and back. If anything crazy happens, get out—this job isn't more important than your life." My boss acts like business has to go on, no matter what. At least when Aria was here they worried more about her than me. Now she's a fancy-pants nurse living her life, and I'm stuck here. I could have moved out after high school, but since I went with online college, there hasn't been a reason. I love my family; I just haven't done the wild stuff I wanted in my late teens or twenties. My 21st was lit, but I heard about it for days after I sobered up. Ugh. Thanks for always listening... now back to writing the most boring paper on the most boring book for English. Ugh.

xoxo – Brynn

Dear Diary,

Well, I complained about the war talk too much and now the shop is closed. I have no reason to leave the house except for store runs. Dad's in full zombie-apocalypse prepper mode—he's bought up all the salt and canning supplies in town. We look like crazy people. The news is telling everyone to prepare for power outages and stock up, but the biggest scare is still that I haven't heard from Aria. I only watch the news to see if there are any prisoner-of-war updates that explain her disappearance. It's been two whole weeks. I know her job pays well, but who can afford a two-week retreat these days? Mom doesn't know where the retreat was, only that Aria said she'd have no service. This war threat isn't just local—it's everywhere. Even my college classes are suspended. Ugh.

xoxo – Brynn

Dear Diary,

It's bad. It's really bad. We lost power days ago. We're living in gas-lamp and bucket-of-water mode. I know we're lucky to be outside the city—the cities are literally rioting for supplies. At least we have everything we need, and our windmill-powered well still works for the cows. No cell phones either—I tried charging mine with the solar bank, but the towers are down so it was pointless. No word from Aria. She could be stuck at the hospital, but who knows. Every time I hear a car on the road, I run out hoping it's her, but cars are so rare now. The military came and started rationing gas and food. It's actually pretty wild. I thought it would take zombies to take us out, but widespread power loss is just as crippling. We don't even know why; the news says it might be a hack on our grids —but every country is experiencing the same thing. I can't watch the news anymore; I have to listen on Dad's radio like it's the 1920s. I didn't realize how much I loved TV until there was none. Or even social media. Ugh.

xoxo – Brynn

Dear Diary,

It happened: the bombs. I can't see anything obviously, since there's no TV. I heard on the radio that all the major cities were hit. They don't even know who launched them. Some came from China, but China was bombed too, and everyone denies starting it. There are conspiracy theories about artificial intelligence, but who knows. Ricky from down the street came home from Chicago to help his parents. He said the journey was terrible, but there were still TV broadcasts in some areas—probably generators or solar panels powering them. He said the world was basically on fire. Everything not bombed has been hit by natural disasters, like nature itself wants us gone. Now I'm living like I'm on Little House on the Prairie—tending the garden by day and learning to can food by candlelight. Ricky's family and ours are teaming up: they had corn planted already, and Dad's garden is thriving. They've also been standing guard; we're the only two houses on this dirt road, so we know desperate people will come for supplies. It's like every apocalypse show I ever watched… except no zombies. Ugh.

xoxo – Brynn

Dear Diary,

It's been eight weeks since I last heard from my sister, and two weeks since we lost Ricky's family. Raiders are a thing now—they burned their house after stealing every last can of beans. I'm actually thankful Dad went full prepper mode; he booby-trapped everything outside our makeshift fence. The raiders never got in—some didn't make it at all, and their bodies drew flies for days before Dad burned them. There are no cops, no military—we're on our own. Even the radio barely works; it's like we're cut off from the world. I don't know how long we can survive like this or how much worse it will get. I always thought the army would step in, but it's like this is bigger than them. Dad is tough and holding it together, but I can tell he's terrified. Mom tries to soothe me, but I remind her I'm an adult and she can be real with me. I told them we should pack up and go… we have trail horses and heard about little settlements popping up—maybe we could find one. Isn't there safety in numbers? But then again, we had numbers when it all went to hell the first time. Ugh.

xoxo – Brynn

Dear Diary,

Nine weeks. Nine weeks of hell. Mr. Tom from the drugstore came by today. He lost his wife to the raiders two weeks ago. He's heading for a settlement in North Carolina with his two daughters and begged us to come along. Dad wants to stay put, but Mr. Tom left a map and all the details. We don't know if it's real, and Dad doesn't want to risk leaving when we have everything we need here. I worry he'll stay stubborn until we run out of supplies—or raiders show up again. Traveling is dangerous too, and we don't know what we'd find. Mostly, I just want to know my sister is okay. Mom says she can feel in her soul that Aria is safe. I don't know if that's real, but it's easier to believe she's alive than imagine the worst. We eat smaller meals to preserve food, and Mom, Dad, and I work the fields together in case someone shows up. Every day feels like a "will we make it?" kind of day. I miss working in the boutique, where all I had to worry about was being nice to customers and looking cute. It seems so silly now that I miss it this much. Ugh.

xoxo – Brynn

Dear Diary,

Intruders are almost daily now. We're running low on ammo. Dad taught me how to use his rifle—I've shot before, but he wanted me to know every part inside and out. He's worried that if something happens to him, I'll be ready. We still have enough food and water, but luxuries are gone. We don't even bathe every day anymore—and when we do, it's freezing. Dad says if things don't improve in another week, we're packing up and heading out. He thinks the military or someone might pull together and save us, but I'm not so sure. I wish Mr. Tom could radio us to say he made it, so we'd know. I guess if we're going to die, I'd rather die trying… or something. Aria—if you ever come home and I'm not here and you find this, I love you and I miss you so much. Thank you for always being the best big sister a girl could have. Mom and Dad love you too, but I know you know that. I pray you're okay, doing amazing things. I hope I get to see you one day. Even if the world is total shit, I'd accept it if I could survive just one day next to you and the family. I love you.

xoxo – Brynn